Totally Bound Publishing books by Jane Colt

Single Books
Treat or Hex?
Red Rock Romance

I0524361

RED ROCK ROMANCE

JANE COLT

Red Rock Romance
ISBN # 978-1-83943-999-5
©Copyright Jane Colt 2021
Cover Art by Louisa Maggio ©Copyright July 2021
Interior text design by Claire Siemaszkiewicz
Totally Bound Publishing

RED ROCK ROMANCE

Chapter One

The tremor in her arm was the first sign Cat was reaching her limit. Her labored breathing was the second. She'd pushed so hard during this climb that every bit of clothing she wore — her long-sleeved gray jersey, her sports bra underneath, her long black climbing tights — was soaked. Sweat ran down from her sopping bandana into her eyes. The salt stung. She clenched her jaw.

I can do this.

The fear she'd fought so hard to ignore disagreed. *'No, you can't,'* cackled the demon within.

She fought back.

Hang in there. Stay here for a minute and rest. We'll be okay. Relax. Just don't look down.

She took a deep breath and gripped the red-hued rock tighter. Her gloves weren't thick enough to protect her from its knife-like edge. It bit back. "Ow!" The burn spread through her arms. She kept shifting her right foot to find a more secure foothold.

Better. Worse. Better. Worse. Damn!

The struggle only added to the strain on her upper body. Now both her arms were shaking. *Stop!* she commanded. They ignored her. She took a series of deep, hard breaths, hoping to get oxygen to her muscles. Her throat burned from the effort.

Put the weight on your left foot to get a better grip.

The black rubber sole slipped off the rock and shot into mid-air. She grunted and instinctively tightened her grip even more, which only increased the pain.

Defying the agony, she pulled herself up a few more inches. Her heart thundered against her chest. Straining, she gasped for air. Safety was within sight. If she could just grab the next handhold, she could regain her balance and give herself a chance. She gritted her teeth and stretched — but it was just out of reach.

She put all her weight on one leg and explored the rough surface with her free foot. Miraculously, she found a foothold that would let her lift herself.

I can do this!

She shifted her weight onto that side.

Stretch! Push! Pull! Fight! Just two more inches.

But the pressure on her leg was too much. The pain in her calf was instant and searing.

Fuck! A cramp!

The muscle tightened with a mind of its own, oblivious to the fact that it was bringing about its own destruction. With her legs now useless, she shifted back to her arms. Drained, they shook. Even her hands had nothing left.

No! No!

She gulped as dread washed over her. But she still struggled.

It will be okay, she lied.

Her heart pounded as her fate became undeniable. Her throat tightened and her face flushed. She didn't know which felt worse — the pain in her hands from gripping so hard? The searing burn in her muscles? The terror at being so high? Shame at having overreached and being the author of her demise? Swallowing hard, she knew that, given what was about to happen, the question was academic.

Her trembling arms told her that she had only seconds before her body betrayed her. She closed her eyes tight, clenched her jaw, kept fighting and prayed for a miracle. But her final bit of energy evaporated.

Even as the cold, merciless hand of Death pried her fingers from the rock and pulled her to her tragic destiny, she refused to surrender.

No! No!

But gravity pulled her backward like a rag doll.

"No! No! Please, God! No!" she screamed into the void.

She plummeted.

Three feet.

The sturdy black safety harness snapped sharply around her. She grunted in reply, and her friend slowly lowered her to the gym floor.

Lauren greeted her with a big smile and a warm hug. "Twenty feet. That's a new personal best, Cat. Congratulations. Of course" — she laughed — "it doesn't change that you just died again. What is that…five times today? But it's still an accomplishment. High five!"

Cat's arms were so spent that she couldn't raise either one in response. As her friend helped her out of the harness, she hung her head and wiped her face. "I know you're trying to be encouraging, but being so weak and terrified only twenty feet off the ground is humiliating. I'm such a failure!" She began to cry.

Her friend covered her in an oversized pink towel to sop up the perspiration. "They've got the AC blasting, sweetie. You're drenched from going all out. You don't want to catch cold." She put her arm around her as they walked to the locker room.

As she and her friend dressed in the pristine locker room after showering, Lauren pointed to the sopping mountain of heavy, colorless, sweat-soaked fabric in front of Cat's locker. "That's at least one problem you could solve in one stroke. You'd be cooler and more comfortable climbing in shorts and a sports bra. All that wet cloth makes you overheat and drains your energy."

Cat winced. She was a failure as a climber. Now she couldn't even dress right.

"I'm sorry, Cat." Lauren hugged her. "You know I'm your biggest fan. I'm just trying to help. Let me treat you to coffee. I'll even spring for a chocolate croissant. The good news is that since you're now nearly a ghost, calories don't count."

Cat mustered a weak laugh.

"Seriously, it takes real guts to face your fears like this. You should be proud. You're a fighter!"

"Sure, a fighter without a punch," she replied dejectedly.

Lauren wrapped Cat in another big hug, and Cat laid her head on the comforting shoulder, took a deep breath and relaxed into her warmth.

"You're the best, Lauren. I'd have given up weeks ago if it weren't for you."

As they left the gym, Cat squinted at the bright sunshine and winced at the heat then she tossed her bag into the trunk of her old canary-yellow Toyota. It was a glorious day in Sedona. The spectacular blue sky perfectly framed the red rocks glistening in the distance. Normally, Cat took comfort in the natural beauty around her — especially the rugged red mountains that reminded her of her heritage and her mission. Today, defeated by the climbing wall yet again, she barely acknowledged her surroundings. Her friend pointed to the mountains. "You have my word," she said resolutely. "You're going to own those rocks." Cat shrugged. She was too tired to argue.

They walked the few blocks to the café arm in arm. Lauren wore cute pink shorts and a tight white sleeveless top. Cat had on long, loose-fitting black track pants and an oversized, long-sleeved, gray, Red Rock University T-shirt. Pressed down by the weight of her exhaustion, the best she could manage was a slow trudge.

As she reached for her coffee on the white stone counter, her arm still shook. She had to use both hands to pick up the red paper cup. She carefully placed it on the sturdy wood table so it wouldn't spill. As she started to sit down, however, her leg began to cramp again. She lost her balance and jostled the table. The cup rocked, but Lauren grabbed the drink before it could tip over and stain the red-and-white checkerboard tablecloth. Despondent, Cat plopped into a chair and stretched out her leg to stop the cramp. Once the pain had passed, she picked up a sugar packet — but tore it so badly that it exploded over a pair of cute guys walking by. As she brushed the white powder off her gray T-shirt, she noticed that they looked her way then chuckled. She flushed hotly, put her head on the table, covered it with her arms and sighed.

"They thought it was cute," Lauren said quietly. "Sit up. They're hanging around. They want to come over and chat."

Cat sat back up, shook her head and mumbled something incomprehensible.

Lauren caught the guys' eyes and shrugged apologetically. They picked up their drinks and headed out. "Okay, the coast is clear."

Cat shook her head in disgust. "See? I can't even manage a cup of coffee and cute guys. I'm pitiful—a pathetic sack of fears destined for failure. I'm an aspiring archaeologist who's afraid of heights. Even after presenting at a bunch of conferences, I'm still terrified of public speaking. I hate it when anyone even looks at me. Those guys were gawking at adorable you. They noticed me only because what I did was stupid. I have 'career fiasco' and 'relationship nightmare' written all over me. I'm hopeless." She slumped again.

Lauren took her hand and gave her a warm smile. "Are you kidding? Bumping into the table and not being able to open the sugar are signs that you went *all out* on your climbs. You don't do things halfway. I admire that about you." She put her finger under Cat's chin, raised it and looked directly in her eyes. "Now, tell yourself you're a fighter…and mean it! That's an order!"

She sighed. "Fine. I'm a fighter," she murmured sullenly.

"Cat!" Lauren replied.

"Okay, okay. Despite my unbroken string of miserable failures and despite the obvious futility of continuing to try, I *stupidly* haven't given up," she said.

Lauren laughed. "If that's the best you can do, I'll take it. And also tell yourself that you're a beautiful, sexy woman. I've seen you naked at the gym. Those guys were checking you out because you're hot—even when you insist on dressing like a nun."

Cat managed a weak smile then the tears started again.

Lauren reached into her white backpack and handed her a tissue. She stroked Cat's arm gently. "I know it doesn't feel like it, sweetie, but you actually had a good day. Once you get past the fear of heights, you won't waste so much of your energy gripping so tightly. And weight work will give you the strength you need."

Cat wiped her eyes and made a face, recalling how embarrassing her recent sessions at the gym had been. "I struggle so much, even with small dumbbells, that I get that pitiful look from everyone around me. They ask me if I'm okay, like I'm coming back from major surgery or something. I've even tried to go when no one else is there, but then the trainers come over. I can see it in their eyes. They're worried I'm going to hurt myself then sue them. I'm so self-conscious that it's humiliating."

Her friend paused, a frown furrowing her forehead, and looked down at the table. She sat quietly for a few seconds, pursed her lips and moved the saltshaker from a red square to a white one as deliberately as if she were playing chess. She glanced back up at Cat. "Maybe…you…" She took a sip of coffee. "It's just…"

"What?"

"Nothing." Lauren looked down and took the pepper shaker this time. Staring in its direction but not really looking at it, she rhythmically tapped it on the table as she pursed her lips.

Cat sighed. "Come on. I can take it. You're going to tell me I'm stupid to think I can do this. I need to face facts and give up." She closed her eyes and covered her face with her hands as though someone was going to punch her.

Lauren gently took Cat's hands and put them back on the table. "Look at me, Cat. I am *not* going to criticize you. You do that too much already. How do you forget so quickly that you graduated *summa*, won a great graduate fellowship and are on a fast track to your Ph.D.? Didn't the school just send you to that conference in Greece where everyone raved over your presentation? You're awesome! *You're* the only one who doesn't know that. I wasn't going to criticize you. Actually" — she looked out of the window — "I *might*...have an idea," she said hesitantly.

Is there hope?

Looking back at Cat, Lauren sat quietly. She leaned in, lowered her voice and spoke. "I have a thought...about a Plan B...to solve your problems. It's unusual, but..." She left the sentence incomplete.

Cat leaned forward excitedly. "A Plan B? Really? Tell me."

Lauren looked into her coffee and stirred. She took a deep breath and sipped. Then her face tightened and turned red. Quickly looking down at the crusty croissant in front of her, she said abruptly, "Boy, this coffee is hot." Flustered, she tore off a piece of her pastry. "And this looks great."

Cat was startled. She didn't believe that hot coffee could make her friend's face turn scarlet. *What is she* not *saying?*

Lauren looked away and pulled her long blonde hair behind her. "Um. Not weights." She looked down and tapped her fingers on the table. Her face tensed, and — to Cat's surprise — she bit her lip and held her breath for a few seconds. When she exhaled, she almost imperceptibly shook her head.

After a few seconds, she looked up and glanced out of the window. "I mean, let's figure out why you're so afraid first. If we can reduce your panic, you'll be more relaxed and will climb better," she said, looking back at Cat. "Then we'll worry about body strength. So, where does the fear come from? And if you're so terrified, why are you so committed to learning to climb?"

Everything—Lauren's cadence, expression, posture—screamed that she'd deliberately changed the topic.

Cat frowned. If there were another way to tackle her fears, she didn't understand why her friend wouldn't tell her. But it was obvious that pressing for an explanation was the wrong thing to do. She'd respect Lauren's wishes. At the same time, she wasn't ready to confide everything to Lauren yet about her embarrassing fears and weird obsessions—at least not in a public coffee shop where she could be overheard. "I promise I'll explain—but let's save it for a day when I haven't fallen to my death so many times."

"Fair enough." Lauren smiled. "But enough with the sad stuff." She leaned in with a naughty smirk and lowered her voice. "Tell me all about the conference. Any cute guys?"

"I told you I'm not interested in anything that could distract me from my work—and certainly not a relationship until after I have my degree."

"That's not what I meant, and you know it. Did you follow my suggestion"—she nudged Cat conspiratorially—"and engage in some wanton revelry? God knows you deserve it after how hard you've been working."

"Wanton revelry?" Cat looked puzzled.

"Sorry. Too much Shakespeare. When you got to the conference and unpacked, you must have found my strapless red dress I snuck into your bag. Did it work?

Did you get laid? Surely there were any number of hot young studs happy to service you."

Cat laughed. "*Hot young studs*? Have you ever seen what archaeologists look like?"

"Sure. Indiana Jones. The hat. The whip. The bedroom eyes. Bedroom hands. Bedroom you-know-what." She playfully raised her eyebrows a couple of times.

"Sorry," she chuckled. "That's the movies. Real life archaeologists are nerd city."

"Wait a minute. Didn't you text me that there was some drop-dead gorgeous guy all the women were drooling over? The one who'd made some sort of amazing discovery?"

"Oh, him. The Brit who found an ancient Grecian vase that's going to rewrite the history of the period. Because my flight got delayed, I got to the conference after his lecture, and he was nowhere to be seen. I don't believe he was as good looking as everyone said. Nobody's that handsome! Even so, I wouldn't be interested. He's not my type."

"Not your type? Handsome and brilliant? He's *every* woman's type!"

"No, I mean he's a hound." She waved her hand in the air dismissively and grimaced. "He pursues women with the same vengeance he uses to look for artifacts. We're just prizes for him. The rumor mill said he was bed-hopping the entire conference. Colin Tucker is the *last* man I'd ever be interested in!"

Chapter Two

The cute red-haired secretary in the emerald silk blouse perked up as Colin Tucker strode into the elegant, wood-paneled office. She sat straight back in her chair — a move that showed off her pert breasts and greeted him with her warmest smile.

Colin was aware that he was the fantasy of virtually every woman at the university. On top of his sinfully handsome good looks, he — unlike his perennially rumpled colleagues — knew how to dress. On this occasion he wore charcoal slacks, a black turtleneck and a burgundy leather jacket that looked so decadently soft that it begged to be caressed.

"Good afternoon, Debra. I have an appointment with Professor More at three."

"Professor Tucker. Good afternoon," she replied professionally. "Yes, I have you in her calendar. She had to step out for a minute and asked that you wait. May I offer you some tea?"

The syllabus he needed to write for his class popped to mind. "No, thank you. I'll go back to my office and work until she's back. If you call me, I'll be here in two minutes." He turned to leave.

"I'm sure she won't be long, Professor." A hint of panic seeped into her voice. "And she did say it was *very* important. Please, let me get you a cup of tea."

Not being his chairperson's favorite faculty member, he decided he owed her the courtesy of waiting. Besides, he'd never seen her PA look quite so fetching. "Sure, Deb. Thanks. Milk...no sugar."

As the young woman got up from behind her desk and sashayed to the other side of the office, his eyes locked onto the sexy slit in her short, stylish black skirt. As she stood in front of the antique sideboard, he drank in the delicious shape of her legs and behind — accentuated by her four-inch black stilettos. *Yum!* "Brilliant kit, Deb. You're really decked out today. Hot date after work?"

"Not a chance." She laughed, as she poured from the silver tea service. "These are just ordinary work clothes."

"Well, you should wear them more often. The color of your blouse really makes your green eyes pop."

She smiled shyly. "You think so?"

"Absolutely." He winked. "And paired with that smoky way you have your eyes done gives you a glamorous *femme de mystère* look. Very classy."

She lit up.

"You're unusually observant for a man. None of the guys I've dated have ever noticed my eyes."

"Then you've been dating the wrong sort. You deserve to be appreciated and told all the time how fabulous you look."

"That's very thoughtful of you to say, Professor." But the way she licked her full, ruby lips and looked at him darkly said she appreciated more than his manners.

Colin continued admiring her as she poured the milk and tea into the gleaming white china cup. After stirring with the tiny silver spoon, she looked right at him and licked it — slowly and sensually.

She's flirting with me. What a brilliant little tart!

As she walked toward him, he noticed the tiny fishnet pattern in her stockings. *Was that a flash of a black suspender belt? I bet she's not wearing any knickers. What a delightful tease! God, I love women!*

As she bent down to put the cup and saucer on the table in front of him, he was the grateful recipient of a perfect view of the tantalizing slope of her creamy breasts and a lace bra that matched her blouse perfectly. Her sexy perfume was an added delicacy.

What a view! And that perfume. Musk? Leather? Orange blossom? Same as that beauty in Venice! He inhaled deeply and smiled at the memory.

"Thanks, Deb. Lovely perfume. It reminds me of a gorgeous Duchess I met this summer. It's even better on you. Any chance you have royalty in your blood?"

She giggled. "No. Unlike you, my family is strictly working class. The fragrance is new from Gucci. Do you really think it suits me?" She leaned in even closer this time, steadying herself by putting her hand on his shoulder. She lingered so he could take another whiff — and another look.

The seductive scent kicked his heart rate up a notch. *Wow! She is sexy. How did I never notice this girl before?*

He placed his large hand on her hip as if to keep her from tipping over. "Absolutely. It says 'I'm sexy, but not easy. And once I get warmed up —'" He gave her a smile that was two scoops charm, one scoop innocence and a huge helping of lust.

She bit her luscious red lip and let out a quiet moan. As she took a deep breath, her chest heaved and her blouse pulled tight against her breasts. She put her finger to her cheek. "Oh, I forgot that we have some pastries today." Walking back to the sideboard, she added a little more sway to her hips. Returning, she bent down even deeper as she put the plate of confections beside his tea. "May I offer you a cupcake?" Her voice was unabashedly sultry and seductive. She added a sexy smirk and a wink.

I swear she undid a button to give me a better view! This is fucking brilliant!

Because she was being so flirty, it was pointless for him to pretend he was doing anything but staring down her blouse. "A cupcake? Absolutely." He lowered his voice so she'd have to come even closer to hear him. "But only if I can have both. Otherwise, one will feel neglected...and that's rude. To be honest, however, I actually prefer the rich taste of a good...*muffin*." He gazed at her naughtily. "You wouldn't have one to offer me, would you?" His eyes drifted down toward the middle of her skirt.

She flushed. He took her hand, and she let out a barely audible sigh.

God. She is so beautiful. And she's good with this.

"Why don't you sit down beside me, and we can discuss the proper way to eat pastries. Do you like them licked or bitten?" As he squeezed her hand, he looked directly into her eyes. Boldly. Hungrily.

She gazed back with equal intensity and yearning. As she sat on the couch, she turned toward him in a way that pushed her skirt higher.

Suspenders! Very sexy!

She tugged at her skirt and pretended to be embarrassed by how high it had hiked up.

Moving closer, he made it clear how much he enjoyed the view. "Please, don't go to any trouble on my part. I think suspenders are the sexiest piece of clothing a woman can wear." He rested his hand on her knee and inched it toward the black clip that was holding the top of her stocking. Her breathing audibly deepened. "And knowing how to unhook them properly separates the men from the boys."

Sliding one finger underneath the sheer black fabric, he let it linger against her skin. He lifted the clip and put his thumb on the top of the fastener. He paused and sank into the delicious moment of anticipation, then he freed the nylon from its shackle.

She let out a tiny gasp as he caressed the silky skin of her thigh. "Oh, Professor" — her voice was filled with desire — "we shouldn't."

"Of course we shouldn't. That's why it feels so good."

As he moved his hand up her leg, she cupped his hard cock. Her eyes widened, likely at its size. Squeezing it, she began breathing faster. She tilted her head and closed her eyes. Her moist lips parted in invitation.

Colin leaned in, eager to devour her delicious mouth.

The sound of the door opening made him look to the far corner of the office, where an elegant white-haired woman in a blue paisley dress was stepping in. Her steely glance their way made the temperature in the room plummet. The warm delight of the forbidden was blown away by the frosty chill of being caught.

A startled Debra blushed and pushed Colin's hand away. She hurriedly returned to her desk. Putting her head down, she shuffled through papers. The woman surveyed the scene, shook her head and sighed.

"Professor Tucker, you're distracting my assistant. You're early for our appointment. But as long as you're here, please come in."

Colin smiled as he walked to Deb's desk and handed her his cup. "I'm so disappointed we were interrupted. We must get together for tea soon and continue" — he leaned down and spoke seductively into her ear — "our *conversation*. May I call you?"

Looking down her blouse again, he saw the clear signs of her arousal — swollen breasts and stiff nipples struggling against the lace of her bra. His imagination ran to other parts of her body.

She licked her full, deep-red lips. "I'd love that, Professor." Her voice was breathless — and hungry with desire.

The look she gave him made it clear that 'tea' and 'conversation' were the last things she had in mind.

"Brilliant. I'll ring you. And please stop calling me *Professor*, Deb. It's *Colin*." He gently stroked her cheek. She held his hand against her face and sighed softly.

He walked into his chairperson's office and scanned the room. He could never enter her *sanctum sanctorum* without being intimidated. The floor-to-ceiling bookcases were crammed with volumes, new and old. He'd lost count of how many his aunt had authored. There were also the awards and photos with important people covering an entire wall. She was a legend in the field with more discoveries than anyone could hope for.

The stern older woman pointed to a chair immediately opposite her desk. "Sit," she commanded. She poured herself a cup of tea. Looking directly at him, she shook her head.

"Really? My *PA*?"

"Sorry, Aunt Clarissa. We were just having a friendly chat. You aren't going to discipline her, are you? It was entirely my fault."

"Your fault? With your history, I could never think otherwise. Friendly chat? Five minutes later and I would have walked in on the two of you *in flagrante delicto*. I've asked you to consider the women at this university to be off-limits. I expect you to be sensitive to their signs of interest in you and not encourage them."

"And I've certainly tried to do so," he replied seriously.

She raised one eyebrow skeptically as she tilted her head toward the brown wooden door leading to Debra's desk. He shrugged and smiled sheepishly. She sat down behind her desk and glared. Sighing again, she looked at the door that led to her PA's office.

"I suppose it's not *entirely* your fault. You couldn't have known that Debra arrived at work in a completely different—and much plainer—outfit. Or that after I asked her to set up your appointment with me, she was on the phone begging a friend to go shopping over lunch. Even *I* didn't know she told you to arrive thirty minutes early and hoped for some sort of rendezvous. However"—she held up her paper cup—"have you ever seen a silver tea service, china cups or pastries here?"

Pleased at the implications, he laughed. "She did all that for me?"

"She obviously doesn't know you as well as I do. Like all your female admirers, she finds your 'Indiana John Thomas' reputation irresistible. And they all harbor the fantasy you'll settle down with them. They don't seem to realize that you're—no offense, nephew, but it's the truth—a Tilt-a-whirl."

He cocked his head.

"A what?"

"An amusement ride—fun for a while, but then it stops. One rider gets off and someone new gets on."

He chuckled. "It's just fun, Aunt. We're all adults. No one gets hurt." He waved his hand in the air.

She leaned forward placing her arms on her desk. She narrowed her eyes. "This may be just a game to you, Colin, but you have a bad habit of creating situations other people have to clean up—which is why I called you in." She pointed at the sleek black telephone on her desk. "Would you please explain the series of angry voices I had to deal with on the other end earlier today?"

He stared back blankly.

"First, an official from Greece. Rumors are floating around that a few objects on the dig you just returned from went missing. I assured her it must have been a cataloguing error." She looked directly at him. "I told her I was sure these stories are the result of academic jealousy. I promised we would become better bookkeepers. I know the paperwork is tedious, but we're guests in that country. Are we of one mind on this, nephew? No. More. Missing. Artifacts." Her stare got harder with each word.

"Yes, Madame Chairperson. We are of one mind." He answered seriously, shifting in his chair.

She nodded. "The second call was from the parents of that American girl from Smith who was on the dig."

"This is about *her*? Lovely young woman. *Very* talented for an undergrad. Has lots of promise. I invited her back for next season. Do you think I should encourage her to take her Ph.D. here?"

Clarissa looked back sharply. "Don't toy with me, Colin. You know what I mean."

He shook his head and chuckled. "Oh that. Her parents are having a typically American, puritanical overreaction. Nothing happened between us until after the dig had ended. She wasn't my student anymore by then. When I walked into my tent after our goodbye party, I found her posed naked on my sleeping bag. We were consenting adults. It was just an innocent hook up, except for her wanting to wear my hat while we —"

Clarissa slapped her hand hard on the large oak desk so forcefully that her teacup jumped. "Colin! I'm both your Chair and your aunt. I don't want details." She shook her head. "It's a good thing you're a brilliant archaeologist. Otherwise, you'd find yourself cut off from research funds. But mark my words... One of these days you'll go too far, and even I won't be able to protect you. *Please* take your dealings with the opposite sex more seriously. This may be fun and games for you, but these young women are certain you're in love with them. They start falling for you, but they don't understand what's really going on until it's too late. Or have you forgotten about that sweet young Italian who started teaching here last year and ended up so heartbroken she took a job at Cambridge?"

Looking down, he rubbed his forehead. "You're right. I'm sorry I cost the department a promising scholar." He held up his hands. "But I didn't lie to her, and I didn't lead her on. And while I've never said I was *in love* with any of the women I see, I really *do* love them. They're smart, beautiful, sexy. I'm helpless."

Clarissa gave him an exasperated look. "No, Colin, you *aren't* helpless. It's worse than that. You're cursed. You probably think you're lucky to have your father's looks and charm. You attract women as easily as you breathe. But that's dangerous for everyone involved. I believe you when you say you love them — but it's only until the next one comes along. You're like Casanova with ADD. It's one conquest after another." She thrust her finger in his direction. "But one of these days you'll meet the woman you truly want, only she won't trust you—precisely because it's all so easy for you. *Please* think seriously about this, Colin. And *stop* creating unnecessary problems for me. It's hard enough to run this department without having to deal with your antics."

He nodded seriously, got up, walked to the window and stared out for a minute. Then he put his hands in his pockets and bowed his head. When he turned back toward his aunt, he was unusually somber. "You're right. I've been selfish and haven't considered the effect my actions have on people like you. I apologize if I've done anything to embarrass you, the department or the university. I'm truly sorry. I promise to do better."

"Apology accepted, nephew." She waved her hand in the air. "Go and sin no more." Then her face softened. She got up, walked over to where he stood and took both of his hands in hers. "We are family, Colin. I promised your mother I would look after you, and I am more concerned about your welfare than you can imagine. I know how hard you took her death, and I probably didn't do you any favors by not intervening as you picked up some less-than-admirable habits. But you don't make it easy for any of us who care for you. More important, you don't make it easy for yourself. No matter what, however, know I'm always here for you."

He was truly touched by her words. He bent over and kissed her on the cheek, happy they'd made peace. Aunt Clarissa was not someone he wanted to be on the wrong side of. He, too, cared about her and was genuinely sorry he'd made her job harder.

"But leave *that* way." She pointed to the door at the far end of her office. "You've distracted my PA enough for one day."

As he walked out and turned down the corridor, a cute student from one of his courses last term approached him. She wore thin, black yoga pants and a tight white T-shirt that appeared to have a reproduction of some sort of ancient mosaic on the front. "Hi, Professor! It's brilliant to see you!" Her greeting was so effusive and her smile so radiant that it was a sign to be cautious.

She gave him a quick kiss on the cheek and blushed. "How do you like my T-shirt? It was a souvenir from my field work in Pompeii." She stuck out her chest. The fact that she wasn't wearing a bra couldn't be more obvious. The shirt featured an image of a couple having sex. It was from the brothel in Pompeii.

"Hello, Fiona," he answered with professorial reserve. He was not about to encourage her.

"I heard you made headlines in Greece! Was that the artifact you said in class no one thought existed? Wow! You showed them, didn't you? Can I hear about how you found it?" She bit her lip coquettishly.

"Of course. You're always welcome to make an appointment with the department secretary."

"Or"—she tilted her head coyly—"we could talk now. Tea? My treat," she suggested nervously. "You were my favorite teacher. It's the least I owe you." She played with her long blonde hair and twirled it around her finger.

"That's very thoughtful, Fiona. I can't today because I'm swamped with some pre-term work. But please make an appointment."

"Oh. Okay." As she looked away, it was obvious she was trying to hide her disappointment.

"But it was lovely to see you. I look forward to our chat. Cheers."

She beamed. "Me too! Cheers!"

He continued quickly down the corridor. He turned right to exit the building using a shortcut through the university's art museum.

Colin congratulated himself on handling Fiona sensitively. He was well-practiced in fending off flirtatious coeds without hurting their feelings. He grumbled about his Aunt's lecture. He understood her position and sincerely regretted any difficulty he'd brought to her as Chair. But she'd misjudged him. She'd called him a Casanova. But he'd never lied to, seduced or manipulated any of the women he'd slept with.

He had a strict code. No student in his class. No undergrads of any sort. *Okay, the Smith student was an undergrad, but she was the exception that proved the rule.* Graduate students were different. They were older and more mature. No woman who was married or in a relationship. Honesty about his intentions. No photos or videos. Strict confidentiality from his side—no bragging about whom he slept with. No threesomes. If a woman was giving the gift of going to bed with him, it would be rude not to give her his undivided attention.

He was especially offended that Clarissa had called his paramours 'conquests'. It was a matter of honor with him that what these women did, they did freely. He was honest with them about his intentions. They always had the option of saying no. *They* had the power, not him. All he could do was *ask* to be with them. He could only open his heart about how desirable they were, how much he wanted to pleasure them, how wonderful their time together would be.

Isn't life too short to deny pleasure when it presents itself, as long as no one gets hurt?

Just then, one of his favorite works of art, Dora Carrington's *Standing Female Nude*, caught his eye. He studied the painting—a naked woman simply standing. And while the body was clearly shown, there was no face. There was nothing sexual about it—no teasing expression, no seductive or tantalizing pose. Its honest, straightforward representation of female nudity struck Colin as a celebration of the female form by a female artist. He could spend hours studying the portrait because he genuinely, truly, passionately, soulfully *loved* women for who they were in an unvarnished state—not the way anyone said they should be.

What can be wrong with loving such a gift from the gods? Thinking about his aunt's request to refrain from pursuing women at the university, he began sulking. *It's not fair*, he grumbled. Then he remembered something else she'd said. *Deb made the first move when she went shopping and had me come in early. Technically, then, I'm not pursuing her. She's pursuing me!* Smiling, he took out his mobile and punched in a text.

Drink after work, Deb? Loved how our conversation started. Shall we continue? Your humble and obedient servant. Colin.

Barely five seconds passed before his phone pinged.

Absolutely! Send me time and place. Can't wait to 'talk'!

Chapter Three

On Saturday night, Cat and a few of her grad student girlfriends were hanging out in her dorm room when Brittany said, "You aren't going to believe this! A story in *Cosmo* says it's all the rage for couples to go to 'gentlemen's clubs' together."

Teresa got up and plopped down on the bed beside the cute blonde. "Seriously? Let me see. I've been looking for something outrageous to surprise my boyfriend with for his birthday. That sounds perfect, especially since he keeps teasing me about being less adventurous than he is. He means bungee jumping and zip lining, but I'll show him what *adventurous* means! Wow! The story even mentions a place here in Sedona."

Karen looked shocked. "You want to take your boyfriend to a sleazy strip club where some skanky cocktease will give him a hard-on? Are you crazy?"

Teresa looked up from the story. "It doesn't sound like that. Here... See for yourself." She tossed the magazine onto the bed beside Cat. "It looks classy and upscale. The strippers don't sound like oversexed 'hos'—just regular girls trying to make a living."

Cat reached for the magazine in a way that was studiedly casual. After scanning the story, she spoke up. "Terri's right. The girls profiled seem a lot like us. In fact, a bunch of them are doing this to pay their tuition. One's a nursing student. Another's in law school. I wouldn't be surprised if somebody isn't putting themselves through Red Rock this way."

Teresa hopped off the bed and started throwing everyone's jackets at them. "Come on. It's settled. We're all going. I want to check this out before I spring it on my boyfriend—and I'm not doing this alone."

Cat had never been to a strip club, but she found Teresa's idea more intriguing than she wanted her friends to know. That was because her absolute favorite sex fantasy was peeling off her clothes in front of a room filled with hunky guys who became hypnotized by the sight of her naked flesh. They were so filled with desire for her that each begged her to let him serve her. They'd do anything she desired. She chose a ruggedly handsome man with curly blonde hair, electric blue eyes and a devilish smile. She led him to a private room where she commanded him to pleasure her in every way imaginable until she passed out from too many orgasms.

She knew precisely why this was her fantasy. In it she could pretend she had overcome her fear of being looked at. The fact that it dominated her life haunted her. It influenced everything from how she dressed to her terror of public speaking to insisting that the lights be out whenever she had sex.

Stripping in real life would obviously look very different from her fantasy...but she was curious.

In a flash, she squeezed into Teresa's bright red VW bug and headed to Satin, the gentlemen's club mentioned in the article. Cat was pleasantly surprised that the parking attendants and doormen were clean cut and crisply dressed in black slacks and bright white, short-sleeved polo jerseys, and she was impressed by how respectfully and courteously they were greeted. When they entered the elegant, softly lit club, a stunning woman in a gorgeous black gown escorted them down a richly appointed corridor and to a booth upholstered in rich brown, baby-soft leather. "Ariel will be here shortly. If there's anything I can do to make your visit more enjoyable"—she gave the entire group a friendly smile—"please don't hesitate to ask."

Looking around the club, Cat expected that she and her friends would be the only women there. But, like the article suggested, there were a few couples in the audience. She admired how sexy the women chatting up the customers were—presumably offering lap dances in the back rooms out of sight. But while the club had a very sexy vibe, nothing seemed sleazy. The woman dancing on center stage was gorgeous, and Cat was impressed with how strong she had to be for the routine she was doing. Cat had always assumed that 'pole dancing' meant just stripping while the dancer caressed the tall, chrome rod in a way that made the guys in the audience imagine it was their cock. She hadn't realized how athletic the dancers were.

She couldn't contain her envy at how comfortable and confident the women appeared. They were walking around nearly naked, as men and women alike admired and lusted after them. And it wasn't like they all had bodies that put hers to shame. She got angry at herself. *How can they do that so easily when I don't feel comfortable wearing shorts and a T-shirt?*

A pretty, young, topless waitress wearing a pair of cute red satin shorts, black stockings and heels arrived and greeted Cat and her companions with a friendly smile. "Hi, I'm Ariel, your hostess. Welcome to Satin." She handed them menus and chatted with them for a few minutes. She probably wanted to make sure they didn't feel uncomfortable and likely was curious about what made a posse of Red Rock coeds come to Satin.

Ariel was about the same age as Cat and her friends, and she explained that her real name was Phyllis. She was married and attended Sedona Community College. She and her bartender husband both worked at Satin.

She pointed him out. "He's the tall, cute one behind the bar." She caught his eye and blew him a kiss. He gave her a big smile and mouthed 'I love you'. "It's the fastest way for us to save money for a down payment on a home while I finish my education. I'm studying to be a web designer. And we don't want to start having a family while we're still renting."

Brittany fidgeted noticeably, having trouble getting her question out. "Ariel... Don't you...? I mean... Please don't take this...um... How do...?" She couldn't quite look directly at the waitress.

"For heaven's sake," Karen finally said, "we're all wondering the same thing. Doesn't it feel weird working topless at a strip club while you're married — and even weirder with your husband right here?"

Ariel smiled. "It did feel strange at first. Being topless with guys obviously checking out 'the girls' is a lot different from waiting tables at a restaurant fully clothed. But the managers here keep a close watch on everything. They're okay if customers engage in a little friendly flirting with me, but they make sure it doesn't go past that. It bothered my husband at first, but now he gets a kick out of knowing that no matter what, he's the guy I go home with. Now we both find it a turn-on. As a waitress, I don't give lap dances. But sometimes, after sneaking a peek at the other girls doing it, I pull my husband into the back room and give him one. Sometimes even a whole lot more." She giggled and blushed. "To be honest, our sex life has never been better."

As Ariel went to check on a booth of guys on the other side of the room, Cat read over the menu. Looking up, Karen said, "I'll admit, the last thing I expected to see at a strip club is a *salad*. In fact, nothing about this place is what I thought it was going to be. Ariel seems really nice — like one of us. And the lap dancing must be done wherever the girls are leading those guys off to — somewhere private — not right out in the open." She tapped Teresa on the arm. "Okay, you have my permission. Your boyfriend's definitely going to be so surprised. But you'd better be prepared for the fact that your Christmas present from him will be a pole of your own! You know what guys are like."

As Cat and her friends shrieked at the idea, the lights dimmed and a deep voice announced, "Ladies and gentlemen. Satin is proud to present *Cassandra*." The stage went dark, and the first demonic notes of Mussorgsky's *Night on Bald Mountain* crept out of the club's sound system.

A bright spotlight lit up a thin woman with black hair, who was clad in a skintight, blood-red body suit made of an iridescent fabric. She sparkled with every move. She had matching red, patent-leather stilettos strapped firmly around her ankles. She wore a mask of the same color. Her lips and nails were painted to match. On top of her head, she sported a pair of red horns. Her costume paired with the music perfectly. It said, '*I am the Devil, and I* invented *sex.*'

Her powerful presence filled the room. Any conversation stopped mid-sentence. Her sexy energy commanded everyone's attention. Cat couldn't take her eyes off the sexy dancer.

As the frenetic music surged, Cassandra spun effortlessly around the pole. Cat was in awe of the strength and control it took. She was also struck by how beautiful Cassandra looked — and how incongruous the athletic character of her movements was with her sexy costume. It was truly a dance, not the strip tease Cat had been expecting.

As the music slowed, the feel of Cassandra's routine changed. Her dance became more sensual and ballet-like. But it also was more overtly seductive and sexy. She shamelessly pressed her sex into the pole and slid up and down against the shiny metal. She then began doing slow turns around the shiny metal rod. Holding on with one hand, she gently fondled her breasts with the other. With each rotation, her nipples became more prominent through the red cloth as she uttered small moans. There was something forbidden about the way she caressed herself and offered her body to the audience. Even though the dancer was still fully clothed, the atmosphere in the club became increasingly erotic.

An electric charge shot through Cat. Her nipples struggled against the satin of her bra. Her sex grew warm and moist. She squeezed her legs tightly together and attempted to hide from her friends that she was breathing more deeply. She loved how illicit the pleasure felt.

Cassandra's spins sped up. She climbed farther up and flipped head down again. All at once, the catsuit was gone. The audience gasped.

Cat's heart raced. Her breathing deepened. The wetness between her legs increased. She'd seen naked women in the locker room and in porn, but no woman's body had ever had this effect on her. It wasn't just how beautiful and sexy this woman was or that Cat was aroused. She didn't simply ache sexually. She longed to have the qualities Cassandra displayed that she so hopelessly lacked—fearlessness, confidence, shame-lessness, power and charisma.

Now beautifully bare except for the horns, the mask, a bright red G-string and heels, the dancer did another series of amazing gymnastic moves in sync with the rhythm of the powerfully dark music. The fact that they took so much strength to perform only added to their sensuality.

Cassandra's dark nipples were now rock-hard. She slid her G-string-covered sex against the pole as she held the gleaming metal with one hand and squeezed her breasts with the other. As she moaned loudly, she began doing another set of slow twirls around the pole. She gripped the shining rod, and her twirls got so fast that she looked like a skater spinning.

In fact, she spun so fast that her mask flew off right before the music had ended. She let out a passionate scream—and the stage went dark.

Cat was stunned. *Wait! Is it possible?* The dancer's face had been visible for only a second, but she bore an uncanny resemblance to her friend Lauren.

The audience was silent for a few seconds—still hypnotized and under the erotic spell Cassandra had cast—then burst into applause and cheers. Cat looked around the table. Her friends' faces were all flushed.

Ariel came back and took everyones' order for food. Cat and the others watched the next dancer. Because she wasn't as athletic as Cassandra, her routine wasn't as impressive. Still, Cat was struck by how confident she looked, and what great upper body strength she must have.

She couldn't stop brooding about how much Cassandra and Lauren looked alike. It wasn't just how similar the two women's faces were. They were the same height and had the same body shape. They did have very different hair, but 'Cassandra' could have been wearing a wig. And there was the fact that the routine looked so much like a gymnastic performance. There were too many similarities to be a coincidence. Cat took out her phone and texted Lauren.

Believe it or not, I'm at a strip club – Satin – with some friends. Either I just saw your doppelganger or there's something you aren't telling me.

A few minutes later, her phone chimed.

Okay, I'm busted – but you can't tell a soul! I still have more shows tonight. Lunch tomorrow? I'll explain.

For the record. You were awesome!

By the time Cat had finished eating, she and her companions had admitted to loving Teresa's idea for her boyfriend's surprise. They stayed for another few dancers then returned to campus.

Cat had trouble falling asleep because she couldn't stop thinking about the evening. She would kill for the qualities Cassandra had. Confidence. Pride. Physical strength. Fearlessness. Bravery. If she could develop even a tenth of what that woman had shown, she could make the discovery she dreamed of. There had to be a way. She owed it to her people, to her mother and to herself to figure out how.

But that wasn't the only reason she tossed and turned. The idea she couldn't shake was ridiculous and embarrassing, she told herself. She wished she'd had more to drink at Satin. That way, she could blame it on the alcohol.

Chapter Four

When Colin stepped into The Jeremy Bentham, a noisy, old-fashioned pub near the university, a ginger-haired man wearing a tweed sport coat and sitting at a table waved to him. As he sat down, his companion placed a glass of ale in front of him.

"I figured you'd need a pint after being called in by Aunt Clarissa. How'd it go, little brother?"

Colin grimaced, picked up the glass and drained it.

"That bad, eh?" He gestured to the waitress, who brought over another. "You can't say you don't bring this on yourself," he chided. "Doing something to get on Aunt Clarissa's bad side? Are you crazy? I warned you about turning down that offer at Oxford to teach here. She's tougher than all the men in your department combined. And don't think being family will protect you. Knowing your history, she'll throw you under the bus faster than if you were a stranger. One of these days—"

Colin put up his hand and nodded somberly. "I know. I know. That's what she said—and she's right."

Ian leaned in and lowered his voice. "You're just lucky you haven't been caught yet. Those artifacts you sneak out of your digs may have no real value, but one day you'll regret it. Do you think our all-knowing aunt suspects?"

"It's pretty clear she does. She doesn't want to know for sure, but she won't turn me in...yet."

He shook his head. "You're playing with fire, lad."

"But I only take duplicates. And it's for research, not entertainment. I study pottery — objects people used in everyday life. I need to know what they feel like on a day-to-day basis. I want to spend time with them and see what they look like in ordinary light. I can't do that in a lab. I admit I'm breaking protocol, but it's for research."

Ian nodded. "I suppose I can't argue with your results. It turns out you're a bloody genius. But some day, little brother..."

Colin just shrugged.

Ian leaned back and crossed his arms. "But I doubt that was the main thing our dear aunt wanted to chat with you about. That American coed, right? So, what about that weakness of yours? You can't call *that* 'research'."

Colin winced and took a large pull on the warm amber liquid. "But they're all so lovely, Ian. And so smart." He was almost pleading. "And so willing. It's not my fault. They're the ones who say *yes* when they could say *no*. They're so fantastic, and they're irresistible. How can I not want them? I'm not a monk, you know."

Ian slapped his hand on the old wooden table and let out a hearty laugh. "A monk is the last thing anyone would take you for, my friend."

Colin punched his brother in the arm and finished off his drink. "Okay. The truth is, the way women respond to me makes me feel I'm the luckiest bloke on the planet. I wouldn't have it any other way. But Clarissa thinks it's a curse. She says I'm too much like Dad."

Ian shuddered. "Ouch! It's never a good sign when our dear aunt leads with that one. But a curse?" A smirk came over his face. "You know, I think she's on to something. You're cursed with 'Colin's Cock'."

Colin rolled his eyes. He pointed at his brother's glass. "And how many of those did you have while you were waiting?"

Ian poked Colin's chest sharply, clearly pretending to be angry. "You ungrateful tosser, you," he growled. "Here I am, trying to give you the secret behind all your troubles, and you mock me?" He frowned, sat back and looked away. "Maybe I'll just keep my ancient wisdom to myself."

Ian smirked. "The Curse of Colin's Cock?" He waited until curiosity got the best of him. "Fine, oh great Oracle of the Empire, I apologize. Please enlighten me."

Ian continued to look offended. "Very well, but only because I'm thirsty, and the next round is on you."

Colin signaled the waitress. When fresh pints had arrived, he motioned for Ian to speak. His brother's mischievous expression said that he was already enjoying himself far too much at Colin's expense. He took a deep breath and adopted a serious, professorial demeanor.

"The Curse of Colin's Cock is like Achilles and his heel. You know the story. His mother dipped him in the River Styx to make him immortal. Except she held him by the heel, which never got wet—so that was his weakness. Our mum must have tried to do the same thing to you, except she held you by your willie."

Colin winced at the image and crossed his legs.

Ian chuckled. "Strictly speaking, we can translate the Greek in a variety of ways. It could also be the 'Tucker Todger Curse' or 'the Professor's Pecker'. Do you prefer either of those to 'Colin's Cock'?" He laughed loudly as Colin scowled. "Whatever we call it, your dick is your fatal weakness. I bet you can't think of one scrape you've been in that didn't involve some beauty your John Thomas couldn't resist."

"Of course I can," Colin protested. "There was…"

Ian sat quietly.

"Give me a minute…"

Enjoying his difficulty, Ian crossed his arms across his chest and grinned broadly.

"Got it! The episode in Berlin."

"You mean with the cellist? Think again."

"Sorry… I meant…"

Colin closed his eyes tightly. Two minutes of silence passed before Colin's face dropped with failure. He ran his hand through his tousled hair and put his head on the table.

Ian howled. "See? I told you!"

"You're as bad as Aunt Clarissa," he told the table, then looked up. "The two of you make me sound like a dog in heat, nothing more than a sport-fucker."

Ian leaned back in his chair, smiled and put his finger on his nose.

"It's like I told her. I *love* women," Colin protested. "I love everything about them. I don't do shag and bag. When I see a beautiful bird, I'm *consumed*! It's not some calculated seduction. I'm genuinely enchanted—and not just by her body. I love everything about her. Sex is a sensual feast for me—the smells, the sounds, the tastes, that magical sensation of merging with an exciting woman."

He got more animated the more he explained.

"And nothing makes me feel more like a man than making a woman explode with pleasure. A *boy* can get a woman into bed. It takes a *man* to make her come. And only the *right* man can let her discover how much pleasure her body can give her. When I show a woman how much I love pleasuring her and how much joy that gives me, she lights up. She loves the pleasure I give her, and I love making her feel like that. And afterward…? Well, is it my fault that God made so many gorgeous beauties that I want them *all* to feel the same way?"

Ian roared so loudly at Colin's earnestness that the people at the nearby tables turned to see what was happening. "Sorry. Just humiliating my brother," he explained.

He turned back to Colin. "You're a piece of work. You make it sound like you're a veritable saint, ministering to those poor girls who are starved for pleasure." He raised his glass in a toast. "So, let us give thanks and praise to Saint Colin, patron saint of the selfless fuck that leads women into ecstatic union with the Divine." He laughed again, paused, then pointed his finger at Colin. "I think you're on to something. *There's* a religion billions of people could get behind. Sign me up!"

Colin joined in the laugh. "Okay. Maybe I get carried away, but I'm serious. It's not zipless fucks. I genuinely *like* women. I *love* having sex with them. And I don't deliberately lead them on."

Ian stroked his jaw as he thought. Then he rocked back on his chair and beamed. "I've got it! You just need them to sign a 'pre-fuck'!"

Colin furrowed his forehead. "Did you say 'pre-fuck'? What the devil is *that*?"

"It's like a pre-nup, but it covers just the one night." Ian tapped his fingers on the table as he stared into his pint and thought some more. He looked up with a big, mischievous grin then stood up and walked over to the bar.

Ian picked up a knife and banged it against his empty glass to get everyone's attention. "*Oi*, lads! Ladies!" he boomed over the din. When everyone in the pub turned his way and quieted down, he stepped up onto the bar. "Ladies and gentlemen, thank you for your kind attention. I am Ian Tucker, a professor of classics at University College, and that sorry fellow over there is my brother Colin, an eminent archaeologist at the same grand institution. The two of us need your help. Colin's basically a good sod, but he really is a hopeless shagger who unintentionally breaks a lot of hearts. I've suggested that if he and his young lovelies simply had a clear understanding of what was about to happen between them, there'd be fewer tears the next day. Therefore, I've proposed that in all my brother's future shagging, he ask his partner to sign a 'pre-fuck' before they do the deed."

The crowd laughed.

"So, I'd like to tell you what I think a good 'pre-fuck' should say. And you can let me know if I've missed anything."

They laughed again and cheered good-naturedly at the idea.

"It would go something like this." He paused for a moment, apparently gathering his thoughts.

"The party of the first part — hereafter known as 'the fucker' — hereby promises to give the party of the second part — hereafter known as 'the fuckee' — a singularly remarkable sexual experience."

All the women cheered.

"The fucker will lavish the fuckee with compliments about her beauty and desirability as he ravishes her and takes her to new heights of sexual ecstasy. The fucker promises that the fuckee's pleasure will be a higher priority than his own during the encounter. He guarantees that the fuckee will experience at least five orgasms."

The women hooted and cheered.

"The fucker promises to perform oral sex on the fuckee enthusiastically" — the women applaud — "with no expectation of receiving the same in return."

The men groaned, but the women cheered again, even louder.

"The fucker will follow any instructions, suggestions or requests from the fuckee about activities that will enhance her pleasure, with the exception of anything that will produce clear harm, undesired discomfort, is illegal or involves farm animals."

Everyone roared.

"If the fuckee persists in trying to get the fucker to do something he's uncomfortable with, the fuckee owes the fucker enthusiastic oral sex and must allow herself to be spanked until her bum is a ruby red" — the men cheered and the women groaned — "although the fucker must then kiss it until it feels better."

The women cheered again.

"In exchange for the 'singularly remarkable sexual experience,' the fuckee agrees that she will allow the fucker full access to her body, trusting that his sole goal is her pleasure. The fuckee will describe any secret sexual fantasies if asked to do so. The fuckee promises that all her orgasms will be genuine. Most importantly, the fuckee warrants that she understands that the 'singularly remarkable sexual experience' promised by the fucker in the initial paragraph of this document is a one-time event unless the fucker and fuckee agree in writing to extend the duration of this agreement, that the fucker is not and never will be 'in love' with her and she promises that she will not 'fall in love' with the fucker."

The men cheered, while the women murmured and groaned.

"Both the fucker and the fuckee stipulate that they are to be considered 'not in their right mind' during this encounter."

Everyone laughed.

"Accordingly, all statements — particularly expressions of love or promises of exclusivity, fidelity, eternal love, marriage or even of a subsequent text or phone call — uttered during this episode will be treated as though they were never spoken."

The men cheered and women booed.

"Finally, the fucker advises the fuckee that, while he is in other parts of his life a responsible adult devoted to Queen and country, when it comes to women, he should be regarded as a worthless hound who is led around by his tallywacker."

The women howled and the men booed.

"The fuckee, thus, must accept responsibility for the consequences of consorting with such a manwhore."

The men cheered.

"For her part, the fuckee confesses that even though in the rest of her life she is known for her good sense and prides herself in being a role model for the many young girls who admire her, her decision to have sex with such a fucker shows her to be a silly ninny."

The women booed.

Ian put up his hand to silence the crowd. "Just wait. Hear me out. As I was saying, a silly ninny who is doing so either because she has a history of colossally bad judgment when it comes to men, is in desperate need of some serious shagging or — in the case of the women in this room — is merely intellectually curious about the fucker's reputation for being able to give a woman a first-class rogering. That is, she is doing this only as anthropological fieldwork."

The women cheered and everyone laughed.

"So, before anyone in here hits the sheets later, make sure you draw up your 'pre-fucks'. Then it's tally-ho with no hard feelings."

He waved his hand with a flourish and took a deep bow. The crowd clapped, laughed and cheered.

As Ian hopped down from the bar and made his way back to their table, Colin noticed a few couples beginning intense conversations, grabbing bar napkins and scribbling on them.

When Ian sat down, his grin showed enormous self-satisfaction. Colin smirked and just shook his head. "You know, if you put as much imagination into your research, you wouldn't be such a crap scholar."

His brother laughed and punched him hard in the arm. "You ungrateful sod. I give you the solution to all your problems, and I get abuse in return. But to show you I'm the bigger man, I'll even tell you how to gild the lily.

"Women appreciate rituals, formality and going the extra mile. So, I suggest you carry copies of your 'pre-fuck' with you at all times — ideally on really good quality parchment. Better yet, roll it up as a scroll tied with ribbon! You'll also want some sealing wax, matches and that family crest do-dah thing dad uses on important documents. After all, we're nobility. Our family has a reputation to protect, and your paramour gets a nice souvenir — a copy of our ancient family seal in wax. And since you'll already have melted wax on hand" — he winked — "you're ready to start with something a little kinky."

Colin rocked back in his chair and frowned. "Dad actually uses that thing?"

"Dad?" Ian let out a disgusted snort. "You mean the Earl of Ye Olden Shire of I'm Too Sexy for My Wives? He can't resist it. Our family is *barely* nobility, and he crows as though he's next in line for the throne. Someday that's going to blow up in his face — because shooting himself in the foot is what Dad does.

"First, he thought he could get away with fooling around behind mum's back. He was convinced she'd forgive him, but his arrogance cost him lots in the divorce. He just married his fifth wife, he's cheating on her already and I bet she suspects. He'll deserve whatever comes crashing down on his head. You've got to be in awe of how consistently he screws up his life. And he never learns. If there's a gene for snatching misery from the jaws of happiness, he's got it, especially when it comes to women!"

Colin got still and somber. He looked at his phone. "Sorry, mate. Gotta go." He abruptly stood and turned to walk out of the door.

"Okay, little brother. What did I say?"

Colin turned. He hung his head and his shoulders were slumped. "Haven't you noticed that our father isn't the only member of the family with that gene? You heard Clarissa. I'm cursed. You said it yourself. My track record with women is no better than Dad's." He took a deep breath then let it out. "There's something wrong with me, Ian."

His brother put his arm around his shoulder and squeezed. "I'm sorry, Colin," he said seriously. "I shouldn't have said any of that crap. It was thoughtless. You aren't Dad. You hear me? You just haven't met the right girl. Trust me."

Colin looked at the ground and slowly shook his head. "No, I don't think so." His voice was filled with resignation. "Real relationships are like marathons. I'm just a sprinter. I need to accept that. Otherwise, I'm just going to make one woman after another unhappy." He took a long pause and pointed at a building that was nearing completion. It was faced with glass and sparkled. "That's me. Flash and style." He pointed to an older one made from red brick. "That's you. Solid. Real substance. You're a husband and father, while I'm a serial shagger." He turned to Ian. "I wish I could be like you and that building. But I never will be because...something's broken. I can't fall in love, Ian. Believe me, I've tried. I've been with some terrific women. I can do charm and lust. But *love*—" His voice trailed off.

Ian squeezed again. "Rubbish! The right woman for you is out there. You just need someone who isn't as impressed with you as you are and who doesn't fall for your silly, seductive bullshit. You'll find her. And when you do, everything will be different."

Colin sighed and looked back, unconvinced.

"But while you're searching for her," Ian clapped him energetically on the back and announced cheerfully, "at least you'll have a good 'pre-fuck' in your pocket to prevent any more misunderstandings. That'll take the sting out of the search."

Colin managed a half-hearted smile.

"In the meantime, it's a beautiful afternoon in the world's best city. I prescribe a nice stroll along the Thames. Short skirts are in bloom. We can enjoy some beautiful sights."

Chapter Five

Cat was so anxious to hear Lauren's explanation about 'Cassandra' that she arrived at the Red Rock Café twenty minutes early. She selected a booth in the back so they wouldn't be overheard. When Lauren stepped in, her hair was its natural blonde color. As soon as she sat down, Cat leaned in, lowered her voice and gave her friend a conspiratorial glance. "So, Lauren, do you have any other secret identities you aren't telling me about? Supergirl? Catwoman? Or do you channel all your superpowers into Cassandra, the sexy pole dancer?"

Her friend blushed. She leaned in as well, speaking quietly. The way she scanned the room showed how nervous she was to be talking about this. "You really have to keep this a secret." Her face was filled with worry.

Cat nodded, rummaged through her backpack and pulled out the copy of *Cosmo* with the story about Satin. With a theatrical show of seriousness, she placed it on the table, put one hand on it and raised the other. "I swear on the Bible that I will never tell anyone."

Lauren smiled and relaxed.

"Thanks. I'd get thrown off the gymnastics team if anyone at school found out. The irony, however, is that being on the team is how I got into this."

"What do you mean?"

"A friend of mine on the team who'd graduated a couple of years ago was doing it and suggested it to me. I'd been complaining about how exhausted I was trying to handle classes and team practices while working enough hours as a barista to make the money I needed to stay in school. I was so tired it was even affecting my performance in competitions. My friend told her that if I worked at Satin, I could earn enough in a fraction of the time I put in making lattés. Since I did ballet as a kid and was a gymnast, I already had the ability. She showed me how to put together a routine, arranged an audition for 'Cassandra', and the rest was history. She graduated, so now you're the only person at Red Rock who knows."

Cat was overflowing with questions. She'd start with something easy. Hopefully it would give her the nerve to work up to what she really wanted to ask.

"Your parents? Do they know?"

"No. They wouldn't be thrilled to find out. But I'm not keeping it from them because I'm ashamed of what I'm doing. They'd understand how it's just for the money. But that would make them feel like failures because they can't afford to help me more. They live far enough away there's no chance of a surprise visit – and the manager at Satin is really good about letting me work around my schedule whenever we have gymnastic competitions."

Cat nodded. "I know what it's like to have to juggle jobs, scrimp and save to get through school. My undergrad years were totally like that. You do what you have to. I'm *so* lucky I have a graduate fellowship. Even so, I'm trying to finish my degree as soon as I can so I can start paying off my school loans. I understand about the money."

She took a deep breath. *Go ahead. Ask her.* She opened her mouth just as the waiter brought their meals. Lauren turned their conversation to school. Cat kept trying to make herself get back to asking more about Cassandra.

Lauren finally tapped Cat's water glass with her knife and raised one eyebrow. "I've never seen you fidget so much, Cat. Go ahead and ask. I can see it in your eyes."

Cat blushed. "Am I that obvious?"

"I'll make it easy for you. You want to know how I can do this—perform nearly naked in front of a room full of people and act so sexy."

Cat leaned in closely so she couldn't be overheard. Her eyes widened. "You were amazing. You were beautiful and athletic and sexy all at once. But guys were drooling over you like a piece of meat. How do you do it?"

Lauren moved her empty salad bowl to the edge of the table, folded her hands and thought for a moment.

"Being able to focus on my routine is the easy part, because I compete in gymnastics. I know how to tune out the rest of the world. The bright stage lights also help, because it's hard for us to see what's going on in the audience."

She took a deep breath. "As far as being nearly naked and doing such a sexy routine goes? Well...this is going to sound crazy... I don't know how else to explain it than to say that when I put on my costume, I become someone else. I stop being 'good-girl Lauren' and become 'temptress Cassandra'." Her face turned red, and she looked down at the table. "More than that," she said, almost in a whisper, "I love it."

She looked up with a naughty gleam in her eye. "I'm not going to lie. It's exciting being Cassandra. I love her. She's a piece of me I've never been able to express in any other part of my life. And I'm grateful she's helped me so much financially. I'll miss her when I graduate, get a job and don't have to perform at Satin anymore. Maybe it's because it's so secret, sexy, risky and forbidden, but I enjoy the excitement."

Cat nodded. She poked at her salad with her fork, trying to get up her nerve again. She ordered herself to ask. She took a sip of water and swallowed, but the words stuck in her throat. *Lauren does pole dancing because she needs the money. She's a gymnast. It makes sense. I'm just caught up in some depraved fantasy.*

When Lauren continued, it got her off the hook.

"But enough about Cassandra. I'm glad you found out, because I wanted to tell you about her the other day. In fact, the Plan B I wanted to suggest for developing upper body strength was you learning pole dancing. But then I would have had to tell you about me at Satin, and I wasn't ready."

Cat's eyes became like saucers. She choked on the last bit of her sandwich and grabbed her glass of water.

When Cat was okay, Lauren continued. "Sorry... I shouldn't have sprung that on you like that. I'm not talking about you stripping at Satin, so don't get all freaked out. I'm simply suggesting pole dancing — with your clothes on — to develop upper body strength. You *did* say you'd do anything to avoid doing weights in the gym. You must have seen that these routines take a lot of strength. And I promise it's fun. I have a practice pole in my apartment. I can't guarantee to turn you into a gymnast, but I can help you put together a series of moves that will be a fun resistance routine. Since I climb rocks myself, I know exactly which muscle groups to target. Pole dancing will give you the right kind of upper body strength. Then you'll feel more confident dealing with your fear of heights. Deal?"

Secretly relieved, Cat was touched at how wonderful a friend Lauren was. She not only trusted her with her secret, but she was also offering to help her achieve her dream of doing the groundbreaking research she had her heart set on. And Lauren didn't need to know the other reason Cat was curious about what it was like being Cassandra.

"Deal!"

* * * *

Lauren developed a series of basic moves and exercises Cat could do to her favorite songs, and she let her use the practice pole in her apartment whenever she was in class, at gymnastics practice or working at Satin. She insisted, however, that Cat dress differently than she did for climbing. She had her wear yoga shorts and a tight, sleeveless tank top. "This isn't like the gym. No one is going to see you. And you can't do this in those loose-fitting track pants and baggy, long-sleeve jerseys you wear. All that cloth will get in the way."

Cat made great progress over the next eight weeks because she found it so much more fun than lifting weights. Using Lauren's pole felt more like playing and dancing than working out, so she didn't mind the long hours she put in.

As she got stronger, she also felt more of the sexual thrill she'd experienced when she'd watched Cassandra that night. She started making the routine sexier. Because she was alone, she let herself play with her fantasy of stripping in front of a bunch of horny guys. She felt silly, but even pretending to have the courage to do it made her feel better about herself.

Turning on a room full of strangers by teasing them as she took off her clothes was the exact opposite of the 'nice girl' Cat was supposed to be. She secretly yearned to be so wild that she'd shock even herself at what she might do. But she was terrified what people would think if they knew about her hidden desires. Being alone in Lauren's apartment made her feel safe enough to let her inner bad girl take over. She'd get so turned on that as soon as she was finished, she'd rush home, pull out her favorite toy and enjoy the *best* orgasms.

As Cat got more proficient and more confident, the sexual thrill got even stronger. She began wearing less. She moved to black bun huggers and a tight red sports bra. Next, she went online and found a sparkling gold stripper's bra and G-string set.

Cranking the music all the way up, she would lose herself in the strong beat, get increasingly aroused and fantasize that she was on the stage at Satin. Because Lauren's apartment was empty, she could be as outrageously sensual as she wanted.

One day, Lauren came home just as Cat finished. "You've been working at this like crazy for weeks. I'd love to see how much you've progressed. What do you say? It's just us dirty girls," she said…and smirked.

It took some prodding, but Cat was so grateful to Lauren that she relented. "Okay. But no criticism, all right?"

"I promise."

She wanted to impress Lauren, so she put everything into her performance. She pushed so hard that her heart hammered in her chest when she'd finished. She stretched out on the floor, exhausted.

"Amazing, Cat! Amazing, beautiful and sexy! You've made so much progress in such a short time. I can't tell you how proud I am of you. Next step, Satin!"

Chapter Six

Colin felt better after a long walk along the Thames with his brother. For all the banter the two of them regularly engaged in, Ian was his biggest supporter. And despite the many 'little brother' lectures, Ian accepted him for exactly who he was. By the time they hugged before heading in different directions to their homes, he half-believed Ian's insistence that the right girl really was out there somewhere.

"Trust me. She's real. She's just waiting for you. And don't be surprised if you meet her when you least expect it. In fact, I bet it's sooner than you think. You know me and my intuition. I have a strong feeling the Fates will bring you together very soon."

As Colin continued walking, he resolved to turn a page in his life. He decided to be more responsible in his dealings with women and less of a pain in the ass to his aunt. *Who knows? Maybe virtue really does get rewarded.* He pulled out his phone and canceled his date with Debra. He patted himself on the back for being mature and responsible.

His flat was in an old building that had been beautifully restored. He found the history and majesty of the architecture in his neighborhood uplifting. But his mood dipped as soon as he opened the door and surveyed the huge stack of mail still sitting on his kitchen table. After returning from a dig, he was always surprised at how much business he still conducted via paper.

He decided to get it behind him. He put the kettle on, brewed a pot of tea, put a large waste basket beside the table and sat down.

Junk mail — *toss.*

Catalogues — *toss.*

Magazines — *skim and toss.*

Scholarly journals — *set aside to read later.*

Flyer from the London Symphony — *save for later.*

Pamphlet from the National Gallery with a picture of a brilliantly colored Native American pot on the cover? *Hmmm. That's an unusual exhibition for them.* He sat back and salivated over the description of the special display. He'd recently begun expanding his research on ancient pottery to include the Americas. This was a perfect specimen.

He looked at the ending date of the exhibition, then at his watch. *Damn! Today's the final day, and it's already closed.* However, the announcement mentioned an invitation-only event that evening. It was obviously meant for wealthy and influential individuals being courted as patrons.

He stared at the pottery on the cover, mindlessly tapped his foot a few times, then he headed to his bedroom closet and pulled out his midnight blue Dior tuxedo. *Since I do research in this area, it would surely be wrong to pass up such an opportunity. I owe it to my students.* He smirked.

When he arrived at the stately museum on Trafalgar Square, he was asked for his invitation by the young, well-dressed attendant. Having been around enough of the 'nobility', he knew how to bluff his way in.

"My invitation? Oh, I'm sorry, my good man. Smithers must have it. Smithers is my driver, you know. He's trying to find a safe place to park the Bentley. You understand how it is."

He aimed for the right combination of the imperiousness and uselessness he saw among too many nobles.

"Surely my name is on your list. I'm Colin Fitzwillans Tucker-Smythe the fifth, son of Edgar Newcastle Tucker-Smythe the fourth, Earl of Linden-by-the-Bridge. We've been members and donors for years. Your director and I play polo on a regular basis. We went to Oxford together. We both read Philosophy, Politics and Economics. Oh, the stories I could tell you! He was such a scamp as a student. He went off to the colonies for his Ph.D. while I stayed here to manage the family trust. Here… Let me call him on my mobile, and we'll clear this up. I wouldn't want you to make an exception for me and put your position in jeopardy."

He slowly and carefully searched through all his pockets for his phone. "No… Not here… Maybe this one… No… Sorry, my good man, my mistake… Let me try…"

Meanwhile, the line of people behind Colin continued to grow, and they were murmuring impatiently.

"That's odd," Colin puzzled. "I had it just before Smithers dropped me off. That's it! I must have left it in the Bentley. As soon as Smithers reports to me, I'll have him retrieve it. Or I have a better idea... Why don't you lend me your mobile, and we can call the director? You do know his private number, don't you?" By this time, of course, the elegantly dressed men and women waiting behind Colin were grumbling, and the attendant was flustered.

"That's fine, Lord Fenster Smythe By-the-Bridge," he stammered. "Please go in."

Colin spent an hour viewing the artifacts, dictating copious notes into his phone, and surreptitiously taking prohibited photos. When he finished, he knew he should leave before his deception was discovered. But as he headed for the exit, he was stopped in his tracks.

He spotted a beautiful chestnut-haired woman walking alone through the exhibit.

She was dressed in a surprisingly sexy way for a stodgy archaeological exhibition.

He loved the way the dress revealed what a rounded body she had. Most women he knew would never have worn such a dress because they'd think they weren't thin enough. But he found her hour-glass figure stunning. *Yes. Curved the way a woman should be.*

He was also impressed with how interested she was in the exhibition. She took her time to read the description of each artifact. Then she'd spend a few minutes leaning over the glass case to study the piece carefully. Circling the item, she'd examine it from all angles.

Beautiful, sexy and interested in archaeology. My lucky day!

He was like Odysseus tempted by the Sirens. A familiar, overpowering pull drew him her way. His pulse ticked up, and his pants felt predictably tighter as the blood began rushing from his brain to…elsewhere.

But just as he was about to speak to her, he noticed a silver-haired woman who resembled Aunt Clarissa. He remembered his resolution. He'd meant the promise he'd made to his aunt to do better. So, he stopped to consider whether there was any reason not to approach this goddess before him.

If a woman so gorgeous were connected to the University, I would know it. In that case, she's not off-limits.

The confidence with which she carried herself in such a provocative dress suggested she was in her mid-twenties. *Okay. Old enough.*

No wedding or engagement ring. *Available.*

"Good evening, Miss. Are you enjoying the exhibition?"

When she turned to answer, he was treated to the sexiest brown eyes he'd ever seen. They were deep, deep, chocolate with tiny flecks of gold. The contrast was stunning. His breath caught.

"*Oui, monsieur.* Thank you for asking." She had a heavy French accent. "*Et vous?* Do you enjoy it?" Her open face and friendly smile were disarming.

French! I love French women. They're so…French!

He took her hand, bowed and kissed it. "*Je suis enchanté de faire votre connaisance, mademoiselle. Bienvenue à notre museé.*" The way her eyes danced when he looked back up told him she was used to getting such attention from men — and loved it. He was impressed she wasn't at all startled at being approached by a stranger. Her confidence only made her more appealing.

"Please, *monsieur*. When I am in England, *seulement* English. You will help me improve, *non*?"

"I shall be delighted. In fact, I am an archaeologist from University College." He handed her his card. "It would be my honor to give you a private tour of the artifacts. Ancient pottery is my specialty."

While he was all courtesy and propriety on the surface, Colin was never one to hide how attractive he found a gorgeous woman — his tone and demeanor, the way he continued to hold her hand, the fire in his eyes, which he made no effort to conceal. She couldn't miss that his offer to be her tour guide was a way for him to spend time with her.

She hesitated for a moment, scanning the crowd as though she were searching for someone. When she turned her attention back to him, the spark in her eyes spoke volumes. Yet she hesitated. "I am not sure that is such a good idea, *monsieur*." He noticed what seemed to be a slightly naughty smile and just a hint of blushing.

A real coquette. Flirty, sexy and a touch of innocence. But does that smile mean she doesn't trust me...or, better yet, herself?

"I am sorry, *mademoiselle*, if I implied something inappropriate. I meant only that a tour would be excellent practice for your English." He looked at her sternly and wagged his finger. "I guarantee that our time together will be entirely educational and not in the least enjoyable. I promise to be such a strict teacher that if you make too many mistakes, I will punish you."

They both laughed. Then she looked directly into his eyes.

"Do I understand you right, *monsieur*? You are saying you will..."

The sexy look she gave him while she paused made him gulp.

"...*punish* me?"

He was stunned — in the best possible way.

Fucking brilliant!

"But of course, *mademoiselle*." He made clear what he was suggesting. "What kind of a teacher would I be if I failed to discipline a student when she makes mistakes?"

Her mischievous smile said she approved.

"*Bien sur, monsieur*. I am Danielle. For the sake of improving my English, I put myself in your hands." She took one of said hands and examined it closely. "Your large, strong hands." She winked, took his hand and intertwined their fingers. "Lead me where you will, *Monsieur le Professeur*." And, *Monsieur le Professeur*, these pieces are fascinating. Perhaps you can tell me more about them..." She looked at him coyly and whispered in his ear, "*after*."

Her boldness made him stop in his tracks.

"Oh, *monsieur*, my English! It is so poor." She put a hand over her mouth. "I meant... *later*. Perhaps we can meet *later* — for coffee tomorrow? — and you can tell me more."

He chuckled at the game. "Of course. *Later*... tomorrow." He winked.

There was so much sexual tension between them that Colin could barely contain himself. He was relieved when they entered the final room of the collection to see the piece of pottery from the cover of the catalog. But this time, something about the object held his gaze even more than the enchanting Danielle.

He studied the piece. It was a reddish-orange water jug with symbols running all the way around it. It was remarkably well-preserved and the colors were striking. The white lines were brilliant. The black-and-gray shapes were rich in their darkness. The blue symbols — *Blue? With those symbols?*

He opened the exhibition's catalog and read the description. "*This is the best preserved, but most controversial piece in this exhibit. Discovered here in Sedona, Arizona, its shape and designs are consistent with the earliest pottery in that area, c. 2500 B.C.E. Carbon dating of organic material from inside the object, however, places it 2500 years earlier. Most archaeologists say this must be a mistake because there is no evidence of any tribe living in that part of Arizona at that time. While the scientists argue this out, we hope you appreciate the beauty of this object.*"

He looked back at the jug and frowned. *Not only was there no pottery in that area before 2500 BCE, but that blue is impossible to make in that climate. The only way the carbon dating can be accurate is —*

His eyes widened as he recognized the central symbol. His heart sped up. He slowly shook his head. *This is astonishing! How could anyone have missed that? The combination of this color with that symbol is possible only if...* He took a small black notebook out of his pocket and flipped through it until he found what he was looking for. *The myth that grad student in the States talked about at the conference. I wish I'd heard her. Hmmm. Could it actually be more than a myth?*

As they finished touring the exhibit, he suggested that since it was such a beautiful evening, they should take a walk outside. Trafalgar Square at night, with its fountains lit up, was stunningly romantic.

Colin took Danielle's hands in his and feigned shock. "*Mademoiselle!* Your hands are freezing! The night is cooler than I thought. I insist you allow me to take you where we can find some brandy to warm you up." He put his coat around her and flagged a taxi. A few minutes later, they were at Colin's favorite watering hole—the bar at the five-star Rosewood London Hotel. Conveniently, his family kept a suite there.

The location was 'romance central'. The magnificent Edwardian building was bathed in light. As they walked from the cab across the courtyard and toward the entrance, the din of the city faded behind them. When they stepped into the bar, Danielle sighed.

He could hardly wait to discover this beautiful woman's desires. He was desperate to satisfy himself by burying his throbbing cock into her wet pussy. But first he needed to take her—body and soul—to new heights of ecstasy.

Chapter Seven

Cat sat with Lauren on the couch as Lauren poured wine into their glasses.

"Me strip at Satin?" Cat laughed. "In your dreams."

"I'm serious. I honestly think you should try it in real life."

Cat looked at her friend, expecting the punch line. Lauren's expression remained serious.

"I mean it. I think it's important you do this."

The very idea of being on the stage at Satin made panic flood through her body. Cat shot to her feet. Her heart pounded. Beads of sweat appeared on her forehead. She began pacing furiously back and forth. "Are you crazy? I can barely keep it together when I present a research paper in front of an audience of academics. And you want me to strip in front of a bunch of horny guys! Just thinking about doing this at Satin makes me petrified." She held out her hand. "Look... My hand is shaking from just talking about it."

Lauren got up, led her back to the couch and put her arm around her shoulder. "Take a breath, Cat. You don't have to do anything you don't want to. But the fact that this terrifies you so much is precisely why you need to do it." Cat looked at her quizzically and frowned. "You want to get over your fear of public speaking and being terrified of heights, right?"

Laughing, Cat pointed at Lauren's wine glass. "If you think there's some connection between pole dancing and fear of heights, you've had way much to drink. That pole at Satin is, what, ten feet high? I need to be able to climb hundreds."

"I'm not explaining it right. Tell me again what you feel when you think of actually performing at Satin."

Cat's body tightened, and her eyes opened wide. "You have to ask? Terror! Panic! Fear! And that's just for openers."

"Precisely. It scares the pants off you. So, don't you think that figuring out how to do something that terrifies you *on the ground* will help you handle fear when you're two hundred feet up?"

Cat leaned back into the couch and frowned. "I never thought of it like that." She sat quietly as she closed her eyes and thought. She opened her eyes, looked at Lauren and scrunched up her face. "I *hate* that you're making me think I should actually do this." Then she shook her head, getting anxious again. "No. Even if you're right, it's just not me."

Her friend reached for the bottle and refilled their glasses. "No, Cat, it *is* you," Lauren pushed back gently. "You're a fighter. You don't back down from your fears. I know it will be hard, but I want you to trust me."

"I do trust you, Lauren. You know that. But this would be *too* hard."

"Look. You're just focusing on the fear — on how bad it could feel. But there's another side as well. Maybe it would help if I told you how it went with me after I got past the fear.

"At first, I'd get turned on from the sense of power I got knowing I could make the guys hard within a minute of walking on stage. But when I noticed *couples* in the audience, it made me want the women to feel something of the power *I* felt. Some women think strip clubs demean women and that we're letting ourselves be viewed as objects. I don't see it that way. The women coming to Satin are open-minded. I'm an athlete. I'm proud of my body — how it looks and what it can do. I think all women should be proud of their bodies and love how sexy they are — no matter what they look like.

"If all that happens after watching me is some woman in the audience gets inspired to go home and dance around naked for herself to her favorite song, that's great. If she feels like putting on a show for her guy, that's even better. And maybe after she finishes and is sitting on his lap stark naked, she says, 'Okay, bucko, now it's your turn. Let's see what you've got and what you can do with it!'"

Cat and Lauren howled at the image of a woman treating her guy as a boy-toy.

"We may have 'come a long way, baby' in some things, Cat, but look at all the times some girl is called a whore, slut or tramp just because of how she's dressed. You could imagine the response if she made the mistake of saying publicly that she enjoys sex. You don't hear guys getting reamed when they say they like getting laid, do you? No, that's the sign of a 'real man'.

You don't hear anyone say that the threesome fantasy that absolutely *every* man has means all guys are twisted. So why the double standard? Being watched stripping is one of women's top fantasies. I get to live it out as Cassandra, *and* I try to make the women in the audience feel it's okay to be as sexy as they want to be."

Cat sat quietly again. Her feelings were all over the place. Just discussing the idea of stripping at Satin terrified — and aroused — her. And if it would actually help her conquer her fear of heights and her dread of getting in front of an audience, she didn't want to close her mind to the idea.

"I can't deny that part of this sounds exciting, Lauren. A piece of me would love to be able to do that. But the rest of me could never work up the nerve to walk on stage. I'd get so nervous I'd pass out before I even got to the pole. Also, I'd always worry my parents would somehow find out. If they did, they'd never speak to me again. If anyone at the university found out, I'd be dead professionally. My career as an archaeologist would be over before it began. That feels scarier than my fear of heights."

"*Right!*" Lauren said excitedly. "That's the point! That's why you *have* to do this! Didn't you take Psych 101?"

Cat laughed. "Psych 101? Now you're really reaching. What does that have to do with anything?"

"Remember that list of everybody's top fears and how public speaking was usually right at the top, with dying being second?"

"Right. So?"

"You can be sure that if anybody had asked, fear of public pole dancing with no more than a G-string on with your career hanging in the balance while worrying about whether your conservative parents will find out would be a whole lot more intense than fear of public speaking. If you can do *that*, don't you think handling *any* fear — including fear of falling off a cliff — is going to be easier? Trust me, Cat. I honestly believe this will help. I think you should at least give it a try." Then Lauren did her best female 'evil witch' impersonation. "Yield to temptation, my pretty. Give in to your inner tramp. Join me, and our naughty asses will rule the world."

Cat had to laugh. She appreciated that Lauren was trying to help. She got up and hugged her. They sat back down on the couch and talked some more. The longer they went, the more Cat's resolve to do whatever she needed to make her discovery came to the surface.

Cat agreed to give it a try — as long as Lauren promised to help her make sure no one could recognize her. She and Lauren discussed different costumes, music and personas until they came up with something Cat was comfortable with.

Chapter Eight

Colin had never been with a woman wearing nipple rings before. *And in the shape of little hearts. She's a secret romantic.* He couldn't wait to take Danielle's advice and explore. "A work of art and a mystery. You are indeed from heaven!" Sucking her right nipple, he was rewarded with a quick shriek of delight.

Yes! I've died and gone to heaven!

As he caressed and kissed her ample breasts, she sighed deeply.

She took them in her hands and pressed both nipples into his mouth. She moved them around so that they were being grazed by his teeth. Taking the hint, he nipped them lightly. "*Plus fort. Mordre plus fort,*" she groaned.

He happily complied. As he carefully pressed his teeth into her stiff pink peaks, she whimpered in delight.

His pulse was racing. His hard cock strained against its confinement. He had to force himself not to rip off the rest of her gown and plunge his shaft into what he knew would be a lusciously tight, warm pussy. But it was a matter of honor to him that she came first. And that meant...

"So now, I search for more treasures."

Kneeling down in front of her, he teased her by inching the rest of the red fabric down over her hips. As each new patch of snowy white flesh appeared, he welcomed it with a kiss. A diamond-studded belly button ring appeared. He circled it with kisses, which caused her to giggle. As the cloth dropped lower and revealed more alabaster skin, the luscious, musky aroma of her sex got stronger. Unable to wait any longer, he pushed her dress all the way off. *What's this?* Looking up, he smiled broadly. "And what have we here?"

She stepped back and proudly let him admire her decorated body. Not only did she have no pubic hair, but a pink tattoo occupied the spot where it had been. He recognized it as the Sanskrit symbol for 'joy'. He kissed her smooth mound repeatedly and ran his stiff tongue along her slit. She gasped in response.

"*Très sexy, mademoiselle*," he said, his voice getting darker and his breathing heavier.

He buried his head between her legs and inhaled deeply. He groaned loudly at her intriguing scent. He lifted one of her legs over his shoulder, grabbed her behind with both hands and pulled her toward him. As she steadied herself, her legs spread wide, revealing her wet pink sex — complete with a genital piercing.

He leaned back, looked up into her face and gave her a naughty smile. "This is a truly delightful discovery, *mademoiselle*. You are indeed a *very* bad girl — and I am a very lucky man."

She answered by impatiently pressing his head into her warm lips.

Because every woman tasted different, he couldn't wait to discover Danielle's unique flavor. He enjoyed the sweetness and slowly ran his wide tongue up and down the sensitive flesh. "You are delicious, *mon choux*."

She groaned loudly and pressed herself against his mouth. As he enthusiastically kissed, sucked and nibbled her lips, she squealed loudly in delight.

Playing with the stud, he discovered it rested right on her clitoris.

She trembled so much that she had trouble standing up. "*Oh, mon Dieu!*"

He held her firmly in place and tortured her by exploring every inch of her sex with his tongue. He sucked her lips. He teased her by probing her opening. When he found a spot that sent her squeals higher, she squirmed — pressing her cunt, hungry for just the right kind of attention, against his mouth. He held her against him and drank her sweet juices with the desperation of someone just rescued from a desert. He moaned loudly, showing his joy.

As he licked the entire length of her sex, her breathing got fast and deep. When he settled on her clitoris, her body tightened. She grabbed his shoulders harder. When she exploded, the passionate, inarticulate noises that burst from her mouth were a mélange of primitive hunger and relief.

He held her shaking body. When her breathing slowed, he put her leg on the floor.

She exhaled, stepped back and leaned against the wall to steady herself. She ran her hands through her hair, reached up and stretched. With a look of feline satisfaction, she sighed and eyed at him seductively.

Colin was transfixed by the glorious sight of this naked woman adorned with her magnificent necklace, perched on stilettos, leaning against the wall. Everything about the way she held herself said she was ready for more.

"You have a most talented tongue, *mon Professeur*. I must repay you. Now you will let me fuck you?"

Looking shocked, he shook his head. "*You*, fuck *me*? *Mais non, mademoiselle*! A gentleman never lets a lady fuck him. That would be rude. And we British are nothing if not polite. No, I am here for your pleasure. So, I will fuck *you*."

She frowned. "You English may prize manners, but we French—especially French women—insist on *égalité*. At the very least, since you undressed me, I must do the same for you."

She walked behind him and removed his jacket from his broad shoulders. When she took the time to fold it and put it on a chair, it was clear she was going to go slowly and torture him. She undid his vest, smirking as she folded it and placed it neatly on top of his jacket. She removed one shoe, one sock, the other shoe, the other sock, and added them to the pile. After unsnapping his gold cufflinks, she finished undoing his shirt. But before removing it, she nuzzled the light-colored hair coating his pecs. Sighing, she then kissed each of his well-defined abdominals.

"*Un…deux…trois…quatre…cinq…six…et.*"

Abruptly changing her pace, she quickly unbuckled his belt and jerked his trousers and navy boxer briefs down. His stiff, red-veined cock sprang out from its straw-colored nest.

"*Et mon préféré*...my favorite...*sept!*"

She licked the pre-cum from its tip. His cock jerked when her pink tongue made contact.

"You have a beautiful penis, *mon Professeur*. Let us see — "

She stood up and leaned against the wall. Her face took on a dark and ravenous look. She ran her hand down her stomach and unabashedly caressed her sex. She was testing him — seeing if he was game for what she had in mind. He'd seen that look from sexually aggressive women before, but never from a woman so young. It said, "*I fuck only one way — hard and without mercy. Can you handle that?*"

Stepping out of the fabric pooled around his ankles, he fished his wallet from his pants and removed a condom. He quickly sheathed his throbbing shaft and answered her challenge. He pushed her hard against the wall, her nipple rings scratching his chest. Grabbing her waist, he lifted her.

She shrieked at being pinned against the hard surface. She wrapped her legs around him, bit into his shoulder and dug her blood red, razor-like nails into his back.

He roared like an animal and gave her an expression meant to show her that she would pay for what she'd done.

As he forcefully plunged his cock into her, she moaned loudly. She squeezed her legs hard and pulled him deeper inside her. "*Baise-moi, cheri! Baise-moi!*"

He pounded into her so intensely that he grunted with each thrust. Nevertheless, the look on her face was ecstatic. Their bodies were so coated with sweat that they slapped when he drove into her.

Grunting, she squeezed her legs around him so hard that he cried out like an angry animal. But the pain made him thrust even harder.

Her rapid breathing and high-pitched squeals signaled that she was about to come. "*Oh, mon Dieu!*" Her sex gripped his cock and pulsed forcefully. "*Oh, mon Dieu!*" she screamed again as she grabbed him tighter.

He was in heaven. This was one of life's best moments — balls deep in a woman's pussy as it gripped and exploded on his cock. The condom prevented him from feeling her wetness, but her warmth and powerful spasms penetrated the latex. His penis couldn't help but swell, twitch in response and explode. It was pure joy.

The sounds they made as they came were guttural and primitive.

As his breathing slowed, he kissed her tenderly. As they continued kissing, Colin grew more passionate. As far as he was concerned, what had passed between them had just been an appetizer.

He pulled out of her then playfully threw her over his shoulder. She laughed as he carried her from the salon to the bedroom. He tossed her onto the bed, took a fresh condom from the bedside table and reloaded. As he joined her on the bed, however, she pushed him sharply in the chest. When he fell onto his back, she straddled him, facing his feet. She positioned herself on top of him so he could not move. Her pussy was just out of reach of his mouth, but he struggled to reach it nonetheless. He drank in the delightful, sinful aroma of her sex.

He felt her rip the condom off his cock and slide her full red lips down his shaft. As she enthusiastically took its full length, he gasped at the warm, wet suction. He was about to come again, but then winced as she ran her teeth up and down his cock. She had clearly practiced this form of torture—*pleasure, pain, pleasure, pain*. Finally, she put him out of his misery. She sucked hard, and he jetted his cum into her mouth. Climbing off him, she settled on the bed and gave him a Cheshire Cat grin.

He was so in awe of just how sexy she was, all he could do was nod in appreciation. She bowed back and let him know the challenge had only just begun. "*Monsieur*, have you forgotten that you promised to help me with my English?" she asked coyly. "How will I learn, if you do not make me correct my mistakes? As an English gentleman, are you not a man of your word?"

She is amazing! Sexy and unstoppable!

He donned a very serious expression and wagged his finger at her. "You are correct, *mademoiselle*. I am shirking my duties. It is time you pay the penalty for being such a bad girl." He grabbed her roughly and flipped her so she was on her stomach. He twisted her long brown hair around his hand. Pulling it tight with one hand, he spanked her sharply with the other. She moaned loudly with obvious glee.

"I apologize, *Monsieur le Professeur*. I insulted you by saying you were going to skip my discipline. I am a terrible person as well as a poor student. I deserve your punishment." She pushed her full, round bottom in the air. "Do whatever you think will help me learn. I am at your mercy."

The message was clear. The game was 'strict teacher and bad student'. Colin yanked her mane and swatted her behind hard. She grunted from the impact, then moaned in gratitude.

"*Oui*, young lady. You are my worst student ever. I must discipline you." *Swat!* "Maybe then you will learn to study." *Swat!*

As he continued, her creamy behind grew to a deep rose hue. Every pull on her hair and sharp spank produced a satisfied squeal.

"Oh, *Professeur* Tucker, you make me *so* sorry I did not study my English. Instead, I went to parties with my friends. You must make me feel *very* bad I was such a naughty girl. *Oui*, you must be *très très dur* — very, very hard — on me. I must learn my lesson. You must spank me even harder so I do not forget."

To Colin's surprise — and delight — her pleasure from such a hard spanking brought his cock back to life. *She is so amazingly sexy!* After letting go of her hair, he quickly re-sheathed his dick.

"You are right, *mademoiselle*. I must be very hard on you." Then he struck her burning red ass repeatedly. "If I do not discipline you severely" — *spank* — "you may forget my spanking you" — *spank* — "and go back to your naughty ways" — *spank.* "But I am going to make sure you will not forget" — *spank* — "my *fucking* you."

He grabbed her hips and thrust his hungry penis into her welcoming cunt. She moaned loudly as he growled and pounded hard — again and again. Delighting in the sound of their sweat-drenched flesh slapping together, he increased the force with which he plunged into her.

All she could do was moan.

He leaned forward and put all his weight on her so she was now face-down on the bed. Pinning her arms so she couldn't move, he used his legs to open her wider. With primeval grunts, he drove into her as hard as he could, her excited shrieks telling him she was heading to a climax. She cried at the top of her voice as she peaked and her sex clenched his penis hard. As her pussy spasmed around his cock, he came as well. Their climaxes were so powerful that they both shook then collapsed onto the passion-soaked sheets.

Colin was exhausted but content. The dreamy look on Danielle's face said she was as well.

When they eventually untangled, Colin fetched chilled champagne and a bottle of aloe skin lotion. After a couple of sips, Danielle lay down so he could minister to her brilliantly red ass. She winced as he worked the lotion into her burning skin, then sighed as it seemingly began to cool her flesh.

Reflecting on the evening, he continued to marvel at her. Despite all the women he'd been with, Danielle was the first who burned with the same passion he did. He'd been with her no more than a few hours, but he was already captivated.

"You are extraordinary, Danielle. Beautiful. Intelligent. And you are the sexiest woman I have ever met. I would love to spend more time with you. I am busy at the university tomorrow, but may I take you to dinner?"

She lifted herself up on her elbows so she could turn to look at him. He was surprised to see what looked like a hint of doubt and shame in her face. She'd exuded nothing but confidence so far. *Where is this coming from?*

"You are sure?" She looked down. "Now that you know how much I like *le fucking et le spanking*, you do not think I am *une souillon* — how you say, a slut?"

He was shocked she could think that of herself but suspected that someone had taken his pleasure with her then berated her afterward. He sat down on the other side of the bed so he could look her in the eye.

"Danielle, that is the last thing I would ever think about you." He held her hands tenderly. "Your enjoyment of sex is a sign of how free, strong and healthy you are. Sadly, many people find that intimidating. If any man ever said that to you, I will find him and see that he is horsewhipped...unless he likes that sort of thing. If that were the case, we'd need to find a different punishment."

She laughed, as he'd hoped, and squeezed his hands

"You are a treasure, and I would be honored if you would go to dinner with me."

She beamed. "*Merci, Monsieur le Professeur*. I would love that."

He lay down beside her, took her in his arms, kissed her tenderly and drifted toward unconsciousness. He sighed, enjoying a new sense of hope about his life. *What a perfect night. I can't wait to find out what surprises the morning has for me.*

Surprises, indeed.

Chapter Nine

Since covering her face was essential, Cat chose an elegant, dark blue Venetian Carnivale mask that concealed her entire face. She also used a few tricks to look taller than her diminutive five feet two inches. The illusion of additional height would make it harder to be recognized. She wore five-inch platform stilettos. She braided and pinned up her long black hair. She wore a feathered headpiece that gave her at least six inches. Each feather was a different shade of blue, and she arranged them according to an ancient Native American myth that she had come across in her research. It was a way to honor her heritage and remind her why she was doing this. And since there were no more than six people on the planet who would know about the myth — and none of them were in Arizona — she was sure this wouldn't risk revealing her identity.

She wore an iridescent, long-sleeved half-bodysuit of the same color — perfect for her light bronze skin. She decided to leave her legs bare to make removing the costume easier. The garment had a wide lace V that started from her shoulders, ran across her breasts and ended caressing her sex. The catsuit's color matched her mask. Under it was a tiny blue G-string. As an additional precaution against being recognized, she added a pair of temporary tattoos — a chain of dolphins that started at the mid-point of the outer edge of each breast, curved down and ended underneath. Finally, she spritzed the rich and spicy perfume Opium in a few strategic places. Cat had always felt it was too heavy a scent for her to wear, but it seemed perfect for the persona she had in mind.

When she stood in front of the mirror, it was the oddest sensation. A stranger looked back. *This* woman looked strong, confident and sexy — a woman who lived life on her own terms. It took her minutes of staring at the reflection before she could accept that it really was her she was looking at. She was 'The Contessa', and she found the sense of power exciting.

The music she'd chosen was Ravel's *Bolero*. The rhythm and pace of the piece matched exactly what she had in mind for her routine. It started with slow foreplay, got more intense then crescendoed at the end. The piece's climax was perfect for her finale.

She'd chosen 'The Contessa' as her stage name. Like Lauren's 'Cassandra', it was a persona — a character she became. The Contessa was elegant, sexy, powerful. Cat had even come up with an entire backstory that helped her truly *be* the character. She'd made sure that The Contessa personified traits Cat lacked but desperately wished she had. She knew it was silly, but she hoped that pretending to have them might help her actually develop them.

She'd deliberately chosen a persona that had no connection with her Native American heritage to throw off anyone who might look for clues to figure out who she was. The Contessa lived in sixteenth-century Venice, where she was the most desired—hence, most powerful—courtesan. She was renowned for her unabashed delight in sex, which led to her being remarkably skilled in the bedroom.

Cat loved the idea that The Contessa was in charge of her own destiny—and especially that she was an expert at sex. Cat saw herself as exactly the opposite—not very experienced and uncertain about the future. She wondered whether she could actually pretend to be The Contessa.

* * * *

Lauren helped Cat perfect her routine and arranged for an audition with Satin's manager. Cat passed with flying colors.

For a couple of weeks before her scheduled debut, she went to Satin with Lauren a few times to see if she could pick up any pointers. She observed from backstage so none of the regulars in the audience could see her. When she realized who was usually there, however, she got so unnerved that she seriously considered changing her mind. Even though Satin was on the other side of Sedona from the university, guys from Red Rock—students *and* faculty—were there all the time. She was terrified that someone would recognize her.

The day of her debut at Satin, she called Lauren in a panic. "I can't do this, Lauren. I'm terrified. But I can't *not* do it. I have to go on stage, but I can't. I don't know what to do." She was so upset that she was literally gasping for air. "If I can ju —"

"I'll be right over," Lauren interrupted. "Try to relax. Take deep breaths."

As soon as Cat opened her front door for Lauren, she said tearfully, "I can't do this! The idea of guys drooling over me as I take my clothes off repulses and terrifies me. If anyone from Red Rock recognizes me, my career will be over before it even begins. But I *have* to do this. I *need* to! But I *can't*!"

Lauren gave her a big hug. "Take a breath and let's talk, Cat." They sat down at the kitchen table. Cat blew her nose, wiped her eyes and tried to regain her composure.

"You're right. There are risks here. If you can face your fears, however, you can conquer them. But if you don't even try, will you be okay with that? Not doing serious rock climbing and presenting your research? What about when someone else uses your theories and makes whatever discoveries you would have? Or worse, what if no one does, and you were the only one who ever *could* have? Hasn't your dream been to be the archaeologist who makes that discovery?"

Cat got up and paced back and forth. "It still is. You have no idea how *much* it is. And I'm desperate to get past my fear of heights. But look at how much I'm shaking." She held out her hand. "You know that if I'm that unsteady, I'll fall off the pole and get hurt — never mind look stupid."

Lauren nodded. "Let me think." She closed her eyes and tapped her fingers on the table. "Sit back down, Cat. I have an idea."

Cat complied.

"Okay, you're scared. I get that. Maybe it would help if you told me *why* climbing means so much to you. I know how serious you are about your work. But you've never told me what's so important that you need to conquer paralyzing fear."

"You're right. I haven't. In fact, I haven't told anyone—because everyone will think I'm crazy."

"You mean as crazy as someone suggesting that stripping and pole dancing are excellent preparation for academic research?"

The two of them laughed.

"Okay, I guess we entered 'Crazyville' a while ago."

"Come on, Cat. Trust me."

She took a deep breath. "It has to do with my mother."

"The nurse?"

"No, my *real* mother." Cat began tearing up and fingered the arrowhead-shaped black obsidian attached to a thick leather thong around her neck. "This stone was in a large animal skin bag in the basket I was found in. There was also a neatly handwritten note that said, 'Please take care of my baby girl, Cocheta White Eagle. My heart is breaking that I cannot be there to protect her. My mother gave me the crystal for protection. Please give it to my daughter.' It's my only connection to her, so I rarely take it off."

"'Cat' is short for 'Cocheta'? I'd always assumed 'Catherine'."

"Most people think that. I even told my department that's what it is."

"But 'Cocheta' is such a beautiful name. Why don't you correct people?"

Cat threw up her hands. "Because whenever anyone hears I'm Native American, they ask me all about my heritage. But it's a total mystery to me. I know nothing about my parents, where I really came from or who I am. 'Cocheta' means 'stranger,' and that's what I've felt like I am my whole life. When I was in high school, I contacted every tribal elder in Montana for help. They knew nothing about a woman at that time having a daughter and giving her up. The most important reason I came to Red Rock was their Native American Studies program. I hoped to find some answers."

"And did you?"

Cat took another deep breath. "Here's the crazy part. My first week here, I hiked high into the mountains. We don't have mountains like this in Montana — not with so much red in the stones. I was at this amazing spot, admiring the view. It was so peaceful and quiet. It was just me and nature. I'd never felt happier. Suddenly, I heard an eagle shriek. I looked up and saw this white eagle soaring above me. It was the first time I'd ever seen one. I was shocked. I didn't think they lived here. As I was intently watching the bird, I heard a woman right behind me call my name. I was frightened because she must have snuck up on me. I turned around and no one was there. But I'd spun so fast that I fell over. My head banged into the rocks, and I was knocked out. When I came to, a beautiful woman was looking after me. She helped me up, then pointed to a ledge we could sit on. There was something incredibly familiar about her and we had a conversation.

"*'I know you. Don't I?'* I asked her."

"*'Yes, I'm your mother. I've been watching over you since I died — just after I left you in the basket. We've been given permission to have this conversation, so I can tell you about your path,'* she replied."

"I'd hit my head so hard that it was throbbing. She touched it and the pain went away. But I felt like I was in a fog. *'If you're my mother, please tell me about who I am.'*"

"She held my hands. *'You are Cocheta for the same reason all the women in our family for a thousand years have been Cocheta. We are strangers to everyone because our tribe has been forgotten. You are the last survivor. You and your partner will keep the people from being forgotten forever. That is your path.'*

"*'My partner? Who is that?'*"

"She ignored my question and pointed at my necklace. *'I'm so happy you wear this. It's how we connect with each other. Do you still have the bag?'*

"*'Yes.'*"

"*'Good. The key to your path is inside it. The women of our family have been its guardians. Protect the key until you are ready to use it. I must go now. Know how much I love you. Now rest, little one. Remember, I am always with you.'*"

"She touched my cheek. It was amazing. I felt completely enveloped by her love for me. Then I felt an overpowering desire to sleep. The next thing I knew, I was waking up on the rocks with a huge bump on my head and a killer headache. I was alone, of course."

Lauren wiped a tear away. "That's beautiful. What do you think happened?"

"The Native American in me says I had a vision." Then she chuckled. "But the scientist in me says that I was knocked out and had a weird dream, courtesy of my unconscious."

"I vote for vision," Lauren said enthusiastically. "Do you know what it means?"

"I didn't at first. I went back and made sure there wasn't an old key—or anything else—stuck in the animal skin bag. There wasn't. So, I didn't know what to think. But a few weeks into the semester, one of my professors was talking about Native American myths. One was about a so-called 'lost tribe' — an ancient people who lived in these mountains thousands of years ago in an almost utopian community. Peaceful. Harmonious. Wealthy. My teacher made it pretty clear that he thought the idea was silly. But he did concede that there was one piece of *possible* evidence that baffled everyone."

"What was that?"

"A set of symbols carved into a rock dating from a time long before anyone supposedly lived in the mountains. A myth said there was a map to the wealth of a lost tribe. Someone had run across the symbols about a hundred years ago. As word spread, treasure hunters chiseled the rock out. All that's left is a grainy photograph of the figures taken by the first archaeologist who paid any attention to them. My teacher passed out copies, and he explained how they didn't make sense. No one's been able to decode them. He thought it was all a massive fraud — a good bar story at best."

"Lost tribe? Is that what your mother was referring to?"

"I couldn't help but think that. Then a couple of classes later, my teacher was describing unique Native American traditions. He mentioned one in which a tribe wrote all their most important communications on the *inside* of animal skin sacks. When he said that, I realized what my mother meant when she said my path was *inside* the envelope. I was so excited that I pretended to be sick and left class. I went home and turned the bag inside out. There were symbols like the ones in the photograph."

"Wow! Is it another copy of the map? Do you think your mother was telling you your path is to find the tribe's treasure? Wouldn't that be great? And what about her reference to a 'partner'?"

She shook her head. "I have no idea."

"I bet it's a romantic partner — the love of your life! You'll be rich, famous and madly in love in one stroke."

Cat smirked. "You read a lot of romance novels, don't you?"

"Sorry. I get carried away. Did you show your professor what you found?"

"Right," Cat laughed. "I'm a freshman who walks into her professor's office, tells him about a vision I had involving my dead mother and shows him symbols she pointed me to. And, oh yeah, I'm the last member of the lost tribe he joked about in class. That's a great start to an academic career!"

"What did you do?"

"I kept everything to myself. But I started working on trying to figure out what it all meant. I told my advisor I was really interested in Native American *mythology*. That way I could work on the 'Lost Tribe' story without people thinking I was crazy."

"Okay, but where does climbing and your fear of heights come into the picture?"

"When I was researching a paper a couple of years ago, I found a footnote in an article that said there were rumors of something akin to a Rosetta Stone for Native American symbols from a bunch of tribes hidden high in the mountains. It was supposedly impossible to reach unless you were one of a tribe's most expert climbers."

Lauren nodded her head. "Got it. You want to find it and decode what your mother left you. Only *if* it exists, it's hundreds of feet off the ground."

"Which brings us to why I *have* to do this tonight. And why I'm in a panic that I *can't.* You convinced me that performing at Satin would help me conquer my fear. And if I can, I have to do this. But now I'm afraid of not only *going* on stage, but of being *unable* to. I'm afraid that if I can't, I'll never be able to climb and learn the truth about my people."

"Okay," Lauren replied calmly, "I hear how important this is to you. And I promise we'll figure things out. If it's not tonight at Satin, no big deal. We'll find another way, and you can forget about Satin. But no matter what, I *promise* you'll climb."

Cat sighed deeply. Her face relaxed.

Then Lauren reached across the table and took her hands. "But this is about more than getting over your fears, isn't it? What about that other side of you that you've gotten in touch with being The Contessa? That woman who isn't ashamed to display her body? Who gets turned on by the idea of letting men and women see her virtually naked? Who is so powerful she can inspire other women to conquer their inhibitions? What about her? How is she feeling right now?"

Cat looked up sheepishly. "Honestly? She's terrified at being found out. My inner tramp is a coward."

"A coward? Are you kidding? I say she's *brave.*"

Cat let out a weak laugh. "*Brave*? That's a joke."

"Look at me, Cat. Tell me the difference between a hero and a coward?"

Cat sighed and sat silently. She had no interest in being on the receiving end of what she was sure was a pep talk Lauren's gymnastics coach had given her at some point.

"Answer me, Cat. It's important."

Cat sighed again. "Fine, a coward is someone like me…terrified. A hero is fearless."

"Wrong," said Lauren strongly. "A hero feels as much fear as the coward. The only difference is that the hero doesn't let the fear stop her. A hero fights through the fear. That's why I think you're brave. You're a fighter, Cat. You're my hero."

Tears welled up in Cat's eyes in response to Lauren's loving support.

"Look at all the fears you've faced to come this far. I think you owe it to yourself to do this at least once. If it's too much, you don't have to do it again. But you've worked too hard and come too far to quit without even trying."

"Cat, I'd love to see my hero on the stage at Satin — at least one time — to see you prove to yourself you're bigger than any fear. You need to look fear in the eye and kick its ass — with your ass, tits and every other part of your sexy body."

Cat got up, gave her friend a big hug and walked over to where her costume was hanging on the door. She looked at it silently for a few moments, then she took it down and turned to Lauren. "Okay, let's do this. Let's kick the shit out of fear."

After helping Cat get ready, Lauren hugged her and said, "Take a deep breath. Everything will be fine. You just need to know what to expect. I remember my first time. First, you're going to be more scared walking out to the pole than you've ever felt before. Once you get to your spot, you're going to feel like you're too afraid to move. But I promise that as soon as the music starts and you focus on your routine, the fear will go away, and everything will be fine. Trust me. Most important? When you're on that stage, you're The Contessa, and you're at your *palazzo*. So, *buona fortuna*, sweetie. Knock 'em dead."

* * * *

Lauren was right. As soon as Cat stepped onto the stage, she felt terrified — of being watched, criticized, laughed at, looking stupid, feeling ridiculous, losing her grip on the pole, being recognized and a million other things she couldn't name but *felt* throughout every cell of her body. With each step toward the pole, her dread surged to the point she felt lightheaded.

Great. I'm going to faint before I even start.

By the time she grasped the cold metal of the shiny pole, her pounding heart and the cold sweat running down her spine signaled a terror akin to looking into the maw of a horrifying, ravenous monster. She reminded herself that as bad as she felt, this was a safer place than the side of a mountain to experience heart-stopping fear. She waited for the music.

When she heard her introduction — "Ladies and gentlemen, Satin is proud to present The Contessa." — she took a deep breath and commanded herself to relax. The instant she was lit by the spotlight and felt the eyes of everyone in the audience on her, something remarkable happened. It was like a cocoon opened and another woman emerged. Cat's fears evaporated.

She stood perfectly still as the music began. The snare drum and the deep sound of the plucked strings established the rhythmic pattern that would continue throughout the piece and serve as the foundation for all her moves. Only when the flute began playing the piece's famous theme did The Contessa move.

Cat and Lauren had come up with a routine that was the perfect marriage of motion and music. Her first moves echoed the soft sound of the woodwinds as she gracefully twirled around the pole. The initial part of the routine was very ballet-like, but as more instruments came in, she tried to match the sexy, Spanish feel of the music. She let the soft melody carry her.

She could never master 'Cassandra's' ability to remove her catsuit in a single move, so she'd had hers designed so she could take it off one piece at a time — first one sleeve, then the other. Next, as she bent back while holding on to the pole with only her legs, she removed *almost* everything else covering her. All that was left was the lace V that crossed her breasts and kissed her sex.

When the music became louder and sexier, it struck an electric spark inside her. As she moved into the most erotic part of her routine, the spark burst into a flame and ignited something in her body. Unfettered desire. She hungrily ran her hands over her breasts, first over, then under the blue lace.

By then, the audience no longer existed for her. The music, her body's movements and the primal yearning had merged to become a single, remarkably powerful, purely sexual experience. When she pulled off the lace V to reveal just the tiny blue G-string, it was with joyful abandon.

As the music approached its climax, she positioned herself at the top of the pole. And at the height of the crescendo, she let herself fly down the rod with her vee pressed snugly against the shiny metal, screaming in a way to make everyone think she was having an orgasm. As the last note sounded, the lights went out and she lay flat on the stage. She was drenched in sweat. Her heart pounded from the exertion. She gasped to catch her breath.

The Contessa faded into the background of her consciousness. Cat returned. The room was silent. *Oh no! They thought I was terrible!* She wanted to slink off stage. Then the audience burst into cheers, whistles and applause.

As Cat drank in the reaction, she felt prouder — and more relieved — than she'd ever felt in her life. If she could do this, she could do rock climbing. She acknowledged the ovation with a formal bow to the audience.

When she stepped backstage, Lauren gave her a big hug. *"Spettacolare, la mia Contessa! Assolutamente spettacolare!* You were amazing! Everyone was spellbound. I've never seen anything like that."

They went to the dressing room, where she gulped down a bottle of ice water. "I'm dying to know what it was like," Lauren prodded. "Tell! Tell!"

Cat took off her headdress and shook her head in disbelief. "It's literally indescribable. I-I... I don't know how to put it but to say I *disappeared.* Someone else stepped into my body and took over. God! I wish I were that woman!"

Lauren lit up. "I'm so happy for you!" She laughed. "And trust me... That woman was you!"

The Contessa did five shows that evening. When the music began, Cat's fears melted and her alter ego took her place.

The character was so popular with Satin's clientele that the management asked her to perform nightly.

Cat's classes and research were too demanding for that, however. She would perform only on Friday nights.

She also limited performing because she remained at war with herself about doing it.

While performing, The Contessa felt no fear. But when not on stage, Cat could never shake her worries. She was afraid of falling off the pole and terrified of being recognized. She was apprehensive about being virtually naked in front of a room full of strangers. Part of her could never get used to the idea that she was a stripper. The good news, however, was that she was learning how to focus on the task at hand and push everything else into the background. Her numerous fears didn't go away, but she could manage them.

At the same time, however, she was intensely unsettled by what happened each performance. Her fears would melt, and a strong, sexy woman would command the stage. She found it difficult to believe she had those qualities buried in her somewhere. The Contessa was everything she was not. She dreaded being looked at, but The Contessa loved it. She was positive that in every dictionary, her picture illustrated the word 'insecure', while The Contessa was fearlessly confident. Cat thought of sex as an intensely private matter, but The Contessa displayed her sexuality with pride – and publicly.

But no matter what she felt when she reflected on the experience in quiet moments, it paled in comparison to the incredible sexual rush her performance gave her. Taking her clothes off and teasing the audience with her explicit moves never lost their forbidden thrill. She loved the physicality and sensuality of her routine. And after each dance, she luxuriated in the pleasure.

More importantly, the experience did indeed make her feel ready to attack her fears connected with climbing. Having conquered a figurative mountain, she now had to tackle a real one. Cat eased herself into rock climbing. Since Lauren also climbed, they went together. Lauren became her mentor in this area as well. Cat made consistent progress but she could never entirely get over her fear of heights — especially the first fifty feet. When she got nervous on a climb, Lauren would remind her to take a few deep breaths and relax. If Cat found herself with a very tough challenge, she told herself The Contessa actually was an accomplished climber as well as a skilled courtesan and pole dancer. Cat knew it was silly, but it helped. And her mission to decode the symbols was so strong that she knew she'd be able to handle any climb the mountains threw at her.

Since she was spending so much time studying and climbing, Cat didn't have much of a social life. She didn't party. As long as she danced at Satin, she was nervous about anything that would reveal her secret. Letting any man who might come to Satin see her naked was too big a risk. But none of that bothered her because she knew that in order to make the discoveries she wanted, she had to keep her focus strictly on her research. She would think about a relationship in a few years.

Chapter Ten

The morning sun streaming through the bedroom windows woke Colin. He gazed at the naked young woman beside him. *Even more gorgeous in the light of day. Such perfect, smooth, white skin and a surprisingly young face for someone in her mid-twenties.*

As she turned over in her sleep, he saw how pink her ass still was from being spanked. Sliding over, he kissed each cheek. When he spooned against her, she began to wake. Without a word, she took his hand, pressed it against her breast and ground her behind against him. His shaft stiffened. Her sounds left no doubt how much she wanted him. *She is fucking amazing. Barely awake and she's horny. I love it!*

"*Un moment, chérie.*" He turned to get a condom.

The doors to the room suddenly burst open. A dozen police officers with automatic weapons stormed in. Stunned, Colin froze. A female officer pulled Danielle out of bed, put a robe on her and hurried her out of the room. When the young woman looked at Colin, she mouthed something he wasn't sure he caught right. *Désolé? She's sorry?*

As shocked as *he* was at what was happened, he was stunned that *she* didn't seem surprised. *What's going on?*

As one officer pointed a weapon at him, another threw him most of his clothes and ordered him to dress as quickly as he could. Astonished at what was happening, he was roughly handcuffed, marched down the corridor into the elevator and pushed into a waiting car. He repeatedly asked for an explanation. His guards sat mute, eyeing him warily.

He was taken to New Scotland Yard, led into a room and handcuffed to a cold metal table. He waited for what felt like hours, running every detail of the evening through his mind, searching for anything that would explain what was happening. Looking at his situation objectively, he reasoned he should be more upset. But the situation was so surreal that all he could feel was bafflement. He'd had an unforgettable evening with a beautiful woman — then he'd been awakened by a SWAT team. He couldn't imagine how the two things fit together.

But she wasn't surprised. And what did she try to say to me as she was raced out? He closed his eyes and replayed the scene in his head. He focused on her mouth. *She said 'désolé' — 'sorry.'* Her expression had been one of embarrassment — not shock and surprise. Obviously, there was more to her than he knew.

Who was she? A remarkable, sexy woman, without a doubt. But who else? What secret did her silent apology allude to? All he could do was wait and hope to find out.

Eventually, a middle-aged man wearing a worn navy-blue suit, burgundy tie and serious expression joined him. He sat down, cleared his throat then he took Colin's thin black leather wallet out of an evidence bag and examined its contents.

He pulled out a driver's license and studied it. "Mister...*Tucker*," he said in a Geordie accent, without looking up. He took out another ID. He glanced up and raised his eyebrows. "*Professor* Tucker. University College. Now this is a surprise. What's a smart bloke like you doing sitting handcuffed opposite me?" He sat back and looked at Colin. "I am Detective Chief Inspector Lewis of Scotland Yard. You are in an impossible amount of trouble. Your only hope is to be absolutely honest with me."

"That is entirely my desire, Chief Inspector." Colin schooled his face to stay open, sincere, cooperative, relaxed. Lewis looked puzzled.

The officer pressed a button on a recorder on the table. "This is an interview with Professor Colin Tucker being conducted by DCI Lewis. This is part of an investigation into the alleged kidnapping and sexual assault of Danielle d'Argenteuil, daughter of the French Ambassador to the UK, and the theft of the Josephine Necklace."

Colin's jaw dropped. "Kidnapping! Sexual assault! Theft! The French Ambassador's daughter?"

Lewis nodded. The glint in his eye signaled that he thought he'd just made a career-defining arrest.

Colin shook his head in disbelief. He stared back at Lewis and laughed. "I'm fucked, aren't I?"

"You've been apprehended red-handed with both the ambassador's eighteen-year-old virgin daughter *and* the Josephine Necklace in your bed. Right now, I am your only friend in the entire world. If you confess and tell me everything that happened, I will speak to the prosecutor and see what I can do for you. If you have any confederates with whom you were working — maybe someone who was going to fence the jewels? — this is the time to identify them. Otherwise, these very serious crimes are all on you. This is your only opportunity."

Colin's head was spinning. *Eighteen! The necklace was real? Ambassador's daughter? Fuck!*

Lewis moved Colin's wallet to the right and looked straight at him. His demeanor was professional but friendly.

"I assume your plan was to seduce the virgin and make off with the gem as she slept. It's a shame you got carried away, wore yourself out screwing and overslept. But I've seen how beautiful she is. You let your John Thomas do your thinking for you. It's a pity. Someone so smart at least shouldn't have gotten caught so quickly... Let's begin. How long have you been planning this, and did anyone help you — perhaps someone from the Ambassador's household?"

Colin couldn't believe what he was hearing. "You can't be serious. How would I think I could get away with something like this? A rare piece of jewelry that can neither be displayed nor fenced? Wait! Did you say 'virgin'?" He laughed. "I can assure you, Detective, that girl was anything but innocent."

Lewis's skeptical expression, combined with the way he settled back in his chair, told Colin he was prepared for a long interview.

Just then, the female officer who had taken Danielle away opened the door and beckoned Lewis into the corridor. As the door closed, Colin heard the woman say, "When I got her away from her father and explained — "

The detective returned five minutes later, holding a sheet of paper. His earlier satisfaction was gone. He sat back down and started the recorder again. "I've just been given some new information which raises the possibility that no crime was committed. Professor Tucker, please describe what transpired last night between you and Mademoiselle d'Argenteuil. Begin with your first contact with her."

Colin happily complied. He explained that he'd thought Danielle was considerably older than eighteen. He also reported how she'd refused to answer his questions about who she was and that she'd told him the necklace was a copy. He was gentleman enough to describe their romp in the sheets by saying simply, "We were intimate." The necklace had been in his bed because it must have fallen off when they were making love.

As Colin spoke, Lewis read over the paper in his hand. Then he turned toward the recorder. "Officer Jones and I have conducted separate interviews with Professor Tucker and Mademoiselle d'Argenteuil. Their accounts of last night's events match. We have concluded that no crime was committed, so the suspect will be released."

The detective unlocked Colin's handcuffs. He looked at him grimly.

"Scotland Yard does not like having its time wasted, Professor. You would be wise to make better choices in the future. You may go."

Colin rubbed his wrists. "I don't want seem ungrateful to be free, but would you please tell me what actually happened?"

Lewis gave him an exasperated look. "Do you have children, Professor?"

It struck him as an odd question. "No, why do you ask?"

The detective shook his head and sighed. "If you had a teenage daughter, you would understand this better. I suppose you deserve to be forewarned, in case you ever do.

"The young woman was upset with her father for making her go to another boring diplomatic event. She decided to annoy him. The Josephine Necklace, a gift from Napoleon to his wife, is never supposed to leave the embassy. However, the men on the embassy staff can never say no when the Ambassador's daughter wants something. Knowing that her father couldn't make a scene at a public reception, she wore the revealing dress and necklace, and she arrived an hour late. The Ambassador was so furious that he snubbed her all evening, which only added fuel to the fire. She decided to leave the exhibition without telling anyone. She deliberately threw her cell phone into the trash so her father wouldn't know where she was. You, my friend, were just a convenient pawn she used to infuriate him.

"When the Ambassador couldn't find her at the end of the night, he was sure she'd been kidnapped and the necklace stolen. It took us a while, but we finally located the taxi driver who took the two of you to the hotel.

"Seeing how relieved her father was that she was safe, the young lady decided to deflect any anger at her by blaming you. She said you'd gotten her drunk, seduced her and stolen the necklace. Officer Jones suspected she wasn't telling the truth. Getting the girl alone, she explained that it was a serious crime to lie to the police and what would happen to you. Frightened, she told the truth. Well, she told *some* of the truth. She confessed that she willingly went to bed with you, but she insists it was her first time. The Ambassador, who is the President's cousin, believes that you violated his daughter's innocence. If I were you, I would stay out of France for a very long time."

Colin sighed. *The piercings, the tattoo, the 'you must spank my naughty bottom, Monsieur le Professeur' game.* He groaned. *She wasn't leaning over those cases to study pottery, she was giving any man in the vicinity a chance to look down her dress.* He mentally kicked himself. *I should have figured it out. She was just being young and stupidly rebellious.*

"Thank you, Detective. I will follow your advice."

As Colin got up to leave, Lewis's cell phone rang.

"DCI Lewis... Yes, Ma'am... Yes, Ma'am... I understand, Ma'am... Yes, *immediately*, Ma'am... Are you sure?" He gave Colin an amused look. "Since you insist, Ma'am, I am happy to comply."

He took out his handcuffs again. "It seems I've been countermanded, Professor. Your aunt has just instructed me to release you into *her* custody and to deliver you to her personally straight away. She gave me very precise instructions about how I was to do that."

Aunt Clarissa. Why am I not surprised that her reach extends even to Scotland Yard?

He was put in a police car and driven to the university, still in manacles. By then, word of his exploits had reached the school. The front page of *The Sun*, Colin's nominee for London's sleaziest tabloid, screamed, *The Archaeologist and the Virgin. Debauchery at the National Gallery! Ancient Discovery Will Bring Napoleon Back to Life!* Two pictures graced the front page. One was of a pig-tailed Danielle wearing big glasses and braces that had been taken when she was a child. Colin's photo showed him on a dig — handsome, tanned, surrounded by gorgeous graduate assistants. He looked devastating — a cross between Indiana Jones and James Bond.

There was a huge crowd of students — mainly female — waiting for him as he was pulled out of the police car. He looked thoroughly disheveled — unshowered, unshaven, crumpled tuxedo, no socks. Despite his appearance — or probably because of it — he was paraded up and down every corridor and staircase. He assumed this was Aunt Clarissa's idea of public shaming, so he wondered how she'd react to the fact that he was greeted with giggles, some applause and looks of palpable desire on the faces of no small number of the women. It was obvious they were taken with how brazen he'd been. They clearly envied Danielle for what seemed like the perfect romantic night — a designer gown, expensive jewelry, amazing shoes, champagne, chocolates, a five-star suite and a night of hot sex with the suave, party-crashing Colin.

When he was deposited in Clarissa's office, the officer handed her the key and left. A teary-eyed Deb hovered, asking if there was anything she could get Colin. Clarissa impatiently shooed her out. When she looked at him, she shook her head. "What is it about young girls' fascination with bad boys?"

Knowing it wasn't a real question, he sat quietly. He was already in enough trouble with his aunt. He didn't want to provoke her. He held up his cuffed hands. "As long as I'm not being charged with anything, may I at least have my freedom, Madam Chairwoman?"

Clarissa reached for the phone and arched an eyebrow. "And let you make my life even more difficult? I don't think so."

She pointed her finger at him. "You, my nephew, have created a full-blown diplomatic incident. The Foreign Office has had to promise the French government that you will face serious consequences. For openers, you've been barred from any government grants for five years. The only thing keeping the president from firing you is the uproar he'd get from the students, faculty and press. Everyone will forget the story in *The Sun* by tomorrow. If you're invisible, you may ultimately be able to salvage your career — and I'm about to make you disappear."

She punched in the number and waited. Her hard glare told him he was to sit silently.

"Professor Medina, this is Clarissa More at University College London. I'm calling in response to your email asking if I could recommend one of our recent Ph.D.s for that last-minute opening you have. Are you still looking for someone? Good. I have someone even better than you were hoping for. Colin Tucker... Yes, *that* Colin Tucker. It turns out our Professor Tucker is very keen on spending a couple of years in the States. He's recently developed an interest in ancient Native American cultures. He was wondering if you'd be willing to consider him for the post... Yes, this is a wonderful opportunity for your students... Yes, he understands you can't match his current salary, but your location in Arizona will make it possible for him to immerse himself in his new scholarly interests... Excellent. I'm sure you'll want to interview him first... No, no, we insist. Professor Tucker wouldn't want you to treat him differently from any other applicant. How would tomorrow be? Wonderful. He'll be there."

Colin was too stunned to speak. *Arizona? Cowboys and cacti? No! Did she say two years?*

Clarissa got up, walked over to the window and took a deep breath. "You know, Colin… I feel as though a great boulder has been lifted off my shoulders. It will shortly hurtle through space and land in Arizona. We're just lucky you actually started doing research in that area, otherwise I don't know what I would have done." She walked back to her desk and buzzed her assistant. "Deb, please send in the other Professor Tucker."

Ian entered, looking as somber as Colin did. Clarissa handed him a credit card and the key to the handcuffs.

"Here's what's going to happen, gentlemen. Colin, I already had Ian go to your flat and pack your bag. He will now take you to Heathrow, where he will put you on the next flight to Phoenix, Arizona. Ian, he is to fly *coach* — preferably a middle seat with a crying baby on either side. You may unshackle him once you're at the airport — but not before. Colin, you will be met by a driver who will take you to the university. After your interview, find a place to live. Spend at least a week there before you return here to pack up. By then, you at least won't be in the news. At the end of two years, you may ask for a reprieve — but I make no promises." Her tone was so frosty that Colin shivered. "Your quick departure from my office is all that I require. I have an ambassador to try to placate."

They nodded obediently and left. As they walked through the outer office, a sobbing Deb saw that Colin was still handcuffed. She wrapped her arms around him and moaned sorrowfully. "Oh, Colin." Variations on the scene were repeated as Ian led him through the sea of weeping young women.

Ian hailed a cab. As they started climbing into the black vehicle, the cabbie saw the cuffs and turned around. "Hold on there, gents. I don't ferry criminals."

"Not to worry." Ian flashed the key and handed the driver a hundred-pound note. "This is a practical joke. It was the only way I could get my brother here to take a holiday. He works too hard." Once Colin was seated, Ian unlocked the cuffs. "Please take us to Heathrow, my friend. My brother's going to America."

Colin rubbed his wrists. He still couldn't believe how a simple tryst had mushroomed into such a disaster. And he was crestfallen that life had snatched away such an amazingly sexy woman — even if she was a bored, horny, rebellious teenager using him to annoy her father. He turned to Ian. "Cast out of London and exiled to America? Please tell me that when we get to Heathrow, you'll say Aunt Clarissa wasn't serious. She was just trying to scare me."

"I wish that were the case," Ian replied glumly. "Be glad you got her on a good day. Otherwise, she would have handed you over to the French Ambassador. *Then*, you'd be on your way to Devil's Island."

Colin sighed and slumped into the seat.

"Buck up. You have our dear aunt to thank that you still have your job. She's going to take an immense amount of heat for protecting you. She is fonder of you than you know, and she understands that this was just bad luck — not a fuck-up on your part. You may not feel like thanking her now, but at some point, you need to. And look on the bright side. America's not that bad a place. Arizona's perfect for your new line of research. And there's great rock climbing where you're going.

Besides, if you get lonely, you don't even have to worry about meeting *American* girls."

Colin looked puzzled.

"Look in your pocket."

He removed a small piece of paper.

Send me your address. I have vacation time. And we still have to continue our 'conversation'.
Deb XXX

It was still damp from her tears.

"Where did this come from?"

"I guess you didn't notice her slipping that into your pocket when she hugged you." Ian clapped him on the shoulder and chuckled enviously. "I wouldn't be surprised if you get even more offers once they all hear where you are. It's going to be remarkable that so many women at the university will discover a lifelong desire to visit Sedona. You're amazing." Ian gave him a mystified look and shook his head. "Women throw themselves at you, even in your moment of disgrace."

Once they got to the airport, Ian took mercy on Colin and booked him into business class. He winked as he handed him the ticket. "The lovely young woman at the ticket counter assured me there were no seats available in coach. A condemned man shouldn't have to travel steerage." Being upgraded allowed him access to the passenger lounge with a shower. He could at least change into clean clothes.

Colin was so tired from the last twenty-four hours that as soon as the plane was airborne, he closed his eyes. *Please tell me this is all a bad dream that I'll wake up from.*

Alas, the next time Colin awoke, it was to the sound of a crying infant in the row behind him.

Seriously, Aunt Clarissa, you couldn't send me into exile without torturing me as well?

He exhaled slowly, accepting his fate.

Banished to the colonies. I guess there really is a Hell.

* * * *

As Colin walked into the office of Oscar Medina, Chairman of the Archaeology Department at Red Rock University, he felt he'd been transported to a foreign land.

Because it was an interview, Colin was decked out in his best 'dress to impress' outfit—a dark charcoal Armani suit with a noticeable pinstripe, stylish purple tie and black Italian loafers. In stark contrast, the portly Medina was dressed in shorts, sandals and a bright green T-shirt that said, *Archaeologists do it in the dirt!*

Okay…so things are a little less formal here than in London.

The Chairman shook Colin's hand enthusiastically. "Welcome, Professor Tucker. We consider it to be a major coup that our field's *wunderkind* wants to spend time with *us*. I can't tell you how thrilled we are."

Colin hoped the salacious slogan on his new colleague's shirt wasn't an oblique reference to his exploits with the French Ambassador's daughter. He wanted to start with a clean slate. It was definitely in Aunt Clarissa's power at least to limit the story's impact. She'd probably told Medina that it wasn't unusual for the Fleet Street tabloids to make up completely phony stories, and that Colin had been a victim of that. He simply replied, "We go where the work takes us, Professor Medina. Don't we? I'm just grateful for the opportunity to be so close to so many important Native American research sites."

"Please, now that I've 'professored' you and you've 'professored' me, let's just go by first names. We're very casual here." He picked up a folder on his desk and gestured that Colin should follow him out of his office. "We're all very impressed that you insisted on going through the interview process. *And* that you got on a plane within hours after I spoke to Professor More. That's very egalitarian for such a well-known scholar."

Recalling the phone call that had sent him here, he smiled politely. "I can assure you that it was unthinkable to do things any differently."

As they walked down the hall to the interview room, Medina described Colin's responsibilities. "Normally, you'd teach two courses in your specialty. But since the semester is just about to begin, I won't assign you any classes until the spring. You can get settled in this term. However, we have a few doctoral students who might be interested in your advice on their dissertations. So, please make yourself available to them. The term starts in a couple of weeks. You have plenty of time to find a place to stay, return to England to pick up what you need and be back for the first faculty meeting." He apologized profusely for the low salary.

Colin was introduced to the other members of the department. It was a hodgepodge of academics with varied specialties, ages and ethnic backgrounds. They were all very friendly — and dressed as casually as Medina. They asked Colin to discuss his most recent research, and he was impressed with the insightful questions posed by members of the group.

Upon returning to the Chairman's office, he was formally offered the job. He accepted immediately, of course, then was ushered to Human Resources, where there was a stack of papers to sign, issued a university ID and given a parking permit—for a car he needed to get.

Yet despite how welcoming everyone was, Colin was painfully aware of the chain of events that had led him to this point—that he had been used as a boy toy by an eighteen-year-old tart to humiliate her father, and that his imperious aunt had exiled him to the Colonies.

From London Town to Cow Town. He sighed.

As he signed and initialed paperwork, it felt as though each stroke of his pen chipped off another piece of his liberty. It was then sucked into a black hole from which it would never emerge. With the last document signed, he twisted the cap back onto his fountain pen, closed his eyes and sat silently for a moment. He was staring into a great empty void. He shivered. *Banished from everything I hold dear and cast into the darkness. May the saints protect me.*

Pleading the effects of jet lag, he asked to be driven to his hotel. Ian had thoughtfully booked him into luxury accommodation, so Colin hoped to boost his spirits with a massage, an excellent meal and a good movie. No masseuses were available, however, and the satellite feed inexplicably had a major glitch. The same program was now displayed on every channel—a rodeo. He stared glumly at the screen. "I salute you, Aunt Clarissa. I underestimated you. I am your prisoner, and you have your revenge." He settled for room service and an early night, sleeping the night through in his comfortable accommodation.

Colin's room at the Sedona Rouge Hotel and Spa had a balcony with a spectacular view of the mountains. The next morning, he ordered breakfast and studied the multicolored layers of the red rocks. Because the air in Sedona was clearer than in London, the light hitting the stone literally made it shimmer. He was in awe of the rough natural beauty of the American southwest. *Breathtaking!* Even he, a lifelong Londoner, had to appreciate the glories of the desert.

When he arrived back at Medina's office, his spirits got another boost. He was introduced to Yvonne, a lovely young woman professionally attired in a crisp white blouse and navy-blue skirt. He was immediately taken with her voluptuous body and her exotic face. She had distinctly Polynesian features. She had been hired by the university to help him find a place to live and to acclimate to the area. She would make sure everything was settled with the immigration officials and would also tutor him about driving on the right side of the road. He was cheered to see no wedding ring on her hand. Perhaps she could be persuaded to comfort him in his time of sorrow.

Colin and Yvonne spent the next few days getting him settled. Because Sedona was dramatically less expensive than London, he was pleased that he could afford a large apartment with comfortable furnishings and a beautiful view of the mountains. He leased a Jeep and practiced driving on the right side of the road. And while he didn't go past flirting with Yvonne in their time together, her enthusiastic response to his playful advances assured him that his punishment for his escapade with Danielle wouldn't include celibacy.

A few hours before his late-night flight back to London, he switched on the television only to find that the system was again showing the rodeo. Grimacing, he picked up the local paper to see what sort of entertainment the area offered. Noticing an ad for a gentleman's club, he thought a visit there would be an appropriate reward for having been on 'good behavior' for the past few days.

Chapter Eleven

Making his way to Satin, Colin settled in. The club was decorated in a more sophisticated fashion than he'd expected, and he was pleasantly surprised at the diversity of people in the audience. It wasn't just men, but couples and even groups of women. America had always struck him as a country of prudes with an unhealthy view of sex. He was impressed that so many women were enjoying the dancers. *First Yvonne...now this. Maybe Sedona will be more oasis than desert.*

Some of the strippers came by and offered him a lap dance. He politely declined, fearing that Aunt Clarissa might be tracking his every movement. *For all I know, those G-strings have tiny cameras that feed straight to her computer.* He was certain she wouldn't appreciate his taste in entertainment. He was already on thin ice with her. He didn't want to anger her before he'd even settled into his new situation.

He watched the pole dancers for about an hour while he ate. Noting that it was nearing time to head to the airport, he paid the bill. As he stood to leave, however, something about the dancer walking onto the stage caught his eye. She wore an intriguing feathered headdress.

The way the feathers are arranged.... The order of the colors... That blue... The symbol on her mask... Could it be...? No. It must be a coincidence. She was gorgeous. He glanced at his watch. He still had time. He'd watch her before leaving.

He was bowled over by her performance. She called herself 'The Contessa'. She wasn't as athletic as some of the other dancers, but she had an enigmatic quality that he found absolutely magnetic and she was incredibly sexy. He couldn't take his eyes off her.

Such a perfect body. Amazing control. High risk moves — and flawless execution. Her dance is a perfect match for the music. And she's sexy as hell! The Contessa. Yes, perfectly named. She has the grace, presence and confidence that I imagine characterized a powerful Venetian courtesan. I must meet that woman!

As she lay on the floor catching her breath after her dramatic final slide down the pole, he raced to reach her before she could leave. He slipped a hundred-dollar bill under her G-string and kissed the inside of her wrist. His Italian was rusty, but he wanted to impress her. "*Miei complimenti, bella Contessa. Grazie mille.*"

When he squeezed her hand, it was as though he'd grabbed hold of a live wire. He gasped as a current surged through him and produced a remarkable set of sensations. Every inch of his body tingled. He was drawn to this woman like he'd been to no other. It was as though he had finally found someone he didn't even realize he had been searching for his entire life, someone who filled him with an extraordinary sense of completeness. He saw image after image of their bodies fused in passion and exploding in ecstasy. The joy and excitement were so intense that he never wanted to let go. It was sexual and spiritual at the same moment, and his head literally spun. He instinctively let go of her hand and grabbed the edge of the stage so he wouldn't fall. His heart pounded and he felt out of breath. When he looked at her, the expression on her face said that she, too, had experienced an electric moment.

By the time his head cleared, she'd hurried off stage. He considered going to her dressing room, but he needed to get to the airport. Fortunately, he'd be coming back soon enough and could meet her then.

The trip to the airport passed quickly, as he couldn't stop replaying his memories of The Contessa.

He boarded his plane with a sense of optimism and wonder. He kept turning over in his mind the question of who The Contessa really was. He'd been to enough strip clubs in London to know that the women who worked there often had interesting stories about why they'd taken such a job — a novelist doing research for a character in a book, a university student, actress or artist supporting herself until she could get established. Something about The Contessa told him that she was no ordinary pole dancer. Her performance had revealed a powerful personality. It said 'self-confident', 'accomplished', 'sexy' — *especially* 'sexy'. It was clear she was comfortable with her sexuality. She didn't dance to please men. She did it to please herself. Any tips she received weren't 'gratuities for services rendered'. No, they were expressions of thanks — even reverence — from her subjects. The more he thought about her and what he'd felt when they'd touched, the stronger the pull to her became.

Too excited to sleep, he continued to replay her performance and recall the sexual electricity she provoked in him. He'd *never* experienced anything like that before. *Amazing! She isn't just nobility. She's a goddess! I must make love to her. The sex will be unlike anything I've had with other women.*

He had no doubt that he could bed her. His gift — or, according to his aunt, his curse — was being so genuinely enchanted by a woman that she found it irresistible to be desired by a man so gorgeous and sexy as he was. To his amazement, he was now counting the days until he could return to his exile.

* * * *

Spotting Ian in the crowded welcome area in front of Costa Coffee at Heathrow, Colin waved and gave his brother a big smile. He walked right up to him and wrapped him in a huge hug.

"For a man who's been banished to cowboy country, you're in a surprisingly good mood." Ian stepped back and pretended to adopt a serious posture. Stroking his chin, he studied Colin's face. "Hmmm. There's something different about you. I'd guess that you had an epiphany and realized you're a grade-A horse's arse. You have resolved to mend your ways and become a respectable member of society. Your high spirits come from knowing you are firmly set on the path of righteousness." Then he burst out laughing. "No. More likely you've figured out a way to con dear Aunt Clarissa into letting you stay in London."

Colin was unfazed by Ian's jibe as they walked toward the parking garage. "If all you're going to do is mock me, sibling, you can shove it. To be honest, maybe you're right about an epiphany. Something did happen. To be *completely* honest, I don't understand it yet—but I can't wait to return to Arizona to figure it out."

Ian stopped and looked straight into Colin's eyes. A few seconds of intense scrutiny later, he shook his head in disbelief. "Fuck me, you mean it. You're okay with being exiled?" He poked him in the chest. "All right, who are you, and what have you done with my brother?"

"Mock me if you want. Maybe I've decided to make the best of a bad situation. Perhaps Arizona isn't the wasteland I'd expected." He pictured the mysterious Contessa and remembered the powerful effect she'd had on him.

Ian let out a hearty laugh. "You tosser! 'Make the best of a bad situation', my arse. You met some sexy woman you assume will ease your pain with endless shagging."

Colin shrugged and smiled. "Maybe. Maybe not. Buy me a pint and I'll tell you all about her."

* * * *

The instant Cat stepped on stage, she sensed something unusual. The atmosphere felt charged. As she walked to her pole, she scanned the crowd and spotted a new face. Mr. More-handsome-than-should-be-legal was obviously from out of town. The way most people at Satin dressed could probably be called 'Southwest dressy casual'. He wore a charcoal suit with a pronounced pinstripe and a purple tie. He was standing as though he was about to leave, then sat back down.

She shivered as she watched him. *Have they turned the AC way up again?*

When Cat performed, she always ignored the audience. Losing her concentration was too risky. But tonight she couldn't help glancing his way when she could. He was mesmerized. From Bolero's first note to the last, his electric blue eyes tracked her. The intensity of his stare was exciting. As she lay on the stage with her eyes closed, catching her breath after her final slide down the pole, the strangest thing happened. She could sense him walking toward the stage—getting closer to her. It was like feeling the pull of a magnet—invisible, powerful, tugging at her. She was positive it was *him*. And the closer he got, the more her body tingled.

When he stopped beside her, she breathed in his powerfully masculine scent and felt a hand slide a bill under the elastic of her G-string. Opening her eyes, she discovered the sexiest face she'd ever seen. He gazed worshipfully at her.

Her heart raced. And a different kind of heat—not her body's reaction to the dance she'd just done—flooded through her.

Amazing eyes. Brilliantly blue. Sparkling. So much fire in them. That mouth. Those lips. What I wouldn't give to have them on me—everywhere!

Hypnotized by her admirer's rugged beauty, she didn't object when he took her hand and turned it over so he could softly kiss the inside of her wrist. Looking deeply into her eyes, he said in sensual tones, "*Miei complimenti, bella Contessa. Grazie mille.*"

As he squeezed her hand, an electric surge of sexual yearning, of a sort she'd never before experienced, tore through her. Her heart pounded and her flesh burned with longing. Every inch of her virtually naked body ached to be touched by this man — even though he was a complete stranger. She felt an overpowering sense of emptiness that only he could fill. She ached for him to take her right there. Images of the two of them joined in ecstasy flashed through her head. She was about to speak to him when he abruptly let go of her hand and stepped back. When he did, it was like she'd snapped out of a trance.

Deeply unsettled by her reaction, she stood up and hurried to the dressing room as the next dancer began. Her body buzzed so strongly that she stumbled on the way.

As she sat down in front of her makeup mirror, her heart still raced from the stranger's touch. Her breathing was rapid and deep. Her body continued to vibrate from the sexual charge. She took off her mask and inhaled a bottle of ice water to cool herself off… in *every* way.

What just happened? No man has ever affected me like that.

She put her face in her hands and forced herself to calm down. As she relaxed, she remembered her admirer had slipped something into her G-string. She looked down and saw a hundred-dollar bill. It was the biggest tip she'd ever received. Yet what filled her mind was the man's effect on her. She was so curious about who could ignite such a reaction with just a touch that she grabbed her robe and made her way back toward the stage. She peeked from behind the curtain while Lauren performed. He had left.

Sighing deeply, she didn't know whether she was disappointed or relieved.

The pull she'd felt to him had been so strong and carnal that she was sure sex with him would be extraordinary. *If just a touch of his hand made me this excited, imagine if he...*

At the same time, the attraction was so powerful that she didn't know if she would be able to resist him if he showed up again. Once they were naked in bed, he would see her for who she really was. Sedona was a small community. He might recognize her. And the last thing she needed was someone knowing her secret. If word somehow got back to the university that she was a pole dancer, she'd become a joke. No one would ever take her seriously as a professional. The fewer people who knew, the better.

After she returned to the dressing room, her body hummed from the sexy jolt she'd felt from the stranger's touch. Her brain was still flooded with a 'sex haze'. And she couldn't stop herself from fantasizing about what sort of lover he would be. She closed her eyes and moved her hand slowly over her aching breasts, pinching her nipples hard and biting her lip. Then she slid her hand down, caressed her moist sex and let her imagination run wild.

The sound of applause as Lauren finished her dance invaded the dressing room and snapped Cat back to reality. Her diamond-hard nipples, soaking pussy and pounding heart, however, testified to the erotic power of her admirer. She looked at herself in the mirror, ran her hands through her hair and shook her head. "A total stranger and you're having amazingly hot fantasies about him already. You need to get laid," she said out loud.

Lauren walked into the dressing room. "Who *was* that guy, and where can I get one like him? You're still flushed, and all he did was kiss your wrist."

Embarrassed at what the color in her face had actually come from, Cat shrugged. "I haven't a clue. I looked over the audience while you were dancing, but he's gone. I wish I knew who he was."

"That good, eh?" Lauren crooked her eyebrow in envy. "Okay. But when he returns, see if he's got a twin brother for me. Hell, if he's that hot" — she giggled — "I might even give a twin *sister* a chance."

Cat still had another two performances that night. While she waited, she paced nervously. She peeked out from behind the curtain regularly to see if he'd returned. At the start and finish of her dance, she looked to see if 'Purple Tie' had come back. He hadn't.

For the next couple of weeks, she couldn't get him out of her mind. She couldn't stop herself from scanning for him — not only at Satin, but wherever she went in Sedona. When she didn't see him, she was disappointed and relieved at the same time. Sex with him would be amazing, but it would also be as dangerous as crack.

Every night she went to bed, however, he dependably reappeared in the most erotic dreams she'd ever had. She even orgasmed so powerfully that her climax woke her up. In the morning, she was both sated and mystified.

When she continued to fail to see him anywhere and the dreams began to fade, she decided that whatever it was had passed. *I guess that's that*, she finally said to herself, with a deep, disappointed sigh. *It probably wouldn't have been that good in real life. It's just a fantasy.*

She confided in Lauren all the details of what had happened — the remarkable impact the stranger had had on her just by kissing and squeezing her hand, her trance-like reaction, her obsession with him. Wanting him so much, she worried about what she'd do. She asked Lauren if she or any of the other girls at Satin had experienced anything like it.

"I haven't. And none of the girls have ever mentioned it. Remember... We're all normal women just working for a living. We've got an audience of regulars and the occasional newbie. Although we sell the *fantasy* of sex, none of us is looking to discover love at Satin. We all want to find it elsewhere. After all, when I have a daughter and she asks me how my husband and I met, I'd rather say something other than, 'Well, Sweetie, Mommy was a pole dancer. Daddy slipped a fifty into my G-string, and it was love at first sight.' I don't know what to say, Cat. Maybe it was like lightning. Sometimes it just strikes."

* * * *

Cat told herself that the 'sexy stranger episode' was just an unusual event she'd recall occasionally in the privacy of her bed. She also told herself that she couldn't remember much about what the man looked like.

But the truth was that every detail of the brief encounter was seared into her brain — and parts of her body that were a good deal farther south. When she closed her eyes and replayed the scene, the excitement she'd felt on stage came rushing back. She saw the tanned, square-jawed, rugged face as clearly as when she'd looked at him through her mask. The tousled sandy hair... Striking eyes of electric blue... Light-colored stubble... Inviting lips... The way his purple tie had been loosened the way guys who don't like wearing ties do as soon as they can... His smell — a delicious combination of his own 'sexy man at the end of the day' scent and an unusual cologne... She was so obsessed that she spent a day going from store to store until she'd found it — Jo Mallone's Wood Sage and Sea Salt. She bought some and sprayed it liberally on her sheets when she fantasized about him.

Two things about him, however, had made a special impression on her.

First, his voice. She knew he wasn't Italian, even though the only words he'd spoken to her had been Italian. He had some other kind of accent. His voice was powerfully sexy — deep in a way that rumbled through her entire body. It was as though the sensitive skin on the inside of her legs — and the even more sensitive point where they came together — formed a tuning fork that vibrated at the command of the dark, rich sound of the man's voice. She shivered and got *very* turned on whenever she remembered how her body had resonated to the timbre.

Even more memorable, however, was what had happened when he'd squeezed her hand. She'd never felt overwhelmed by sexual desire before. Her hunger for the man had been so powerful that she would have done anything he'd asked.

Every time she thought about his touch, an exciting, surprising, delicious, sexy, electric, liquid charge surged through her and made her body ache for him.

So, she thought about it often.

Chapter Twelve

"It's very straightforward." The gruff voice on the phone was obviously being disguised with some electronic device. "This is a test run for which I will pay you ten thousand dollars. Frankly, I don't care what you steal. In fact, keep it. I just want to see if you can get past the security system there. If you're successful, I have a series of jobs for which I'm willing to pay ten times that...*each.*"

Frank, he taller of the two men, looked at his companion and raised his eyebrows. "You did say *each*? That's a hundred thousand dollars per job," he said into the phone.

"You get one warning from me," the voice barked. "Treat me again like an idiot who can't multiply, and I'll find someone else. Yes. One hundred thousand dollars."

Frank was unfazed at the rebuff. "And the procedure for payment?"

"I'll watch the local papers for an announcement of the theft. Thirty days after the story, I'll wire the money to whatever account number you give me—assuming you haven't been caught."

"Remember who we are," he laughed. "Being arrested is the least of our worries. It also means you don't even think of double-crossing us. We'll be in touch."

"No, we won't," the voice said sharply. "You will *not* try to contact me. Do this job successfully, and I'll transfer the money. I'll contact you about the next one when I've worked out some of the risks connected with the second job. Goodbye."

Frank stroked his chin and looked at Vincent, the shorter man. "Encrypted satellite phone. Disguised voice. I'm not sure whether I should be impressed he's covering his tracks or worried we could be hung out to dry."

"You did vet the buyer, right?"

"Yeah. He was cleared by Harrington. So, if it came to it, we could always throw him to the wolves. What do you think?"

Vincent stared at the mountains in the distance and frowned. He spat into the fire. "It seems too good to be true, which means..."

"Right. We need some players who are *disposable*. But I say we go ahead and do this first job. Then we reassess."

His partner nodded. "Good by me."

They doused the fire, climbed into the black Hummer and drove west.

* * * *

Cat's next encounter between The Contessa and her admirer was in the unlikeliest of places.

Oscar Medina stood in front of the meeting room on the scorching August day. Everyone was crammed into the small room for the first department meeting of the year. The faculty had all the seats, and the grad students were squeezed against the back wall. The air conditioning wasn't working, and the room was stifling.

"And now for the two last items on the agenda," the chairman intoned. "The Bureau of Indian Affairs has asked us to do anything we can to help them work against the ongoing pillaging of Native American archaeological sites. This is especially serious, given how rich the mountains are. I'm sure we all agree this is a scourge that can't be tolerated. Fortunately, I can announce that the Bureau has assigned some of their best agents to this."

Everyone murmured appreciation.

"On a brighter note, I'd like to introduce the newest member of our faculty, Dr. Colin Tucker. He's on loan to us from University College in London for the next two years. I doubt there's anyone in this room unfamiliar with his groundbreaking research — especially his find this past summer in Gr — "

Knowing Medina would drone on forever, his colleagues headed for the exit as soon as they could get away with it. They waved their welcome to Colin as they escaped the heat.

Cat had arrived at the meeting late, so she stood behind her taller classmates at the very back of the room in the doorway — which meant she couldn't see a thing. When the exodus began, people wanted out so quickly that someone bumped into her, and she lost her balance. As she struggled to stay upright, her tan backpack went flying to the other side of the hallway. Books and papers shot out and covered the floor.

As she knelt on the floor picking things up, she was stunned to see 'Purple Tie' walk out of the room. At first, she couldn't believe it. *No. It can't be him.* But she had fantasized about him so often that every detail was etched into her memory — his rugged face, his amazing blue eyes, his tousled, sandy hair, his scent, but most importantly, the fire he lit inside her with just a touch. *It is him! What's he doing here? Is he the new faculty member just introduced? That's Colin Tucker?*

Colin was a rising star. She'd hoped to meet him at the conference in Greece, but her flight had been delayed and she'd missed his lecture. She'd heard he was drop-dead gorgeous and catnip to all the women there. He'd supposedly spent the conference bedding grad students and impressionable junior scholars. He stood beside the chairman, and they were chatting amicably with some of the faculty. The female grad students were fawning over him already. All the pieces snapped together. *Of course. That accent. The pinstriped suit. Purple tie. The visiting prof from London.*

Her feelings raced.

Panic. *Please don't recognize me!*

Excitement. *It is him!*

Astonishment. *I've been fantasizing about someone who I know is a pig?*

Disappointment. *What's wrong with me?*

Apprehension. *His just being here threatens my secret.*

Reassurance. *It's okay. He only knows my stage persona.*

Worry. *What if the next time we touch, he feels something that reminds him of The Contessa?*

Terror. *What if the next time we touch, I feel nothing?*

As her emotions roiled, her body took control. Her heart raced. She felt warm and electrified all over. Unable to do anything but stare at the tall, handsome Brit, she noticed him look her way. For an instant, their eyes locked. Her breath caught, and her heart kicked into overdrive. Fearing he'd recognized her, she looked away and stuffed her things into the backpack as quickly as she could.

Before she could finish and escape, however, he came over and knelt beside her. "May I help? My mum always said to aid a lady in distress."

Any English accent would have made her go weak in the knees, so she was lucky to be sitting on the floor. But Colin's voice set off an even more powerful reverberation that penetrated deep inside her. She tingled and squirmed in the most deliciously embarrassing way. She tried to hide how her face was heating, so no doubt turning red.

"Sorry about my mates. I guess Yanks can be short on manners. I'm Colin Tucker, by the way." He extended his hand.

"Cat White Eagle. It's an honor you meet you, Professor Tucker." She hesitated to take his hand. She was afraid her body would react the same way it had the last time they'd touched. But refusing would be rude and suspicious. And her ability to resist temptation had evaporated as soon as he'd approached her. She gulped as his large, warm hand enfolded hers.

She tried hard to control the effect he had on her but couldn't. Letting his musky scent mesmerize her, she dove into the azure ocean of his eyes and gasped softly. She felt the same sexy charge that had raced through her body when he'd kissed her hand at Satin — the same desperate hunger and the same sex haze.

Colin froze for a few seconds. His face mirrored the painful yearning she was feeling, but it also showed confusion.

She panicked. *Damn! He recognizes me!* The terror of being found out cleared her head. *Quick! Leave!*

"I'm sorry." A clearly flustered Colin abruptly let go of her hand. Sweat was beading on his forehead. Seeming disoriented, he took a deep breath and loosened his tie. "I don't know where my mind went. It must be a combination of that hot room and jet lag. I just got off the plane earlier today."

Bracing herself for, 'Haven't we met somewhere before?' she was relieved when he simply said, "Charmed. Lovely name. I'm sure you're proud of your heritage. Native American cultures are fascinating. I've recently been shifting my work in that direction." He picked up the rest of her books and papers and put them in her backpack.

She exhaled. She hadn't realized she'd been holding her breath. *We're side by side, and no sign of recognition. I am so lucky.* She commanded her body to settle down. Thankfully, it obeyed. *But what did the way he looked at me mean?*

He helped her up. "Allow me to apologize for your being run into by a herd of stampeding archaeologists. It was so bloody hot in there. Everyone couldn't wait to get out."

"Yes, I know. I'm a grad student in the department. I finish my work this semester. I got to the meeting late and was listening in the doorway. So you're the famous Professor Colin Tucker?"

He laughed. "Please, just call me Colin." The two of them walked outside into the cool air, with Colin carrying her backpack. She put on her oversized sunglasses and made sure not to look at him. She regained her composure and clicked into 'grad student' mode.

"Everyone's abuzz about Red Rock's snagging such a distinguished scholar. How did we get so lucky?"

"Distinguished scholar? Hardly. I just turned thirty, and I haven't had my degree that long. I had amazing luck making some important discoveries quickly and getting the job at UCL. Then this opportunity came up, which will let me follow a new area of interest. To tell the truth, I applied on a lark," he said conspiratorially. "I thought the interview might be a good way to snag a free holiday to the States. But I flew in a fortnight ago, chatted with Oscar and his mates, and—Bob's your uncle—they offered me the job. I was so shocked that I pulled out my mobile and called the lads at the Swan and Thistle—my favorite pub. When I told them about my good fortune, they were as surprised as I was that the post didn't go to someone more qualified. All they could say was '*blow me*'!"

It was bad enough that Cat had to contend with the inexplicable sexual pull. The combination of professional humility, boyish charm, devastating good looks and killer accent was irresistible. Fortunately, his womanizing reputation and her knowing that he frequented strip clubs helped her keep her guard up. She decided his British slang merited a poke.

"Okay there, King Henry," she joked, "let me give you some advice—otherwise, your students are going to make fun of you mercilessly behind your back. You're going to want to blend in with the natives. Ditch the Saville Row 'interview suit'. It's 'vacation', not 'holiday', and 'colleagues', not 'mates'. We have 'cell phones', not '*mó*-bi-les'. It's 'two weeks', not 'a fortnight', a 'bar', not 'Swan and Thistle' or 'pub', and 'friends', not 'lads'. '*Bob's your uncle*?' What's that all about? And 'blow me'" — she flushed — "means something *very* different here."

Colin lit up.

She was surprised that he enjoyed being taken to task by her. "So, let me tell you a story that will save you from your most embarrassing moment ever. Last year, one of your countrymen was visiting for a term. The first day of the semester, he walked into the classroom, took out the roster and started calling out names to take attendance. He found a couple of mistakes on the sheet, and when he went to fix them, he discovered that the eraser on his pencil was worn all the way down. He looked up at his students... All ninety of them... All ninety horny, sex-obsessed twenty-year-olds, and said, '*Does anyone here have a rubber?*' The room fell silent. The class was sure they'd heard him wrong.

"He said it again, more emphatic this time. '*I say, does anyone here have a rubber? I need one before I can move from Miss Belle to Mr. Brandt.*' By now, everyone was sniggering. They didn't want to be rude, so they were trying not to laugh out loud. '*Surely someone in this room has a rubber. I'd very much appreciate it if you'd all look in your pockets and purses to see if one of you has a rubber you can loan me. I promise to give it back right as soon as I make my way through all of you and finish with Miss Zelinski.*'

"His final comment was too much, and the class burst out laughing. Thinking this was just a bunch of rude Americans who were making fun of his accent, he packed up his books. He was going to leave in a huff. Fortunately, one of the students who understood what was going on went up to him and quietly explained that while in England, 'rubber' means 'eraser', in America, it means 'condom'. Red-faced, he thanked the student and went on with class."

The two of them burst out laughing. "Thanks for the lesson. And may I rely on the beautiful and helpful Miss White Eagle to be my guardian angel so that I don't do something similar?"

Even though he hadn't touched her, Cat's body buzzed simply from being close to him. His scent whispered, *Sex! Sex! Sex!* to her. She got warm and excited—everywhere. She stumbled taking her next step. He grabbed her to keep her from falling, which only made things worse. She ached from a desire that could be sated only one way—and that was out of the question.

"Uneven stone pathway," she thought to say quickly, letting go of him before the lust clouding her mind made her do something foolish. She struggled to ignore his effect on her.

"You said you're almost finished. What's your dissertation on?"

She was relieved by the direction of the question. "I'm working on the myth that says there was a 'lost tribe' who lived in this area thousands of years earlier than most of the evidence suggests."

"I've heard about that!" he said excitedly as they walked along. "A friend of mine told me about a presentation at the conference in Greece. Was that you? I'd wanted to go, but something came up at the last minute."

Cat rolled her eyes behind her dark lenses. *Something came up? No. Something came down. Some girl's panties. Don't be a tart, Cat. It makes you sound jealous.*

Refocusing, Cat played down the presentation. "Yes. But it was just a preliminary paper."

Colin inquired offhandedly, "Is it true that when someone asked you if you thought there was some truth to the myth—that there actually was a 'lost tribe'—that you didn't give a straight answer? Do you think there really was such a tribe?"

She began to panic. *Be careful. The wrong answer will make him think you're crazy. Your career will end here and now.*

"I believe I said,"—she spoke very deliberately—"that *'all ancient myths ultimately grew out of something factual. They just get blown out of proportion and become bigger than life.'* I should have been clearer. I don't think there's any truth to the myth," she lied.

He nodded, looked around and lowered his voice. "What if I told you I'd recently seen a piece of pottery that could suggest it's *not* a myth after all?"

She stopped abruptly and looked directly at him. She opened her eyes wide but attempted to hide her excitement. "Are you serious?"

"It's probably nothing, but—" He looked around as though he wanted to make sure no one was listening to them, then leaned in conspiratorially. "It was a piece at an exhibition I visited recently in London. It had an unusual combination of pottery shape, a specific color and decorative symbol I'd never seen before. If nothing else, it had been mislabeled. I find it all *very* curious. Why don't you let me take you to dinner, and I'll tell you about it? I remember how little money grad students have. I can even show you some unauthorized photos I managed to take at the museum." He winked as though he was offering dirty pictures. "How can you resist the temptation?"

She froze. This was good news *and* bad news. If he'd seen genuine evidence about the tribe, she *had* to hear about it. But this was *her* path. If she told him the truth and showed him her years of research, she didn't know how he'd react. He might even muscle her out and take over.

As far as the flirting went, the last thing she wanted was to spend enough time together for him to figure out that she was The Contessa. And the longer she stood by him, the more her body tingled and the harder it got to resist his invitation. *Just leave! Decide what to do later. Alone! When you're not thinking with your vajayjay!*

She abruptly took her backpack from him. "That's very interesting, Professor, but you'll have to excuse me. I have an appointment with a reference librarian."

"Understood," he nodded, then paused. "You're doing pioneering and courageous work, Ms. White Eagle. You're an interesting and intelligent scholar."

She was struck by the respectful tone of his voice and how quickly he morphed from boy-on-the-make to serious academic.

"I have very much enjoyed our chat, and I would be honored to be able to share my reflections about the pottery with you. Please stop by my office whenever it's convenient." His smile was sincere.

"Thank you, Professor."

"Please. 'Colin', not 'Professor'. And perhaps you can give me more advice about living here in the Colonies." He took her hand and squeezed just long enough for the sexy spark to fire again. "It's been lovely to meet you, Ms. White Eagle, my guardian angel."

Another wave of hot, liquid desire surged through her. She pulled her hand back and hugged her backpack to her chest. She smiled politely. "Thanks for helping me, Professor. But really...gotta run!" She hurried into the nearest classroom building, Geronimo Hall, and hid until he walked away. She leaned against the cool stone wall, hoping it would draw the heat out of her body. Her heart was pounding so hard, and her mind was racing in so many different directions that she felt dizzy.

This guy is dangerous. I've got to stay miles away from him. But when he touched me – She shivered with excitement. *Which means absolutely no more touching, not even a handshake, or he's going to suspect.* Nonetheless, she couldn't stop smiling. *He called me 'interesting and intelligent'. My work, 'pioneering and courageous'. He said it was 'lovely' to meet me. He likes me!* Then the smile turned to a frown. *Wait! He likes The Contessa too. What a hound. He likes both of me.* She giggled at the strange idea. *No, this cannot go anywhere,* she lectured herself. *A grad student and faculty member – even if he's not that much older than me. It's such a cliché. I'd lose any professional credibility before I even started. But what about the evidence he mentioned? I've got to find out about that.*

She took out her phone and called Lauren.

"Hey, Cat. What's up?"

"You aren't going to believe who I just saw," she said excitedly.

Lauren laughed. "Let's see. The way you skipped 'hello' and 'how are you' tells me it's a guy. That nervous, breathy quality to your voice tells me it's a hot guy. And since you got struck by lightning two weeks ago, I'm going to guess 'Mr. Sexypants with the purple tie'."

Cat laughed. "Am I that transparent?"

"Transparent? No. Horny? Yes. Tell me everything! He's really back? You know it's him? Where'd you see him? Did he recognize you?" Lauren peppered her with questions until Cat interrupted her.

"Just meet me at my place. I'll open a bottle of wine."

* * * *

Puzzling over what had just happened, Colin couldn't take his eyes off the young woman as she disappeared into the building. She was dressed conservatively — navy blue shorts and a sleeveless white top. But he was struck at how sexy she seemed, nonetheless. He was particularly taken with her beautiful face, with its high cheekbones and almond-shaped eyes.

Cat White Eagle. When we shook hands, it was remarkable. The same thing that happened with the stripper. I saw this image of the two of us going at it in bed with incredible passion. I could barely control myself. But she can't be The Contesssa. They're not only different people, but they're also complete opposites. Cat is shorter. Her clothing is modest. No makeup. I can't imagine her having tattoos the way the stripper does. And while The Contessa is sex on stilettos, nothing about Cat even hints at sex. But why do I find her so sexy? I've heard that Sedona is the site of some powerful energy vortices. Is that it? Is the famous 'Sedona energy' sexual? Is this place Lust Central?

He shook his head as he shifted gears.

That 'lost tribe' theory of hers is fascinating. The way she looked away when she answered my question, I bet she believes the tribe actually existed. She thinks this is more than a myth. That would be an amazing discovery. It takes real guts to chase an idea like that at the start of your career. I bet she's not telling me everything. Did she lie to me? At least there's no question that I'll see her again. She tried to play it cool, but she could barely contain herself when I told her about that pottery.

He sat down on the stone bench in the shade, removed his tie and let himself survey the campus. The library, the girls in the fountain, the Quad, the…. He did such a sharp double-take that his neck cracked. The fountain in the center of campus was overflowing with lovely coeds escaping the heat. *Bloody hell! I have died and gone to heaven! To see this much skin in England, I'd have to go to a strip club. Look at this! Short shorts. Crop tops. Tight T-shirts. No bras. Cracking birds as far as the eye can see. Thank you, Jesus, I have arrived in Shag City! And what a selection! Everything from young, curious, untouched nubile flesh to adventurous and experienced young women… Beauties of every race, color, creed, shape and size! Thank you, Arizona! If this is exile, I'll take it.*

Chuckling, he turned to the juniper tree to his right. "Don't worry, Aunt Clarissa. I promise to be on my best behavior. I'm just admiring the natural beauty of the American Southwest."

He sat in the shade, brooding about the unusual and powerful experiences he'd had with the two dramatically different women. However, gentleman that he was, he thought it was rude to turn his back on the bevy of young lovelies in the Quad. He turned their way and drank in the view. He sighed contentedly as he watched them frolic in the fountain.

Over the next few days, he couldn't get Cat out of his mind. He texted her an invitation to hear about the piece he'd seen. She thanked him, but said she'd meet with him after she defended her dissertation later in the semester.

Being put off only made him more curious. He decided to find out everything he could about her.

Because he was a faculty member, it was easy to get information from the department secretary. He also discussed Cat's work with her advisor and some of the other faculty. They all respected her as a hardworking student and they expected to be able to approve her thesis, but they weren't enthusiastic. "Mythology," Medina said dismissively. "We're trying to train scientists here, not poets. I've tried to talk her into doing *real* archaeology dozens of times, but she's too stubborn to listen."

Colin was impressed. Most grad students let themselves get pushed around because they were afraid of alienating senior faculty. *A woman of conviction, as well as smart — and very sexy in a way I still don't understand. An irresistible combination! But a grad student in the department — best to put her in the 'no shagging' zone. She's close to finishing, however. Maybe when she's done? So back to The Contessa! Nothing off limits there.*

Chapter Thirteen

Cat was right that Colin couldn't stay away from Satin. He became a regular and never missed one of The Contessa's dances. He always dressed the same way — suit and purple tie. She assumed it was so that she'd notice him.

On Friday nights, she would perform five times. At the end of her last number, as Bolero's last notes faded with her lying on the dark stage catching her breath, she would feel him slip a hundred-dollar bill into her G-string. When she opened her eyes, he'd simply say, "*Grazie mille, bella Contessa*." She would nod in thanks, making sure never to speak. And even though he wouldn't kiss her hand and squeeze it as he had the first time, he'd always touch her thigh when he slid the bill into her G-string. It might be only for a second, but it was enough for her to feel that electric charge fire through her body. He'd pause for a few seconds, as though he was about to say something, but she'd get up and exit the stage as quickly as she could.

The other girls at the club kept pestering Cat. Did she know the guy? What was she doing that he kept giving her hundred-dollar tips? "Come on, Cat. You're the only dancer he tips that generously. Spill!"

Pretending she didn't know Cat's secret, Lauren chimed in as well. "Are you sure you aren't moonlighting on us, honey? Come on, girlfriend. Share the wealth. You know, guys, the more T&A, the better. Ask him if he'd like a few of us to join you and entertain him at his place."

Cat could honestly say she had no idea why he'd singled out The Contessa. But, as Lauren knew, she'd lied when she'd said she didn't know who he was. "It beats me. While I'll take the tips, he's wasting his money. He's not getting anything for it but the show. And he's not going to guilt me into giving him a lap dance or more than that. For all the cash he's dropping on me, he could have a pretty good time with a call girl. I don't know why he's throwing so much my way. I don't even talk to him. Monique, you're saving up for a new car. Why don't you make a play for him?"

When she danced, Cat could tell from the look in Colin's face that he stayed for all her shows and tipped so generously because he was mesmerized. He had to be feeling something like the electric jolts she experienced when he touched her.

The weekly sexy shocks had her fantasizing about him like crazy. And as each week progressed and Friday night got closer, she'd get more and more excited—and more and more hungry for him. When she walked on stage, she was ready to explode.

But her dancing felt different now. It was like she performed just for him. She couldn't risk having sex with him—yet. But she definitely made him the target of her sexual energy as she stripped off her costume, caressed herself and flew around the pole. And despite her cool exterior, she couldn't wait until his hand brushed her skin at the end of the night.

At the same time, part of her was disappointed that he kept showing up. 'Cat' didn't like the idea that the guy she fantasized about screwing her silly spent his Friday nights drooling over the naked body of his favorite stripper and tipping her extravagantly.

When Cat confided this to Lauren over coffee, her friend scrunched up her face. "Let me get this straight. You're upset that some guy whose bones you'd love to jump is so taken with you that he comes here every week to watch you dance and tips you a hundred dollars. I'm sorry... I mean *The Contessa*, not *you*. So, you're jealous that he likes this other woman, even though this other woman is *you*?"

"Right, but *he* doesn't know that."

"But *you* do. So, you know there's not *really* some other woman. And if you — I'm sorry, *The Contessa* — weren't dancing there, he wouldn't be coming to watch *her* in the first place." She chuckled. "I bet if The Contessa quit, we'd never see him again. It sounds to me like this is more *your* fault than his, honey." Her smile showed how amusing she found Cat's predicament.

Cat had expected more understanding from Lauren, but she had to admit the whole situation had a bizarre ring to it. But because the Contessa had such a different personality from Cat's everyday self, she had an easy time thinking of the stripper as someone else.

It was all too confusing. She told herself to go to the library.

* * * *

At the same time, Colin had his own dilemma. Every week he'd go to Satin, intent on asking The Contessa to join him at his table so he could invite her to dinner. But he'd always lose his nerve. It wasn't that he'd never dated a stripper before. He had, in London. Some were coeds working their way through university. Others were single moms who would go to work after putting their kids to bed and leaving a sitter in charge. Stripping was simply the best job they could get, given the shape of their lives. They were all perfectly normal, lovely women he'd had a good time with, and who appreciated his particular flavor of seductive charm.

But there was something different about The Contessa. He'd never seen a stripper who gave off such a powerful vibe, who *loved* what she did so much or who got so turned on by dancing naked in front of a room full of strangers. She was a true exhibitionist. He was in awe of how comfortable she was being so powerfully sexual without a hint of shame. The magnetic pull of the amazing woman was overpowering. He was literally unable to stay away from Satin, knowing she was performing on Friday night. He also thought about her daily.

Nonetheless, despite the long list of women he'd had sex with — and the randy adventures he'd shared with his more daring lovers — he hesitated whenever he tried to approach her. He didn't understand why. He had no shortage of sexual self-confidence. What was going on? She was a beautiful, sexy, mysterious and irresistible woman. He typically thrived in such circumstances. But every time he'd try to work up the nerve to speak to her, her commanding presence made him hesitate just long enough for her to leave the stage. And Satin had a strict policy of not allowing customers in the back.

While he struggled with what to do about The Contessa, he fell off the celibacy wagon. Unable to move forward in meeting the sexy pole dancer and determined to do the right thing by not pursuing Cat White Eagle, he was so sexually frustrated that his cork was about to pop. He approached the lovely Yvonne, whom he'd met on his interview trip, but she was already dating someone. So, he yielded to temptation.

Since his original area of research was ancient Greek pottery, he decided to sit in on a graduate Greek history class. He knew the course was filled with beautiful, smart young women. He was from a different department, wasn't their teacher and everyone was over twenty-one. He was confident that he wouldn't get into any trouble.

After he'd slept with a few of the women in class, word spread quickly. His lovers cautioned the other grad students. The women he'd bedded didn't have hard feelings. They'd enjoyed the seduction, how great he was in bed and the excitement of being with a 'proper Englishman' who turned out to be such a 'bad boy'. They understood that he would never be a one-woman man. He was just a great lay – and he knew it.

But they were insulted to discover he used the same seduction on all of them.

The women felt he deserved some payback, so they posted some flyers in the women's rest rooms in the academic buildings. This included Geronimo Hall, where the archaeology department was located. On it were two saucy limericks designed to warn off the undergrads.

Once the flyers went up, it didn't take long for Colin to get called in by the chairman. When Medina showed him one, he was terrified. If he lost this job, he had nowhere to go. And he'd meant it when he'd told his aunt he would stay out of trouble.

Medina explained that because none of the women were his students, he hadn't broken any university rules. But this sort of attention didn't help the department or his reputation on campus.

He apologized and promised to mend his ways.

"Well, maybe some of this is my fault," Medina admitted. "I spoke to your chair in London. She told me what *actually* led to your interest in the job. I thought it was too good to be true that someone with your reputation would want to come here.

"You're thousands of miles from home. You don't know a soul, you're one of those guys women fall over and I didn't assign you any courses to teach this term. 'Idle minds' and all that... Although," he added, shaking his head, "it's not really your *mind* that's getting you in trouble." He paused and thought. "Let's do this, then. A couple of doctoral students are on the verge of finishing. You can ride herd on them."

He directed his attention to his computer screen, called up the list of students and started reading. Colin breathed a sigh of relief. His job was safe. Then, in a flash, he couldn't believe his luck. He had the perfect opportunity to spend time with Cat White Eagle. He could get to know her better and learn about her research at the same time. The semester was more than half over. Cat was in the last stages of her dissertation. If he could establish a good professional relationship with her, it might even lay the foundation for 'something more' after she was no longer connected with the university.

Cat had made a strong impression on him in their only conversation, but she remained a puzzle. Other than the stripper, she was the only woman he'd felt such an electric jolt with when they touched. Given how plain she looked, it made no sense. He couldn't stop ruminating about what it meant. Maybe spending time with her would tell him.

"What about that student working on the Lost Tribe myth?" Colin asked innocently. "I have a strong background in paleo-archaeology. I'm happy to make sure her thesis is respectable enough so she gets through her defense."

Medina looked into space and tapped his finger on his desk. "Lost Tribe mythology... Ms. White Eagle... Not a bad idea." Medina called up Cat's file and stroked his chin. "I've worried that her enthusiasm could get the best of her, and her primary advisor doesn't know what to do with her. He keeps giving her good advice and she ignores it. I'll make you her secondary advisor. Your job is to be a stabilizing influence and make sure her dissertation passes." After clicking away on the keyboard, he looked up. "I just sent her an e-mail about this and told her to make an appointment to see you."

"Thanks very much, Oscar. You won't be disappointed. I love a challenge."

Medina sighed as they shook hands. "That is precisely what I worry about with you, Colin."

Chapter Fourteen

Cat wasn't surprised to get an email from her chairman, because there were lots of details connected with finishing her degree. When she read that she had to work with Colin, however, she had a mixed reaction.

Damn! I've done my best to stay away from him so he couldn't recognize me as The Contessa, and so I wouldn't be tempted to do something stupid because of the attraction, as well as to make sure he wouldn't poach my research.

On the other hand, she couldn't wait to find out more about the 'possible evidence' about the Lost Tribe he'd referred to when they'd met. She didn't want to give that up just because his magnetic pull on her was so powerful that she regularly fantasized about fuck-me-senseless sex with him. She made the appointment but resolved that the encounter would be all business.

The day of the meeting, she stood in front of her bathroom mirror and gave herself instructions. "You're to look as unsexy possible—clunky glasses, not contacts, oversized red Cardinals' jersey, baggy navy sweats and old white running shoes. Wrap your hair and stuff it under a baseball cap. If he mistakes you for a guy," she laughed, "so much the better."

She was so successful that Colin didn't recognize her when he answered her knock on his office door.

"My apologies, Ms. White Eagle. I'm usually better at remembering faces." He held her chair as she sat down before he settled in behind his large oak desk.

Oooo, manners! What a change from the guys here.

He immediately started talking about the piece of pottery he'd seen in London. But as difficult as it was, she said she didn't want to hear about that until after she'd defended her thesis. She was impressed that he didn't argue.

Being in his presence, however, was torture. He'd taken her advice about his wardrobe and was wearing boots, tight jeans and a deep burgundy shirt that hugged his chest just right. He looked even taller and more handsome than he had in his suit. It killed her that she had to pretend not to notice him. It bothered her even more that he was responding exactly as she'd wanted — showing no interest in her. Trying to avoid the distractions, she buried her face in her notes, explained her thesis and told him what stage she was at in writing it up.

He responded with genuine interest. At one point he even said, "This would make a great book. When you're finished, if it's okay with you, I'll talk to my editor at Oxford University Press."

She was bowled over by his generosity. She appreciated his respect for her topic, which other professors dismissed as 'soft and literary'. Relieved that he gave no sign of recognizing her as The Contessa, she relaxed.

After a while, he suggested they move to the sofa so he could spread out some maps and charts on the coffee table. As they got engrossed in the drawings, their knees bumped whenever he enthusiastically pointed to locations critical to her theories.

The sofa ploy! Same as with the history girls. Jerk! Can't you come up with something else? Despite being annoyed, she couldn't deny how aroused she got just from sitting beside him. Every time she caught a whiff of his spicy, masculine scent, she got more turned on. A few minutes later, Colin reached to point out something on the map. His arm not only brushed against her breast hidden inside the bulky sweatshirt, but it also slid against her nipple — which was erect from arousal. She panicked. She wanted to slap him — and also kiss him. Since both would be a mistake, she grabbed her bag and ran out of his office.

Colin was stunned at her abrupt departure. He really had been on his best behavior. Their knees bumped occasionally, but it was entirely accidental. Red Rock was a small school, so he was sure she'd have heard about his escapades. She must have thought he was coming on to her. He picked up his phone and had flowers sent to her home. The card simply said, *Sincerest apologies. CT.*

* * * *

When Cat found a bouquet of purple hydrangeas waiting on her doorstep, she knew immediately they were from him. According to the women he'd bedded, Colin was an incurable romantic with impeccable manners. In the days following their night together, the woman would receive flowers and a beautifully wrapped present. The gift was lovely lingerie, expensive perfume — always the perfect choice — and, as he explained in a handwritten note thanking her for the special evening, an original poem in which he tried to capture something of their night of passion. The poetry was making its way around Cat's fellow students. The lucky recipients were genuinely impressed that Colin put such thought and feeling into them.

For example, Cat's friend Wendy had received a haiku —

Goddess with brown eyes
Healer of my loneliness
Through rapture divine.

Wendy, who specialized in goddess symbols in ancient religions, told Cat that before she and Colin had gone to bed, she'd shared with him about how some cultures believed that sex was a powerful spiritual force that could heal troubled souls. In Wendy's mind, then, the haiku showed that he had been listening to her. And since he had actually seemed lonely, she'd taken the sentiment of the verse to be genuine — or so she told Cat.

Cat wasn't surprised, then, at the flowers or that Colin knew hydrangeas symbolized an apology. The fact that he'd acted so quickly warmed her heart. When he called later that night and apologized again, she melted.

"I'm not sure what I did during our meeting, Ms. White Eagle. Whatever it was, I'd like to sincerely apologize." He sounded like the proper English gentleman. "But I meant it when I said I find your thesis fascinating, and I'd like to help make sure that you defend your dissertation and publish it as a book. If meeting in my office is a problem, please choose some public place where you'll feel comfortable. What do you say, Ms. White Eagle? For the sake of Anglo-American relations, will you forgive me?"

Cat was glad they were having this conversation over the phone and not face to face. Otherwise, he would have seen her blushing and struggling to resist the temptation to kiss him. The warmth she was feeling was dangerous. *A tall, handsome star professor with a beautiful head of tousled, sandy hair, bedroom eyes and a killer smile asking a lowly, frumpy grad student to forgive him? These guys usually have egos the size of Everest.* As had happened the night of Colin's first visit to Satin, the rich tones of his voice—and his killer accent—penetrated deep inside her and cranked up her thermostat. She felt as turned on as she did whenever she saw his hungry eyes feasting on The Contessa's virtually naked body.

She bit her lip and forced herself to cool down enough that her voice didn't have that breathy quality that it got when she was aroused. "Thank you, Professor. It was a simple misunderstanding. Let me think about a good place to meet. I appreciate the offer. I'll text you."

Thinking about their next meeting, she looked for a place so public and so unsexy that she would be able to resist any temptation. She decided the Rodeo Clown Café was the perfect choice. As soon as someone walked in, they were given a big red nose. If they didn't wear it, no one would take their order. When Cat sent

Colin the details about where to meet, he responded with a reply she found gentlemanly, but also cute.

RCC it is.
Yee haw! See you there.
Your obedient servant.
Cowpoke CT

She thought seeing him with the red nose would make him look less attractive. It didn't. She found the incongruity of a famous scholar wearing it adorable. That he'd done it for her was endearing. All she could do was plead with herself to ignore the wet heat between her legs, her swelling breasts, stiffening nipples, tingling skin. *Cut it out! Focus on your thesis, slut!*

Each time they met, Colin was generous and helpful. He seemed sincerely interested in her research, and he made excellent suggestions about how to frame her ideas so she'd end up with stronger answers for the most skeptical members of her examining committee. He never complained that she would meet him only at Rodeo Clown—or that he had to wear the red nose every time.

Despite his I'm-too-sexy-for-my-pants reputation, he consistently behaved like a decent guy. *Professor* Colin was charming with a good sense of humor. He couldn't have been more courteous or professional. He even stood up when she arrived and held her chair out when she went to sit down. He treated her as a professional equal, not as just a grad student who should be grateful for the help of a world-famous scholar. He complimented her regularly on her insights. Also, he didn't initiate any physical contact between them, not even a handshake. But he did seem genuinely pleased to see her each time they met.

Cat was reassured when they settled into a professional relationship that was more than mutually respectful. Conversations never veered from academic matters to the personal. But the looks on his face when they met at the café made it clear that he enjoyed her company as much as she enjoyed his. His thoroughly decent and helpful behavior only made her want him more.

Colin's conduct should have made Cat feel better about him. Instead, she felt confused, distrustful and jealous. Just below the surface was the *other* Colin — the one who showed up at Satin every Friday to lust over The Contessa, the Colin who eyed the stripper hungrily and tipped her a hundred dollars at the end of the night. The Colin who'd happily bedded a bevy of grad students.

She even had to confess to being annoyed that he hadn't made a move on her. If he was such a hound and wanted The Contessa and virtually every other woman he crossed paths with, why didn't he want her? What was wrong with her? *Has he put 'Cat' in the friend zone? Does he only want women who go to bed with him immediately or, like The Contessa, seem so sexy they're worth the wait?*

Even more discouraging was that Cat was positive he was trying to get up the nerve to ask out The Contessa. As he slipped the hundred-dollar bill into her G-string after her last dance each week, he'd linger just a bit. He'd clear his throat as though he wanted to say something — then he'd hesitate, which gave Cat just enough time to make a fast exit. After a couple of weeks of that, Cat found flowers from him when she arrived at her dressing room. The card would have a snippet of poetry — usually a haiku. Something like —

Dancer of the air.
Lifted by the music.
A female Daedalus who reaches the sun.

He signed the cards, *Your humble and obedient servant in the purple tie.* When she walked on stage, she'd nod his way, but that was as much of a response as she allowed herself to give him. However, it didn't change how much she actually wanted him. What would she do if he confronted her — directly, honestly — with his desire for her? Giving in would be a terrible mistake. But could she really resist the temptation?

* * * *

For someone who projected an unflappable and easy charm, Colin was having the toughest time. The combination of celibacy and a powerful yearning for two women who couldn't be more different made his head spin.

The more time he spent with Cat, the more interesting she became. She wasn't just smart. She was brilliant. He was sure she thought the Lost Tribe was real and not a myth, even though she never admitted it. He suspected she'd done research on the topic that she was keeping secret. If she were right, it would be a revolutionary discovery. Whenever he tried to steer the topic that way, she'd bring it back to mythology or specific questions she had to address in her dissertation. Her focus and determination were infuriating — and intoxicating. He respected her professionally and liked her personally. He looked forward to their meetings.

And despite her decidedly plain appearance, she struck him as even sexier the more time they spent together. Even with no physical contact, merely being in her presence was enough to make him think about sex. What kind of body hid beneath her modest attire? What was she like in bed? During their appointments, he had to force himself to concentrate on her research.

In the past, the amount of time that elapsed from meeting a woman he wanted to seeing her naked had ranged from a couple of hours to a couple of weeks.

To his amazement, Cat was, without question, the most captivating woman he'd ever met. She was strong, sharp and bold. She was committed to a high-risk research project that was fueled by intense loyalty to her heritage, but she was also unassuming, curious and secretive. She was keeping something from him, and he found it intriguing. He looked forward to their meetings in a way that surprised him. With other women, the excitement of anticipation followed by the pleasure of being with her was all wrapped up in sex. This type of relationship was new for him.

She was also the most frustrating woman he'd spent time with. No matter how comfortable things were when they met, Cat remained distant. Even little things enforced the 'this is a professional, not personal' relationship boundary. She would call him only 'Professor'. There was no idle chit chat about their personal lives. He would try now and then to direct the conversation that way, but she politely deflected his questions and brought their focus back to work. And she was serious, serious, serious.

He was also exasperated that she didn't show any sexual interest in him. She always showed up for their meetings in frumpy, sexless clothes. She wore no makeup, jewelry or fragrance. She was never the least bit flirtatious. *How can I want someone so much who's not the least bit drawn to me?*

With other women, Colin experienced sexual desire as a two-way street. The attraction would be mutual and open. It was a game the two of them happily played. He'd stoke the flames until they couldn't control themselves. In the past, if he were interested in someone who didn't respond, he'd move on. Cat was the first woman whose lack of interest was a turn-on. It was confusing and unsettling for him, as he was used to being the alpha-male who orchestrated assignations and had sex with virtually any woman he wanted.

The situation with The Contessa was just as difficult — except in a very different way. She was pure sex. He got rock-hard as soon as he thought about her. When he watched her perform, he wanted her so much that it literally hurt. *This is crazy*, he told himself. *I know her job is to turn on anyone in the room — men and women alike. But I swear she's looking right at me and offering me her body. It's like she's saying, 'If you could read my mind, you'd know what I really want is for you to grab me and fuck me without mercy on the stage right here in front of everyone. That's how much I want you. That's how much I want you to want me.'* But something kept him from pulling the trigger with her. Watching her without having the courage to act was torture — but agony so delicious that he couldn't stay away.

Finally, after another Friday of losing his nerve at the last minute, Colin decided to 'man up'. Before his next trip to Satin, he reserved a suite at the five-star

Sedona Rouge Hotel and Spa. It had a huge jacuzzi and a romantic view of the mountains. He ordered bouquets of roses placed throughout the suite.

His plan was to watch The Contessa perform as usual, then wait until she'd changed and was leaving Satin. Since all the girls who worked there used stage names and wanted their privacy protected, customers were not allowed backstage. But Colin figured he'd been to the club often enough that he could identify all the girls as they left. He knew their heights, builds and the way they carried themselves. Besides, he was sure that if he got within a few feet of The Contessa, even though she was out of her costume, he'd feel the magnetic sexual attraction between them and know it was her.

Meeting her in the parking lot would let him feel that they were equals. He wouldn't be hypnotized by her nudity or intimidated by the majesty of her mask and headdress.

Using all his British charm, he'd introduce himself. He'd suggest a late dinner — in a suite he'd reserved at the hotel. He would project his trademarked sexual energy and confidence — the energy that had been easy to access before Cat and The Contessa had thrown him off his game. He was positive she'd accept his invitation. But even if she wasn't sure she wanted to sleep with him, she wouldn't turn down dinner. Refusing would suggest she was afraid of something — and he could tell from the sexy, aggressive way she danced that she liked a challenge.

It would be his adventure with Danielle all over again — only minus the early morning invasion by a SWAT team and international incident. He'd already checked in at the hotel and left an overnight bag with everything the two of them would need—plus a fabulous piece of lingerie he'd had beautifully wrapped. It was an elegant silk charmeuse of the same deep blue as The Contessa's bodysuit, with black lace for the bodice.

It would be a night to remember, and they'd have spectacular sex for a few weeks. But she struck him as a woman who liked variety. By the time Cat was available, he was sure The Contessa would be looking for a new lover anyway.

* * * *

"Cat, it looks like you have a fan waiting in the parking lot," Lauren said, looking out of the window just as they were about to open the door and leave Satin. "Looks like you-know-who. My guess is that he wants some *return* on his investment." She laughed.

Cat peeked out of the glass, making sure she couldn't be seen. She smiled to herself. She'd wondered how long it would take before Colin would do something like this. "That's him, all right. Luis!" she yelled. "Plan B!"

"Be right there," answered Satin's chief bouncer.

Because it often happened that customers wanted to date the girls, the club had a variety of tactics to deal with any unwanted attention.

In Plan A, Luis—a six-foot-five-inch giant of a man—would go outside and ask the gentleman why he was waiting. When he named the object of his affection, Luis would tell him that she was happily married but appreciated the attention. Luis then would give him a coupon for a free lap dance.

If the guy tried a second time, it was Plan B. The girl gave Luis her car keys. He walked out, started the car and drove it around to a different door where she would make her escape. The suitor generally got the point when he was the last person in a dark parking lot.

But if Plan B didn't work, Luis would be a little more direct and give him a 'time out' from Satin. He would be banned for two weeks. Any additional infractions meant a permanent ban. The threat of not being able to drink in the sight of Satin's naked beauties was serious punishment indeed. That always did the trick.

"Wait a minute, Cat. We haven't used Plan A on this guy yet," Luis said, looking out of the window. "He's a regular and tips the staff really well. Don't you want to start by going easy on him?"

"No, I'm going for 'woman of mystery' with this guy. Trust me. He'll get the message. Plus, he'll love it." Using her Italian accent, she explained, "Vanishing into the night is absolutely what The Contessa would do."

"Okay, *Contessa*. You're the boss. Keys?"

Five minutes later, Cat and Lauren sped away from Satin. Giggling, she wondered how long it would take before Colin figured out what had happened.

Since it always took Luis about an hour to close after the staff and dancers left, Colin waited until the building went dark and the parking lot lights were turned off. He'd dated strippers before, so he concluded that he'd been 'Plan-something-or-other-ed' by The Contessa. "Her loss." He put down the top of his jeep and got in. "Spectacular night. Billions and billions of stars," he observed as he gazed into the diamond-filled sky. "It would have been a perfect night for romance. But if that's the way she wants to play it,

I'll have to up the ante." He smiled confidently as his car's engine roared to life. "Game on, *la mia bella contessa.*"

Chapter Fifteen

"Then, after I finally get up my nerve and set the stage for the perfect evening by reserving the most romantic suite, she sneaks out." His voice was filled with exasperation. "Of course she knew what she was doing, Ian. We've been doing this flirtatious cat and mouse thing for weeks... You're right. She is more of a challenge than any woman I've ever met... I'm glad you find this amusing, brother... Fine, if it will make you stop laughing. 'Being humbled now and again is good for me. It builds character.' Satisfied? What do I do next? She likes to play games. I'll stay away for a couple of weeks. Let her think I've lost interest... Ian! Please stop laughing... Fine. But I have office hours starting in a couple of minutes. Let's chat later. Cheers."

Cat was sitting on the bench just outside Colin's office. With her dissertation defense a little less than three weeks away, she'd decided to drop by his office to discuss an article that had just been published. The door was open a crack, and she heard the entire conversation.

How irresistible he found The Contessa.

How sensual her dancing was.

How 'limber' her body was — and what he imagined it would be like to have sex with her.

How sure he was that she wanted him as much as he did her.

How intimidated he'd been to approach her.

His plan for that evening.

How frustrated he was that it had failed.

She felt pulled in opposite directions. As The Contessa, she loved the effect she'd had on him. *The Sedona Rouge. Best suite. Yum! Roses everywhere. That's so sweet and romantic! Lingerie!* She was thrilled — and aroused — by the fact that she'd ignited such uncontrollable desire in him simply by her dancing. She was also delighted to confirm that it matched her own passion for him.

But as Cat, she felt hurt and, as crazy as it seemed, even more jealous of her alter ego. She was fuming. She didn't know whom she was angrier at — him, for planning this elaborate seduction for a woman who was a total stranger, or herself, for wanting him nonetheless. She was so upset that she got up and left as he hung up.

As she walked out of Geronimo Hall, she called Lauren and asked if they could meet for lunch in a few minutes.

Luckily Lauren was available, and Cat met up with her right away.

Frustrated, she ran her hands through her hair and exhaled. "I don't know what to do! I'm furious, confused and disappointed. He's been great these last few weeks. He's been a helpful mentor. He's a brilliant archaeologist. He has behaved like a perfect gentleman. He even holds my chair! I didn't think there was a guy alive who still did that. It may seem old fashioned, but with him, it's charming. He treats me as an equal. And he's so, so, so sexy. I *really* like him. And the way he smiles when I arrive, I think he likes me. But he's shown zero signs of interest beyond that."

Lauren looked confused. "Wait... Isn't that what you wanted? You told me he was a pig. He was the last man you'd be interested in. And you're angry because he has treated you with respect?"

"Yes!" She threw up her hands in exasperation. "Because acting that way has made me want him like crazy—which is ridiculous! How can I want someone so much who shows no interest in me—especially someone who's a hound? I should be grateful I'm not one of his targets. Instead, I'm hurt and jealous. I'm being stupid." She put her head on the table and pounded it softly against the dark wood. She looked back up and sighed. "Maybe I had him wrong from the beginning. Maybe he's more than his reputation—and his fixation on The Contessa—suggests. Or maybe"—she squirmed—"I'm too horny to think straight. He's sexy as hell. Just being around him gives me a lady boner! It's been so long since I've had sex that I'm climbing the walls!"

Lauren smiled sympathetically. "That's a tough one. Is he a chronic and incurable manwhore you're drawn to because he's a bad boy? Or does he turn out to be a sexy good guy—who's not making a move because you're his student and you've made it plain that you're not interested? He plays around—but only when he's unattached."

Cat sighed. "I guess that's what it comes to."

"What about his fixation on The Contessa? Could you make your peace with that?"

She pressed her lips together, played with the salt and pepper shakers some more then looked up. "Yes. If he wanted a real relationship and agreed to put all that behind him, I'd be interested."

"What would you do if you were sure he was just another guy led around by whatever makes his cock stiff?"

Cat groaned. "I'd take cold showers and spend a week in bed with my Magic Wand and hope it's enough to get him out of my system."

"You wouldn't be tempted to have a one-nighter? Just to see if he's as good as rumored?" She winked slyly.

"Tempted? Absolutely! But at this stage in my life, I want something real."

"So," Lauren replied, "how do you figure out what kind of guy he really is?"

Cat went back and forth with Lauren through lunch, discussing all the options. When Cat settled on a solution, her friend said, "Ingenious!"

When she pushed her long black hair behind her back, leaned forward and started making notes on a napkin, Lauren laughed. "Super organized Cat White Eagle even has a plan, right? How many parts does it have?"

She flushed. "Three," she said sheepishly, "over the next few weeks."

"Okay…details!"

"Step One—you and I need to go shopping so I can see if 'sexy Cat' gets a reaction from him."

"Shopping! Yay!" Lauren shouted, and they high-fived.

"Step Two—I tease him enough to keep things simmering while seeing that he can keep things professional and not think this is a come-on.

"Step Three—put him to the real test—to see whether he wants me or just sex."

"Test?" asked Lauren. Cat leaned in and whispered in her ear. Lauren raised her eyebrows, and her eyes went wide. She gave a naughty smirk at what Cat had described. "That's just mean!"

"Only if he fails." Cat laughed. "But if he passes, we talk about whether we're on the same page."

Lauren chuckled. "And if so, and if he wants to consummate the new relationship right then?"

"As much as I want him, I've never been a 'sex on the first date' girl. We've gotten to know each other as professor and student. I need at least one date as equals."

* * * *

After a weekend of shopping, Step One began a couple of days later. Cat called the department secretary and booked a two-hour appointment to see Colin that afternoon. She explained that with her dissertation defense just around the corner and she wanted his advice on some important parts of her research—which, conveniently, was true. But instead of dressing in her standard 'nothing says sex' clothes, she would show up in the outfits she and Lauren had picked out. The ones that said, 'too sexy to be true'.

After showering and applying a body crème with a luscious, floral scent, she sat down at her makeup table.

"First, my contact lenses. We lose the studious, good girl, clunky glasses. Next, we're going for a natural, sweet, but sexy look," she explained to her reflection. Once done, she put in her black-gold belly ring with a petroglyph design. She squeezed into tight denim shorts—ones that rode low on her hips and fastened considerably below her navel. Then she chose her unlined white lace Aubade demi-bra and an elegant white lace boho top. The combination was close to see-through.

When she looked at herself in the mirror, she simply appeared to be a beautiful young woman wearing shorts to deal with the unusually warm November day. It was just coincidental that they revealed her toned, light-bronze legs. Her top was modest, but as she moved around, Colin wouldn't be able to ignore her nipples visible through lace of her bra and the gaps in the boho. The petroglyph belly stud would catch his eye—and so would the tight, smooth skin between her navel and the top of her jeans, and especially the way the denim hugged her mound. Her experience at Satin and the progress she'd made rock climbing gave her a new self-confidence. She felt like a beautiful butterfly about to emerge from its cocoon. "Let the games begin," she said to her reflection.

She gathered her things and hurried to her appointment with Colin.

When he opened his office door, he was stunned. She walked in and spread her notes out on the coffee table to make sure they sat right beside each other on the sofa. She made a point of being unusually animated so that he'd see plenty of flesh. Nonetheless, her plan was just to *dress* sexy, not to *act* sexy—no flirting, lingering looks or suggestive comments.

As she'd hoped, he was distracted and seemed confused the entire meeting. She couldn't stop giggling as she left Geronimo Hall. She was thrilled that he couldn't take his eyes off her the whole time. *Yay! He's definitely interested. But interested in what? Pussy Cat — or just pussy?*

Step Two — teasing and simmering — would now come from the fact that she would return every couple of days in a different — and hotter — outfit. She always used the same pretext. "There's just one more thing I need to talk to Professor Tucker about." As much as Colin would want to feast on the delicious sight in front of him, if he were going to act appropriately, he couldn't be obvious about it. He'd have to act as the consummate professional. But she hoped it would *kill* him to do so.

Wednesday... Super-tight, boot-cut jeans with red cowboy boots, a pretty red camisole — no bra. Her makeup was darker, emphasizing her high cheekbones and dark, almond-shaped eyes. She added a cologne rich with leather highlights.

Friday... A low-cut yellow sundress with a flowing skirt that somehow always seemed to slide up her tan legs whenever she shifted position on the office couch, sandals that showed off her manicured toes, understated makeup, but a strong jasmine fragrance. Throughout the meeting, Colin noticeably squirmed, trying to find a more comfortable position.

She didn't see him at Satin that night. He was apparently carrying through on his threat to skip a couple of weeks to worry The Contessa. His frustration was taking its toll. When she arrived Monday and saw what Colin was wearing, she smirked. *It's working.* Instead of his tight jeans, he had on a pair of much looser khaki chinos. *I guess someone's cock is tired of being squeezed.*

For her part, Cat wore a short navy skirt which, like the sundress, didn't want to stay in place. She wore it with an elegantly embroidered, sheer, light-blue long sleeve blouse — since it was a cooler day — over her navy lace La Perla bra, a more sophisticated look — smokier eyes and redder lips — and a businesslike, slightly spicy cologne.

Wednesday... Thin, black running tights and a bright red sports bra with 'Just Do Me!' emblazoned across the front. For an added twist, she'd put on a temporary tattoo just below the bra strap. It was a tiny, but clearly visible outline of a couple having sex. *"Sorry to dress like this, but I'm meeting my girlfriend so we can squeeze in a run. I knew you wouldn't mind,"* she'd explained. She wore a crisp citrus fragrance and just enough makeup to give her face a healthy glow.

Friday... Tan shorts that showed off her legs again. A see-through, light-blue blouse with a lacy, unlined bra of the same color. Instead of buttoning the blouse, she tied the ends together so her tight abs and diamond stud belly ring were on display, and wore sandals again, but with her toes painted the blue of her blouse and bra. She decided to slowly start darkening her makeup over the next three times she met with Colin. Then she'd reverse course and be all 'good girl and professional' for her exam on Friday. She began using Colin's wood sage and sea salt cologne, wondering whether he'd notice.

Monday... Because this followed the second weekend he'd skipped Satin, Cat decided that today would be psychological warfare. Everything was 'Contessa blue'. Tight yoga pants and a body-hugging sweater to bring to mind The Contessa's costume—heavier on the makeup, Contessa-blue eyes, Contessa-blue nails, the darkest lipstick she could get away with and The Contessa's signature scent—Opium.

Wednesday... Because she would be wearing a business suit for her examination on Friday, she chose low-cut, black 'bun huggers', no bra and a white sleeveless T-shirt so thin and tight that she may as well have been competing in a wet T-shirt contest. "Just trying to get one last run in to calm my nerves before the big day!" she said enthusiastically. But she'd taken pains to apply a musky body crème with a pronounced glitter, dark, sexy eyes and deep red lipstick.

* * * *

Colin was amazed, puzzled, thrown off-balance...and *very, very* aroused...by Cat's transformation from tame kitten to *Pussy* Cat over the last couple of weeks. After every appointment with her, he'd watch her out of the window, shake his head and pose the same question to himself. *Fuck! What is that all about?*

After their final appointment, he got up and opened the window to cool off. He furrowed his forehead as he paced in his office. He needed some plausible explanation.

We've been getting along really well. Is this a signal she wants to move things to the bedroom? Life suddenly felt a hundred times better. *But there's been no flirting, 'accidental' touching or sexy talk. She may look hot, but her behavior is as chaste and serious as ever.* He'd been with enough women to know the signs they sent out signaling their interest in men. His hopes faded. *What the fuck is going on?* After a couple of more minutes of pacing, he stopped short. *Damn! She's met some guy! They're hitting the sheets as often as they can. She feels like the Queen of Shag City and wants everyone to know it. Fuck! Fuck! Fuck!*

He sat down at his desk and banged it hard. He narrowed his eyes as he pictured Cat's new lover taking her. He was sure it was some fellow student who was rough, clumsy and inexperienced in the art of love. Someone like that didn't deserve a glorious woman like Cat. Anger and jealousy ate away at him. He felt sick knowing he'd waited too long and missed his chance.

He reached for his phone. It took forever before his brother answered. "I know it's in the middle of the night, Ian. I just needed to talk to a mate."

He had told Ian about The Contessa, but he'd never said anything about Cat. He recounted the whole story. "Fuck! I'm such a tosser. I could kill myself for waiting too long."

Ian listened quietly. This was apparently a conversation with Colin that he'd been hoping to have for years. "I'm truly sorry you feel so bad, Colin, but I'm proud of you. You knew that since she was your student, she was off limits. But instead of saying, 'Fuck it. I must have her,' you respected the relationship. For once in your life, you did the right thing."

Colin sat back, took a deep breath and chuckled. "So this is what 'doing the right thing' feels like? Angry? Depressed? Frustrated? Jealous?"

"Pretty much." Ian laughed as well.

* * * *

Cat's attire for the Friday defense was all business—tan linen pant suit, light-blue silk blouse, minimal makeup, no fragrance. She was taking no chances. As much as she enjoyed winding Colin up, she was a serious professional. She wasn't going to continue the game she was playing with him until she'd taken care of business.

Despite being nervous about her dissertation defense, Cat handled herself extremely well throughout the two-hour ordeal. The only tense moment came when the most skeptical member of the committee removed a sheet of paper from his folder and slowly read off a long list of reservations. "I will be happy to reconsider this dissertation when—and I mean *if*—Ms. White Eagle is able to address them and show that she's doing *science*, not poetry," he intoned condescendingly. It would take months of extra work. That was the point.

It was a ploy to fail her without doing it directly. This particular professor was notorious because of his belief that women didn't belong in archaeology. He threw barriers in the way of the female grad students whenever he could.

As her mouth went dry, Colin stepped in. "Dennis...may I?" He took the piece of paper and reviewed it. "Not to worry." He put it in his pocket with a smile and turned to his chairman, who was in charge of the defense. "Professor Medina, I *personally* guarantee that Miss White Eagle's work will address all *genuine* issues."

"That's fine with me," Medina said to the group. "Given Professor Tucker's stellar reputation in the field, I'm sure we are all happy to defer to his judgment in this matter. Shall we start to wrap up?"

The face of Cat's adversary contorted so it looked like he'd swallowed something that tasted so horrid he was about to throw up. She noticed that everyone else around the table was struggling to suppress smiles.

She left the room while the committee discussed her performance. After twenty agonizing minutes, the chairman stepped out and beckoned. "Will you please join us, *Doctor* White Eagle?"

A million-ton weight dropped off her back. Her head spun from excitement. *Yes! Yes! Yes! I did it! I did it! I did it!* She screamed inside. She stood calmly. "I'd be happy to, Professor," she replied professionally.

The committee gave her high marks for thoroughness. She was asked to make some minor revisions to deal with some of the issues that had come up during the exam then received warm congratulations from everyone on the committee.

She was thrilled as she walked into the hall and called her friends with the good news. Colin was the last member of the committee to leave the conference room. As junior member of the examining team, it was his responsibility to fill out the paperwork. When he stepped out, he saw Cat and extended his hand to congratulate her. "Congratulations, *Doctor* White Eagle."

She shocked him with an enthusiastic hug. "I can't thank you enough for what you just did."

"It was nothing. Everyone knows Dennis is a horse's arse. If I hadn't put him in his place, someone else would have."

"Even so. It was *you* who did. I insist on buying you a drink. Right now. I won't take no for an answer. Meet me at the Desert Cave in twenty minutes."

* * * *

Colin was in agony. Cat's suggestive wardrobe had been torturing him over the last two weeks. Feeling her soft body against his only made things worse. Add to that the fact that it had killed him to miss The Contessa's performances for the last two Fridays. It was no surprise that he was so horny he could barely see straight.

His celibacy had to end. He would go back to Satin that night and work his magic on The Contessa. Cat's transformation from sexless scholar to hot girl only added fuel to his sexual hunger. Since she obviously had a boyfriend now, she was off limits. He didn't ask women to cheat, and he didn't break up couples. But The Contessa was fair game.

When Colin arrived, Cat was already there. He was surprised she'd picked the Desert Cave. It wasn't a student hangout. It was an upscale, romantic establishment with lots of dimly lit corners. It was where someone went to set the mood — dark wood, fine crystal, delicious food and wine, and sexy jazz playing softly in the background.

She was in a booth in the darkest corner. It was crescent-shaped, and she was sitting in the middle. He sat down at the far end, as a gentleman would. He noticed she'd removed the jacket to her suit and undone a couple of buttons on her blouse.

She shot him a brilliant smile. "Slide over here, Professor. We're celebrating." She pointed to a bottle of champagne in an ice bucket. "Would you please do the honors?" He complied and filled their glasses.

"Hold on. I think it's time you stop calling me 'Professor'. We're professional equals. So it's 'Colin'. Okay?"

"I'd like that, Colin," she said, smiling warmly.

"I can't tell you how proud and impressed I was with how well you did, Doctor White Eagle. Here's to you."

She beamed as they clinked glasses and drank. "And here's to you." She touched her glass against his. "I couldn't have done this without you."

As they sipped their way through half the bottle, Cat couldn't stop saying how grateful she was for his help. She pried out of him what had gone on when she was out of the room and joked about the nightmare scenarios she'd had about how the defense might go. And she did a hilariously snarky impression of the faculty member who had tried to torpedo her.

Colin was amazed at how funny she was. The very serious Cat White Eagle actually had a lighthearted side. He found it delightful.

"I couldn't have done this without you, Colin. To thank you, I want to invite you to dinner tonight. I'm preparing it myself. A few girlfriends are taking me out for drinks first, so we'll eat on the late side—ten o'clock? I know I should have said something about this earlier, but I didn't want to jinx things. It means so much to me that it would break my heart if you say no."

He was surprised at the invitation. He'd assumed the champagne was his 'thank you'. Then it registered that Cat made no mention of the B-word. On such an important day, surely she'd include her boyfriend at some point. *Unless...* He needed to be respectful and diplomatic in how he handled this. "Will your boyfriend be joining us? I'm looking forward to meeting him. Is he another archaeologist?"

Cat stared back blankly for a few seconds, then smirked slyly. "*Boy*friend? What makes you think I have a *boy*friend?" She let her face drop enough to suggest being offended.

His jaw dropped. He'd never imagined that as a possibility. *You tosser! Apologize!*

As he scrambled to find the right words, Cat let him off the hook. "I'm sorry. I couldn't resist." She laughed. "It's the champagne. I'm a lightweight. It makes me misbehave. I was just teasing. I don't have a boyfriend or a girlfriend. So, dinner? It will just be us." She put on a playful, wide-eyed, pleading expression. "Please say yes. Pretty please?"

Everything about the moment — their mutual delight in her success, the frisky effect the champagne had on her, her sudden availability — made her irresistible. "I'd love to, Cat," flew out of his mouth without a moment's hesitation — or thought. Never having seen this side of her, he was enchanted. He took her hand and kissed it. An electric current ran through him when his lips touched her skin. The charge was so strong that he froze.

The silent gasp she let out signaled that something similar had happened to her. She pulled her hand away and quickly took a large sip of champagne. Red-faced, she looked at her watch and jumped up. "Tonight at ten. My place." She reached for her phone. "There. I've texted you the address. I have a million things to do. I've got to run. But please stay and enjoy the rest of the champagne." As she walked away, she turned, waved and smiled. "Can't wait!"

As he watched her leave, his body simmered down. He puzzled over what had just happened. *What's going on? That was like the first time we shook hands — and every time I touch The Contessa. It was like holding a live wire of sexual energy. But the two women are opposites. Is this a butterfly coming out of a cocoon? Or was she always that way but hid it? I knew she was brilliant – but funny? Irreverent? And above all – sexy as hell! Where did all this come from? Her suggestive clothes were never about a boyfriend. Is she giving me the green light?* He couldn't wait to see what the evening would bring.

Then it hit him.

Today's Friday! The Contessa! Colin the Hound returned. *Fuck! I cannot give up the chance to bed her. But I also can't miss my opening to start something with Cat.* He quickly made a plan. The Contessa first performed at eight. He'd speak to her after her first dance. Given his absence, she'd surely see him. He'd invite her to spend the following night with him. He was so confident she'd melt when he finally made his move that no other possibility even crossed his mind. She'd agree. Then he'd head to Cat's.

Chapter Sixteen

Cat was on top of the world. Not only was she now 'Doctor' White Eagle, but she also already had the perfect job lined up. She was hired to be the solitary researcher for the Sedona Museum of Native American History and Culture. She could basically do whatever she wanted. She was expected to familiarize herself with the current collection and decide what additions to make. Because the Museum had a small budget, the director encouraged her to do her own collecting in the nearby mountains—working on her own, exploring. She would finally be able to follow up on her theory about the Lost Tribe. It was perfect.

The museum told her she could start whenever she wanted, but she needed it to be as soon as possible. She'd successfully kept her pole dancing a secret. The sooner she could afford to stop, the better.

After drinks that night with Lauren and her other girlfriends, she returned home and prepared dinner.

All she'd need to do was warm things up after Colin arrived.

She went to her bedroom and got her costume, makeup and temporary tattoos. She sat down on the bed, double-checking that she had everything. She fingered the sensual fabric of The Contessa's body suit. Thinking about what the night could bring, she shivered from the excitement, struck by how surprised she'd felt. She had so successfully walled off Cat's relationship with Colin from The Contessa's that she'd almost convinced herself they were two different people—and that it was The Contessa who felt the remarkable sexual charge when their skin touched. Gazing at her big bed, she yielded to the temptation, closed her eyes and pictured the two of them in the throes of passion. She grew warm all over and squeezed her thighs together.

No! This is date one! she chided herself, opening her eyes. She forced herself to stand up. *Or is it?* She sat back down. *Doesn't all the time we've spent together count for something?* She closed her eyes and drummed her fingers against her jeans. *Slut! You're just looking for a rationalization.* She sighed. "You're right," she said out loud, getting up again. *But*—she sat back down—*you vowed to christen them on a special occasion. You've just had an awesome day! You've been so nervous that you haven't slept well. You should put them on just to make sure you'll get a good night's sleep.* She nodded firmly. *Right. To get a good night's sleep. Definitely not to have sex in.*

She took the Egyptian cotton sheets out of her closet. She rubbed the lush, brilliantly white fabric against her face and sighed. *Oh my God. The thread-count must be twenty-five billion!* She quickly made the bed. Then it was off to Satin for The Contessa's final night.

* * * *

When Colin headed out, he picked up a bouquet of flowers and a bottle of champagne for Cat. When he arrived at Satin, he was greeted warmly by Melanie, the hostess. "It's good to see you again, Professor Tucker." She kissed him on the cheek. "We've missed you these last couple of weeks. The Contessa was hoping you'd be able to share her final night here. In fact, she's reserved a special table for you. Let me escort you there."

Colin was startled. "Final night?"

"That's right." The hostess walked him to a table right in front of The Contessa's pole. "You weren't here two weeks ago when we announced she's been offered a job in Las Vegas. She would have been disappointed if her favorite admirer weren't here for her swan song."

The idea that The Contessa would leave Satin hadn't occurred to him. *This is my last chance!*

After a few dancers, The Contessa appeared and gave a spectacularly sexy performance. As the final notes to the *Bolero* faded and she lay on the stage catching her breath, Colin prepared to get up and slip a note into her G-string. It said—

"Mi Contessa,
In honor of your final night at Satin, and in gratitude for all the joy you have brought me, I request an audience in your dressing room. Please tell the staff I have your permission to come backstage."

But just when he should have been getting out of his chair, he found himself holding back, distracted. He realized that the whole time The Contessa was dancing, he'd been thinking about Cat. Now that she was available, The Contessa's sexy body made him wonder what Cat looked like naked, and what a naked Cat would look like doing a pole dance just for him. *You wanker!* he yelled at himself. *What's wrong with you? Move your bleedin' arse out of this chair and slide the fuckin' note into her knickers!*

Before he realized it, The Contessa was up off the floor. But instead of walking off stage, she stood right in front of his table, undid the side ties of her G-string and tossed the sexy garment to him. Although most of the lights were still off, Colin could make out the highlights of her beautiful, athletic figure — the luscious curves of her body, the hard nipples that peaked her breasts, the tattoos that circled them, the tiny dark triangle that her G-string usually hid. This was the first time he'd seen The Contessa totally naked. Even in the dim light, she was spectacular. It wasn't just how beautiful she was nude. It was also how confidently she stood completely naked. He was transfixed. In an instant, she pivoted and quickly walked off the stage.

As the lights came up, he panicked. He hadn't given her the note! She wouldn't know to tell the staff to let him go to her dressing room. But she'd given him her G-string and let him admire her naked body. What was that supposed to mean? Was it a good-bye present? Or was she offering herself to him — finally confirming his belief that they had a powerful mutual hunger? Was the next move up to him? He told himself that she was in her dressing room waiting for him, feeling the same yearning for him that he was feeling for her.

As he scrambled to decide what to do, he felt a hand on his shoulder. The hostess handed him a note. Beautifully handwritten on expensive stationery, it read, 'I believe you have something of mine. Melanie will escort you to where you can return it to me.'

"You should know this is a first for The Contessa," Melanie said as they headed toward the curtains to the left of the stage. "This is quite an honor." Pushing aside the heavy red velvet cloth that separated the bar and dance area from the private VIP rooms where the girls gave lap dances, Melanie led Colin down the hall and into a lusciously appointed room. "The Contessa will be here in a moment."

Colin couldn't believe his good fortune. *A sexy woman who's not afraid to go after what she wants. My kind of woman. It's a shame she's moving.* The same luxurious red velvet hung on all the walls and across the entrance to the room. It gave a sense of privacy with low lighting, scented candles, a luxurious sofa and chairs — and assured that any sexy sounds wouldn't be heard outside the chamber. It was perfect for...well, everything Colin could imagine. Soft, classical music. *Italian opera? Very sensual aria. No doubt she chose it especially for our rendezvous.*

"*Buonasera, Professore* Tucker," said the heavily accented voice. Colin hadn't heard The Contessa enter.

As he turned, he saw she still had on her mask and headdress. She was wearing a long blue silk robe decorated with an elaborate floral print — which she immediately untied and let fall to the floor. Naked, she extended her hand, palm up. "I believe you found something I've lost. *Per favore*, I am going to need that lest I catch cold."

Finally seeing her naked in decent lighting, Colin held off returning her G-string for fear she'd immediately put it on. He decided to take the role of one of The Contessa's Venetian courtiers. He made a deep bow and said, "How may I serve you, *mi Contessa*?"

"I am leaving Venetia in the morning. I would like us to be able to say a proper goodbye. I require your presence at my *palazzo* this evening so that I may thank you for being my most devoted admirer."

She walked up to him, standing silently just a few inches in front of him as she let her spicy fragrance envelop him. Taking her G-string from his hand, she pressed her full breasts and hard nipples against his chest and placed a card into his jacket pocket. "The location of my *palazzo* is on the card. I shall see you at ten o'clock, *si*?" She kissed one cheek and purred seductively. "I promise you a night of unparalleled ecstasy in my bed, *Professore*." She kissed him on the other cheek, turned around and walked out of the room.

The Contessa radiated such confidence and sexual power that Colin was paralyzed—as though he was under a spell. When she'd kissed him, the familiar electric shock he felt every time he brushed against her flesh had surged through his body. And before he had the presence of mind to speak to her, she sashayed her beautifully shaped, naked behind out of the room.

He swore under his breath. *What a cock up! Get it together, mate!* he lectured himself. *Fuck! What now? Regroup! See her after the next dance. Tell her you can't meet her tonight. You'll fly to Vegas any time she wants. If you blow off Cat, you'll never get another chance. Keep your priorities straight.*

Colin walked down the hall, pushed the velvet curtain aside and stepped back into the main part of the club. He watched the other dancers do their second numbers. Where was The Contessa?

He went over to the hostess. "Excuse me, Melanie? Where's The Contessa?"

"Oh, she left. She twisted her ankle a little and didn't want to risk ruining her opening night in Vegas."

Damn! He sat back down and ran his fingers through his hair.

Now he had a dilemma. How was he going to be in two places at the same time? He took out the card The Contessa had slipped into his pocket. The address was for the Sedona Rouge Hotel and Spa. He'd expected to see her home address. But since she was leaving in the morning, it made sense she'd moved out of her place and was treating herself to a luxurious last night in Sedona. Still, the coincidence wasn't lost on him. *The Resort. I wonder. Could she have known?*

As he sat and watched the next dancer, he decided to call Cat and 'finesse the truth.' *There's no way I can pass up a night of unparalleled ecstasy with The Contessa.* He closed his eyes and tapped his fingers on the table. *A mild case of food poisoning. That should work. I'll invite her to dinner tomorrow.* He got up and went outside so there'd be no background noise on the call. He looked at his watch. *Nine-fifteen. Hopefully, she's still with her girlfriends. If I'm lucky, I'll get voicemail.*

He stood in the crisp Arizona night air, rehearsing the call. He had to sound just sick enough to beg off for tonight, but not so sick that she'd hesitate rescheduling for tomorrow. *Lead with an apology. Sound pathetically disappointed.*

He punched the keypad. A second later, he hit 'end'. *You can't do this. Grow up. It's not 'massaging the truth'. It's a barefaced lie.* He paced. The Contessa's promise played over and over again in his head. "*A night of unparalleled ecstasy in my bed.*" *It would be amazing! That has been obvious since we first touched. Are you really going to pass that up? There's no guarantee you'll get a second chance.* He stopped and stared at his phone. *It's just a white lie. Say it with conviction and Cat will believe it. The Contessa leaves for Las Vegas tomorrow. Cat will never find out. You'll be home scot-free.*

He took a deep breath and hit redial. *You do know that with The Contessa, it's just sex. Great sex – but just sex. It could be more with Cat. She's remarkable. Do you really want to jeopardize that? You respect Cat too much to do this.* Again, he ended the call before it could go through.

He paced back and forth, a man at war with himself. He picked up his phone and dialed a different number.

"Ian, what's love supposed to feel like?"

After listening for five minutes, he rang off, let out a deep sigh and slid his phone back into his pocket. "I am so fucked."

When Colin arrived at Cat's, he felt proud for doing the right thing. Working with her on her thesis had revealed her to be the smartest and most interesting woman he'd ever met. He still hadn't learned much about her past, but he recognized her drive, focus and relentless pursuit of answers. Intellectually, she was clearly his equal – although he hadn't admitted that to her yet. In some ways, she outstripped him – although he also hadn't confessed that to himself yet.

Discovering that she was available sexually was a gift from the gods. She was everything he could want in a woman. As much as he lusted after The Contessa, he wanted Cat more. He'd made a promise to her and he would keep it. And as far as the scary possibility that he was falling in love with her went, he'd hope for the best and follow his brother's guidance on their call. *"Listen to your heart. You have one, even if you don't think you do. And remember, your heart is different from your pecker."* Then Ian had laughed.

* * * *

After hurrying out of Satin, Cat sat in her car. She wanted to see what Colin would do, knowing he was desperate to sleep with *both* of her.

If all he wanted from her was sex, he'd leave a voicemail with some silly excuse. He'd go to the resort, where he'd find a note at the front desk—'Life's greatest pain comes from regrets at having made the wrong choice. Contessa Elisabetta Cavaleri.' When he called Cat the next day to reschedule, she'd simply tell him he'd made the wrong choice. There wouldn't be anger in her voice, only disappointment. She'd offer no details about how she knew about his other rendezvous. They could still collaborate professionally, but there would be no personal relationship.

She watched him pace in the parking lot. Her heart sank every time he put the phone to his ear. It bounced back up when he quickly pulled it away and punched it. He did talk to someone for a few minutes, but her phone failed to ring. *Is he choosing me over The Contessa?* Her heart did a cautious flip when he finally drove off. *Is that because he wants a relationship with me? Or will he just go to the resort, stand me up and give me some stupid explanation tomorrow?*

The 'test' she had designed would answer all her questions.

* * * *

When Cat opened the door, Colin showed surprise at how she was dressed. She had on an oversized pink terrycloth robe and slippers to match. Her head was wrapped in a towel, as though she'd just stepped out of the shower.

"I'm sorry. Things ran late with the girls. I only just got back. I need another fifteen minutes upstairs to take a quick shower. They thought it was cute to pour champagne over my head."

"No problem." He handed her the flowers and champagne.

"Thanks. Wow. A suit and purple tie. Very fancy. Hand tailored?"

"Anything I can do to help?"

"Actually, there is. It'd be great if you started a fire. And please open the champagne and get a head start on me while I finish getting ready."

When Cat went upstairs to her bedroom, she breathed a deep sigh of relief. Colin had actually passed the first part of her test. He'd chosen *her*, not The Contessa. And while she knew he was standing The Contessa up, at least he'd had the manners to leave a message for her at the resort. A friend of hers who worked the front desk there had the note from The Contessa, in case he'd showed up, and he'd texted her that Colin had called to apologize.

She went over to her CD player, adjusted the timer, pressed the play button and turned up the sound so it sounded like her shower was running. Grabbing her 'gear,' she silently snuck downstairs without Colin seeing her.

Colin walked into Cat's living room and admired how nicely it was decorated. It had a sophisticated but comfortable feel to it. It was feminine but not girly. And it definitely had a sexy vibe. There were small pieces of erotic art from various cultures sprinkled around the room.

Right in front of the fireplace was a huge, thick, white faux polar bear rug. And there were all sorts of pillows — large, small, soft, firm — in a pile right beside the rug. The sight was too tempting. *Making love in front of a fire. Very sexy. Maybe?* He knelt in front of the fireplace and set to work.

At the very instant he popped the cork to open the champagne, he could have sworn the front door opened and closed. Listening for a moment, all he heard was the crackle of the fire and the water running from Cat's shower. He shrugged his shoulders and focused on tending the fire.

Then he detected one of his favorite scents — a powerful, dark, lusty perfume. *That sexy minx! Not at all a 'good girl Cat' fragrance. Isn't that what The Contessa wears? What a coincidence.* "I smell something deliciously sexy. It that a sign of things to come?" he asked hopefully.

"I certainly hope so, *mi Professore*," said a heavily accented voice.

Colin spun around. He was stunned.

Chapter Seventeen

The Contessa stood at the other end of the living room looking exactly the way she did at Satin — from the headdress to the blue silk robe to her high heels — but not for long. As she slowly walked toward him, she untied her robe, let the sensual fabric fall to the floor and, wearing only a G-string, stood before him. Pressing her hands against his chest, she said, "I see you are...how do the Americans say it — 'directionally challenged' — *no*? You made a wrong turn and ended up in this lovely home. This is very nice." She gestured around the room, then pointed at the fireplace. "And a *fire*...so much more romantic than a hotel." She looked at the bottle and glasses on the table. "Ah, *champagne*. I would love some." She walked over, poured herself a glass and stretched out on the cream leather couch.

Colin had never been closer to passing out from hyperventilating in his life. This felt even worse than when the British SWAT team had broken in on him. At least then he'd been hungover, half asleep and in such a fog that it had taken him some time to process what was happening. Cat would be down any minute. He had to get The Contessa to leave—and quietly. His mind was racing. Hopefully, this was just a prank on her part. *Right...a prank. Let's go with that. Because that's so much better than her being a crazy stalker. Okay, so she was angry I stood her up. This is her way of getting even. How'd she know I was here? Someone who can do a GPS trace on my phone? The Contessa would have all sorts of friends in influential places happy to do her a favor. Now I get it. This is payback. Get a grip. You can handle this.*

Cat's shower was still running, so he had some time to work with. He turned on the charm. "You're absolutely right to be getting even with me, *mi Contessa*. I apologize for canceling."

"You are rejecting me because of the young woman whose house we're in?"

He gulped. *When all else fails, tell the truth. It's going to come out anyway.*

"Yes, because of her."

"You have genuine feelings for her?"

He hesitated. He'd barely admitted this to Ian. He gulped. "I think I do. But these are new feelings for me. I don't know what is possible between us, but I would like us to be able to see what develops. I'm sure you can understand that if you remain here, that will be impossible."

She smiled warmly. "So you are asking me to leave in the name of *amore*?"

He frowned. "*Amore*? To be completely honest, I cannot say... Perhaps... But I am finally ready in my life to see if this is *amore*."

She nodded approvingly. "A truthful seducer. You remind me of Casanova. He too was a rogue, but he never lied to women. To their fathers and husbands, yes. To his lovers, no."

At that moment, Cat's shower turned off. A few seconds later, she called down, "I'll be there in a bit, Colin. Why don't you put on some music? And please pour me a glass of champagne."

His stomach clutched. But then The Contessa smiled. "I am happy for you, *mi Professore*, In the name of *amore*, I will respect your request."

He had never been more relieved to get out of a jam. "*Grazie mille, mi Contessa. Io sono in debito.*" He made a deep bow in front of her. "Please allow me to escort you to the door." He picked up her robe and held it out for her to put on.

"No, *Professore*, I am in your debt," she said seriously, ignoring the robe. "I came tonight to humiliate you in front of your young lady, thinking you were merely a rogue. You responded with grace and spoke of *amore*. You are a romantic. What I had planned was wrong of me. In Venetia, I am known as a woman of honor. I must set things right. I know nothing about this young woman. But if *you* are interested in her, she must be very sexy. However, I doubt she is as experienced as you are. *Si*? And you hope to be her teacher in the joys of the body. Yes? I see that in your eyes. How appropriate, *Professore*. The Contessa thinks that is sweet. But, as a man, you can teach her only so much. I must remain."

Colin's head started swimming, his heart pounded and sweat gathered on his forehead. *What's she up to now? Just get her to the door!*

"No man can know a woman's body as well as another woman. And I suspect your young lady has never been with a woman. I will help her discover the special pleasures that come from two women exploring one another's bodies. Then I will join the two of you in your lovemaking. I am sure *you* have been in bed with more than one woman at a time, but I doubt *she* has. I will act as teacher and servant to both of you. I will teach *you* how to satisfy two women so that each feels she has been worshipped all night. I will teach *her* how two women can give a man unimaginable pleasure. And I will show her how only another woman can take her to a level of ecstasy so remarkable that it is a religious experience. It is settled," she said firmly. "I will do everything I can to make sure this is the most memorable night of your lives. I will tell your young friend that you invited me here because you care so much for her that you wanted to make the evening remarkable... *Sessualmente fantastica!*"

At any other time, with any other woman, Colin would be ecstatic at what The Contessa was proposing. His lovers were always adventurous. But this would absolutely ruin any chance he might have with Cat. All it would do was confirm to her the worst part of his reputation.

"I will fetch her," The Contessa announced. She got off the couch and walked quickly toward the staircase leading upstairs. Colin shot after her, but he froze in place when she stopped short at the base of the stairs and held her hands up in surrender. "Please do not be startled, *Dottore White Eagle.* I am *La Contessa Elisabetta Cavaleri di Venetia.* I must explain something to you and beg your forgiveness."

Colin steeled himself for whatever was coming — knowing it would be bad. *Fuck. I'm dead and buried.* Cat must have been coming down the stairs and had now seen their visitor — a tall, naked woman with a

Carnivale mask and headdress who pretended to be from sixteenth-century Venice. Understandably, she was spooked. *She's probably heading to her bedroom to lock the door and call the police.*

There was no way this could end well. He'd have to beg like crazy to keep from losing his job. At that moment, he wished with all his heart that somehow the earth would open up and swallow him.

"Please wait," said The Contessa, looking up to where Cat must be standing. "This is rude of me. You cannot even see my face. How can I properly apologize for entering your home when we cannot look eye to eye, woman to woman?"

Colin breathed a little easier. Cat hadn't immediately bolted. Counting on some version of 'sisterhood', he decided to stay on the sidelines for now. Perhaps The Contessa could manage the situation so he'd have a chance of repairing the damage with Cat once she left. For now, with The Contessa facing away from him, he just stood and admired her remarkably toned body — and spectacular ass — as she removed her mask and headdress and held them in her left hand.

The first thing Colin noticed was how much shorter The Contessa seemed without the headdress. Then he saw that her hair was tightly wrapped. As she began to unfasten it with her free hand, Colin realized that it was long, straight and black, just like Cat's. But he couldn't see her face.

"So you are the newly minted *Dottore* Cocheta White Eagle. Please allow me to extend my congratulations," The Contessa said, extending her right hand. Cat was obviously making her way down the stairs.

Cocheta? Cat's first name is Cocheta? The department file says 'Catherine'. How does The Contessa know this — or that

Cat just defended her dissertation? Colin was feeling increasingly confused. There was too much about the situation that he didn't understand.

"As I said, I am *La Contessa Elisabetta Cavaleri*," The Contessa continued. "And this" — she gestured with her arm toward Colin without turning her head — "is the *Professore* Colin Tucker."

She turned toward Colin, holding her mask up in front of her face so he still couldn't see it. As she slowly walked toward him, she kicked off her heels, held her hand out and said, in a voice that now had no accent whatsoever, "There are no need for introductions, Contessa. Professor Tucker and I have met." She removed the mask.

A host of emotions crashed through Colin. He was astonished, nonplussed, gobsmacked, disoriented. He frantically tried to process the scene. The Contessa stood quietly, wearing only a naughty smirk.

Cat's The Contessa? No. Impossible. Cat's upstairs. This can't be Cat. The dolphin tattoos circling The Contessa's breasts. Cat doesn't have those. I would have seen them when she started dressing so sexy these last couple of weeks.

He closed his eyes. *Think! Think! What's going on here?* Then it hit him. There was only one logical explanation. *Twins! What a fucking brilliant con!*

He chuckled then shouted loudly enough that his voice carried to the staircase. "Very clever, Cat. And the *other* Ms. White Eagle?" He bowed. "We've never formally met. I'm Colin Tucker. And you are?"

"Winona, the *beautiful* one. Cat's the *smart* one. Charmed." She made a slight curtsy and giggled.

"Okay, Cat," Colin called out again. "You can come down now. Nicely played. Game over."

Winona put on her robe, walked back to the staircase and called upstairs. "He's right. Come on down so I can go home. I have to get up early and head to Vegas. He figured it out pretty quickly. Looks like you've got a smart one here, darlin'." Then she turned back toward Colin and eyed him. "So, you have the hots for Cat. Wow. She's definitely punching above her weight class with you. You aren't looking to just get into my little sister's pants, are you, buster? What's going on?" She grimaced and shook her finger at him.

He looked her straight in the eye. "Cat is simply the most enchanting woman I've ever met. Obviously, I've been very attracted to you as well. But we both knew that had no future. With Cat, it's different."

"A future with Cat?" 'Winona' raised her eyebrows and struggled to look somber. "In that case, since I'm her only family present, you need to explain something to me, young man. What are your intentions?"

He laughed, grateful that the atmosphere was now relaxed. "My intentions are to see what's possible between us. This was to be our first date. I honestly don't know what we feel toward each other. As your sister has probably told you, I have no history of real relationships. I don't know what I'm capable of. But Cat is the most remarkable woman I've met, and she has made me want to try. I can promise I will never deliberately hurt her. I care too much for her to do that."

'Winona' smiled. "That's good enough for now. You have my approval." She headed toward the door. "Oh, Cat said there's some old map upstairs on her office wall that you'd be interested in. Turn right at the top of the stairs. While you're waiting for her, go check it out. I've got a flight to pack for."

Having dodged a bullet, Colin relaxed. He couldn't stop himself from asking. "So, earlier, at Satin. Was that part of this stunt? What would have happened if I'd gone to the resort to meet you?"

She turned around, walked back until she was right in front of him and frowned. "Let's just say that you would have been very, very, very disappointed for a very, very, very long time when you realized what a stupid mistake you'd made." She punctuated each 'very' by poking his chest with her finger. "Now go make my sister happy. I'm leaving."

Colin had to hand it to the 'sisters White Eagle.' *Twins. Same DNA.* That was why he'd get that same electric surge whenever he touched either of them — one a scholar, the other a pole dancer. Such different lines of work that he'd never believe any resemblance between the two of them, even if he'd imagined he saw one. And the mask, headdress and shoes made The Contessa look a foot taller than Cat. A truly brilliant plan. He deserved all the panic and confusion it had given him.

He went upstairs and walked down the hall to her office. It was indeed an interesting map — the sites of ancient settlements in the surrounding mountains. But he didn't want tonight to be about work. He called out Cat's name a couple of times. When she didn't answer, he assumed she'd already gone downstairs.

When he got back to the fire, Winona was still there. Wearing her blue robe, she was stretched out on the sofa sipping champagne, enjoying the fire and listening to the romantic music. "Sit," she said to Colin before he had a chance to say anything. She made room for him on the sofa and handed him a glass of champagne.

"Hi," she said, extending her hand with a big smile, "I'm Cat. I can't tell you how nice it is to put an end to all this secrecy — or how pleased I am with myself that you never suspected. So now I can finally tell you that if you want to be less noticeable at Satin, go for something more casual than the suit and purple tie. And I prefer iambic pentameter over haiku. And if you still wonder whether it's really me, I'll be glad to spend the next couple of hours over dinner telling you about my theory of the Lost Tribe. But frankly, I'm hoping for something a little more personal on a first date."

It was enough information to make Colin accept that this wasn't 'Winona' and that Cat was the master of a very elaborate deception.

"No twin," was his simple reply.

"Nope."

"The sounds from upstairs. The shower? You calling down?"

"I recorded them on a CD earlier today. I just hit 'play' and let you think I was upstairs."

"The tattoos?"

"Temporaries. They wash off in the shower."

"*You…Cat…*really *are* The Contessa. This isn't some stunt?"

"I am The Contessa."

"The move to Las Vegas?"

"My cover story for why The Contessa won't be at Satin anymore. She's served her purpose. Now that I've finished my degree, I can start a job in the field. It would be professional suicide if anyone had known I was a stripper. So as soon as I could leave, I did."

"So, what was tonight's drama all about?"

Cat laughed. "To be honest, part of it was just for fun. Somebody needs to give guys like you a hard time now and then. But mainly it was because of your reputation."

He nodded. "How would you know if I was genuinely interested in you if I wasn't forced to make a choice?"

"That. And I had to hear you explain to someone else what your plans were."

He smiled and held up his champagne glass. "I salute you for your cleverness, Cocheta White Eagle. It is worthy of Aunt Clarissa."

"Aunt Clarissa?"

He laughed. "Trust me. It's a compliment. I'll explain over dinner."

Cat went back upstairs to dress and sat on her bed. She was happy with what Colin had said. If he'd made some declaration of undying love, she would have been suspicious. But he'd been honest. He didn't really know what he was capable of. Her challenge was to be sure she paid more attention to what her heart wanted than what her body craved.

She changed into her favorite little black dress. It was flattering but not overtly sexy.

She'd prepared a simple but interesting dinner. She used a number of recipes she'd come across in her research about the Lost Tribe. During the meal, Colin asked her all sorts of things about herself — her family, how she'd gotten interested in paleo-archaeology, what had brought her from Montana to Arizona. Her favorite books? Music? Movies? Shows on the 'telly'? Color? Flower? Had she ever been to London?

She was very surprised that his first question wasn't how she came to be The Contessa. She was touched at what felt like genuine interest in her.

They had dessert — a rich double-chocolate souffle — in front of the fire.

She licked the last bits of chocolate off her fork and looked at Colin. "I'm surprised."

He smiled. "Good surprised or bad surprised? Don't worry. I can take it."

"*Good* surprised. You've been a perfect gentleman. Between your reputation and all the foreplay at Satin with The Contessa — "

"You expected 'the hound' to show up at some point."

"Exactly."

"I meant what I said, Cat. You're an amazing woman. I honestly want to see what can happen between the two of us. I'm not going to lie. You and The Contessa are the same amazingly sexy woman. The two of you" — he laughed — "are driving me crazy because I want you so much. But I'm willing to take this slowly."

Cat smiled and felt warm all over. "That means a lot to me, Colin."

He looked at his watch. "It's late. I should go." They got up off the floor. "If it's okay with you, Doctor White Eagle, I'd like to call you tomorrow to arrange a second date."

"I'd like that," she said sweetly.

They hugged briefly, and he left.

As she closed the door, she leaned against it and sighed. She hugged herself, feeling content all over. *A perfect first date! He showed genuine interest in me. He understood why I pulled the stunt I did and wasn't resentful. Despite The Contessa flaunting her body for weeks, promising a night of amazing sex, and the powerful chemistry bubbling just below the surface — aching to explode* — she groaned audibly — *there was no pressure about sex. I can't wait for date two!*

She looked at her watch. A very naughty expression filled her face. *Hmmm. It is 'tomorrow' already. It would count as a second date.* She shook her head. *No, I couldn't...or could I?* She smirked, then gestured dramatically. "The respectable *Dottore White Eagle* of Sedona couldn't," she pronounced boldly in a sensual Italian accent, "but *la Contessa Elisabetta Cavaleri di Venetia* is not subject to such conventional restraints." She picked up her phone, sent a text and hurried upstairs to get ready.

Colin stepped outside and headed toward his Jeep with an unfamiliar sense of pride. Despite how much he wanted to sleep with Cat, he hadn't made a single move on her. He'd let her set the pace. Frankly, when she'd explained the point of the Contessa-Winona theatrics, he'd known sex was off the table. Both Ian and Aunt Clarissa had warned him repeatedly that once he finally met a woman he was genuinely interested in, he'd have his reputation to overcome. This was a situation of his own making, so he was prepared to take his medicine. Not having to think about how he would orchestrate a night of playful seduction, however, let him relax. He and Cat already had a good working relationship. There wasn't that big a difference in their ages. It was easy to relate to her as an equal and be on an actual 'date' with her. He could also take comfort in knowing it was just a matter of time before they'd end up naked and tangled in the sheets.

The starry sky was spectacular. The natural beauty around him sparked a sense of hope. *I guess Ian's right. Doing the right thing occasionally goes unpunished.* He laughed. His phone buzzed. *Speak of the devil. He couldn't wait until tomorrow to see how things went.* He looked at the screen.

You forgot to say goodbye to The Contessa. She's waiting upstairs.

Chapter Eighteen

Cat stood beside her bed wearing only a blue silk mask, matching G-string and heels. A rich, sensual aria was playing. A few scented candles gave the room a soft glow.

She was so excited that she could barely contain herself. Her heart raced. Her breathing was rapid and shallow. Her skin felt electrically charged. She was warm all over — and deliciously, sinfully wet.

She stood proudly, shamelessly. She savored the new sexual confidence she'd gotten from being The Contessa. She couldn't wait to let go completely. It had been more than two months since Colin had first touched her at Satin. Her deep yearning had only grown since then — and it continued to grow as he climbed the staircase and got closer.

Just as he was about to enter, she had a moment's panic. *Is this really a good idea? You just said you wanted to wait and now you're seducing him.* When he stepped into her bedroom, however, his face showed he could barely stop himself from simply taking her. His desire was every bit as strong as hers. Her own arousal kicked up a notch. Tonight would be everything she'd dreamed. They had both waited long enough. Slow, sensitive foreplay and languid lovemaking could wait for some other time. Tonight was about satisfying a deep, primitive hunger.

He bowed deeply. *"La mia Contessa. Come posso servirti?* How may I serve you?"

After stepping out of her heels, she pulled off her G-string and slid onto her bed. She cupped her breast and ran her hand down her body until she reached her wet, swollen lips. Caressing them, she parted her legs just a bit. There was no need for words.

Colin stripped. When his stiff cock sprang from his black boxer briefs, Cat's breath caught and she opened her legs farther. He put on a condom then kissed her.

She groaned as she welcomed him inside her. She'd been waiting for this moment forever. His rock-hard penis penetrated her and sent shivers up her spine. Any barriers she'd built to protect her heart crumbled. Completely vulnerable, she was joined to him in every respect. Her body stretched to handle the girth of his cock. He filled her with a single, powerful stroke. She delighted in never having felt so complete.

Because of the way she had reacted so strongly to just his fleeting touch at Satin, she'd wondered what it would be like when their naked flesh made contact, and it was every bit as powerful as she'd imagined. Every cell of her was flooded by pleasure so electric, so primal, that it couldn't be expressed in words. She moaned desperately.

She wasn't prepared, however, for the range and intensity of the emotions racing through her — relief at having finally found the person fated to complete her, a deep yearning to meld with him in every way, undying love for him, joy at being able to give herself to him completely and confusion at how she could feel so much for someone she hadn't known for that long.

As she looked up at his face, she saw raw hunger. But it was a desire for every part of her, not just her body. As he pounded into her repeatedly, she sank into the primitive pleasure of being the object of this man's longing and the wonderful sensation of being possessed by him.

At the same time, she knew The Contessa would not be passive in bed. She pushed her hands hard against his chest and flipped them over. Straddling him, she grabbed his hard penis, put its head against her opening and slid down roughly. He grunted at being taken by her so forcefully. Her breathing was rapid and passionate. Leaning forward, she put all her weight on his chest and took control. She moved up and down on his veined cock, which was now coated with her juices, with the fierceness of an Amazon. Never had she so selfishly pleasured herself on a lover like this. Being in control was exhilarating. Her heart thundered in her chest from the excitement. Her skin glowed from the sweat covering it. The aroma of sex filled the air.

She'd expected him to try to regain control. Contessa or not, he would want to dominate her in bed. But she was prepared. When he reached for her, she surprised herself with just how strong she'd become. Pushing his arm away, she leaned down and commanded him to minister to her swollen breasts with his mouth. He obeyed, as she knew he would. She moaned deeply as he kissed them. Jolts of pleasure shot through her when he ran his teeth along her dark, stiff nipples and sucked hard.

Sitting back and grinding against him, she soared toward a climax. She needed so badly the release this man could give her, so she wasn't going to delay the ecstasy. She squeezed his cock as hard as she could. He thrust up sharply into her, and she shrieked and exploded. Hot, liquid joy flooded every cell. Her entire body shook. Throaty sounds of pure, animal satisfaction emanated from her mouth. Her pussy instinctively gripped his cock and milked it. He moaned loudly and spun them so he was again on top. As he rammed into her, their bodies smacked together from the sweat of their furious fucking. With a final grunt, he bellowed. His cock swelled, twitched and pulsed. He wrapped his arms around her as his body shuddered.

Cat's climax had been so powerful that her head was spinning. Being the object of such desire made her feel more like a woman than ever. Joy at having been taken as never before by a man filled her body.

As she closed her eyes to let her body calm down, she was disappointed when he pulled out of her — but pleasantly surprised when he kissed his way from her breasts to her stomach to her sex. He explored her soaking lips with his mouth. He tasted every inch, every fold, every crease of her pussy with his warm, wet tongue. He licked, stroked, kissed and sucked. Pressing his firm, pointed tongue into her soaking cunt, he drank her juices with the fervor of a man who'd just been rescued from the desert. She gasped, squirmed and groaned as her body tensed and begged for release again. Arching her back, she pressed herself against his mouth, desperate for more. When he finally focused on her clit, her body shook, and she again screamed in delight.

Spent and sated — physically and emotionally — she lay with him on the tangled, newly christened sheets, which were damp from having been baptized with the sweat from their passion. The bedroom was filled with the heady scent of wanton coupling. Colin pulled her against him so they were spooning.

While the physical pleasure of afterglow lingered for Cat, the intense emotions of unrestrained love she'd felt began ratcheting down. Some hesitation and wariness seeped in. Colin cupped her breast tenderly. She would worry some other time about whether these feelings meant anything.

She sighed, closed her eyes and began drifting off to sleep. The only other time she'd felt so content and so protected was when, as a little girl, she'd been wrapped up in a patchwork quilt her grandmother had made for her right before she'd died. It had given her so much comfort after the old woman had passed that she'd worn it out. She'd slept under it every night. She'd used it as a tent to play in. She'd pulled it around her any time she felt cold. She'd cried when it was so threadbare that her mother had thrown it out and replaced it with something from a store. Cat hadn't realized how much she'd missed the feelings the blanket brought. She sighed again and thanked her grandmother for helping her find them.

In addition to the first bout of *ohmygodfuckinglyamazing* sex, she and Colin went at it a couple of times in the middle of the night. Eventually, they were unable to do anything but collapse into sleep.

* * * *

Cat had the best night's sleep she'd had in months. She stretched and purred contentedly. She'd finished her doctorate. An ideal job awaited her. Looking to her left, she saw that Colin wasn't in bed. She smelled coffee and bacon, so she assumed he was making breakfast for the two of them.

He walked in with a tray and placed it in front of her — coffee, toast, juice, omelets, fruit and a small red rose from the flowers he'd brought her the night before. She was impressed at this thoughtfulness. She was also famished from their night-long romp, so she dove right in.

"This might sound like a busman's holiday, Cat, but I've heard about some interesting ruins a couple of hours from here. I thought it would be nice to spend the day together."

She raised an eyebrow and said teasingly, "I'm not getting the 'when it comes to relationships, I'm a sprinter, not a marathoner' speech? This breakfast isn't the condemned woman's last meal before heartbreak?"

He laughed. "Do women tell each other *everything*? No, Cat. No speech. I was serious last night."

"I know," she smiled. "I was just having fun."

"So eat up, get your incredibly sexy ass in gear and put some clothes on. Otherwise, I'll be tempted to ravish you again."

He took the tray away and she hopped out of bed.

She blew him a kiss as she headed for the bathroom. "Or vice versa!"

Chapter Nineteen

Cat and Colin got out of his Jeep and grabbed their backpacks. He kissed her on the top of her head and smiled. "Make sure you have your water. It's a difficult hike in."

Thirty minutes later, they arrived at the ruins and immediately shifted into professional mode. Their conversation was all business — what sort of a site it was, what was the best plan for digging, which kind of artifacts were likely buried there... The longer they examined the site, the better Cat understood why Colin was such a star in their field. He was remarkably perceptive about the significance of tiny details. She couldn't believe how much he knew about the weather conditions of ancient times and how that would influence the design of whatever settlement had originally been here. Cat had already found Colin impossibly attractive. The fact that he was the smartest archaeologist she'd ever met made him even more irresistible.

What surprised her most, however, was that in the middle of a 'typical-guy' archaeologist fixation on measuring the length of an arrowhead she held, he pointed behind her. "Just look at that! The red in the mountains is remarkable! I've never seen that in any other part of the world. It's breathtaking. I could stand in this spot forever. *This* is what I love about fieldwork—the beauty, the grandeur." The look on his face—a deep appreciation of the magnificence of her ancestors' homeland—made her melt.

Unfortunately, the moment ended when he pointed at a cloud of dust in the distance and growled. "What is it with you Yanks? A fucking monstrous Hummer tearing through the desert! Have you no respect?"

Cat shielded her eyes and looked. "More money than taste...or sense. On behalf of the non-ugly Americans, my apologies."

When the vehicle was out of sight, Cat pointed to a rock and they sat down. "You peppered me with questions during dinner. Now it's my turn. What's your story?"

"Me? I'm a cliché." He tried to laugh, but there was more sadness than amusement in the sound. "I was born into a well-to-do family—manor house, nanny and all that—but my mum died when my brother Ian was ten and I was eight. My memories of her are all great." He closed his eyes for a few seconds and his face beamed...then it darkened. "My father is a piece of shit. He cheated on my mother then tried to screw her in the divorce. He married a gold-digging trophy tramp within a year, whom he cheated on whenever he could. She was willing to tolerate it because of the money, but she had no use for two boys. Ian and I got sentenced to boarding school. Dad also had no real interest in us except when we got into trouble. The school would ring him up and insist he come talk to us. Although he said it was a giant pain in the arse, Ian and I could tell he got a kick out of our rule-breaking.

"We were holy terrors and got thrown out of two schools. We finally made it through the third because by then we'd figured out that the best way to escape our past was going to uni rather than jail. Once we got to Oxford, we straightened out. Now, everything's great. We're both at University College. I live in the world's best city! Well, I used to." He wrung his hands and looked away.

"And before you ask—" He took a deep breath and told her the whole story—sneaking into the exhibition, Danielle, the hotel—although as a gentleman, he edited their adventures in bed appropriately. The SWAT team. The fallout at the university. His 'exile' to the U.S.

As soon as Cat heard 'manor house', she assumed Colin's life was going to be the equivalent of an episode of *Downton Abbey*. As he continued, the tale had become heartbreaking. She found the 'Danielle episode' amusing, however. She couldn't muster any sympathy for Colin's exile, because, without it, they would never have met. She found his roguish side exciting. After all, she had a secret wild side herself, but she'd never pushed the envelope as far as he had.

Then Colin shifted on the rock and took a deep breath. "Cat, there's something I want to talk to you about. I meant what I said last night." He turned and took both her hands. "I want something real with you. I confess that women have been like hot fudge to me— sweet, warm and irresistible. And I've done my share of talking a girl out of her knickers for a night of fun. But I've honestly never met anyone like you—and your *twin sister,*" he chuckled. "And I'd really like to see what can happen between us."

Cat beamed and her heart leapt.

"But…" he continued.

Then it teetered.

"I'm not going to lie. This isn't going to be easy for me. I've never done a *real* relationship. It just may not be in my DNA. I *can* promise I'll never cheat on you. I *can't* promise I can go the distance." He squeezed her hands. "But if you're willing to try under those conditions, I'd really like to see where we can go."

Colin's touch made the familiar electric spark run through her. She studied his face. It confirmed that he'd just confessed one of his deepest fears. It also said he was afraid his honesty had just cost him his chance with her. She squeezed his hands and looked down.

She had a real dilemma. He hadn't said, 'Thanks for the great sex. Bye.' It also wasn't, 'I'm madly in love with you, please be mine forever.' It was something in the middle. But it was *real*. Did she want to take a chance? Her guard had gone back up after they'd had sex. Part of her instinctively worried about her heart.

She knew herself well enough that if the two of them continued seeing each other, she'd fall in love. He wasn't just amazingly sexy — as the tingling in her body reminded her. He was smart, sophisticated and exciting. He had 'bad boy' qualities she couldn't resist and was super-confident, unpredictable, willing to take risks and break the rules. He also had the 'good guy' qualities that 'bad boys' lacked — sticking up for other people, the way he had during her exam. Generosity. Honesty. Compassion.

She would fall hopelessly in love with him. If it didn't work out, breaking up would be agony.

Her silence made him uncomfortable. "I know I'm asking a lot, Cat, but I'm not talking bollocks here."

Cat looked up at him quizzically.

"I'm sorry. Let me translate that into *American*. I'm not bullshitting you. I think you're amazing. I'd like to try."

She felt so many different things — joy, doubt, hope, fear, a dizzying desire to jump in with both feet, an intense impulse to step back lest she fall to her destruction — that she struggled with what to say. "I appreciate your honesty. It definitely helps. But before I say anything one way or the other, we have to talk about The Contessa."

He relaxed. "Cat, you can tell me about that whenever you want. I'm not going to pressure you. And, for the record, I'm not the kind of guy who judges women who work as strippers. I don't think any less of you for having been The Contessa."

She frowned. "You don't understand. We need to talk about *you* and The Contessa. For weeks, you've been going to Satin every Friday to lust over a pole dancer and leave a hundred dollars in her G-string. You even reserved a suite at Sedona Rouge and had an elaborate seduction planned."

His eyes went wide. "The suite? How did you know about that?"

"It doesn't matter. The point is that even last night, if The Contessa had offered for you to have sex with her at Satin rather than the hotel, you would have. Then you would have come to see *me* — hoping for a double header."

He looked away and shifted his posture the way someone caught in the act did. He grimaced, then looked back at her. "But you and The Contessa are the same person."

"So?" she asked.

"You're telling me you're upset that I liked watching you pole dance and wanted to sleep with you because of how sexy you were."

"No," Cat objected, "I'm telling you that because you didn't know it was me, you would have had sex with another woman then hoped to have sex with me."

He squirmed some more and frowned. "But *you* knew it was me. And I didn't go to that rendezvous with The Contessa. I admit I was tempted." He ran his hands through his hair. "Come on, Cat. I'm a *bloke*. A man would have to be dead not to be tempted by The Contessa coming on to him. But in the end, I chose *you*. Come to think of it, either way, I was choosing you. You know what I mean?" He put his head in his hands. "*Christ*, this is getting confusing. Is this clear to you? Because it's *anything but* to me. Wait!" He wagged his finger at her. "Your secret identity as The Contessa… Don't you think there's a pattern of deception here *I* could be bothered about? I went to Satin to see only you. You were there to turn on every guy and girl in the audience while you pretended to be my chaste advisee. Perhaps we aren't as different as you think."

She sat silently and scrunched up her face. "Maybe you're right. Let's just put all this in the past and start with a clean slate."

He leaned over and kissed her. "Wonderful idea."

"And as long as we're cleaning the slate, I want to be as honest with you as you've been with me." She told him about everything—her fear of heights, her secret sexy side, The Contessa, obsessing about him after his first visit to Satin, recognizing him on his first day at

Red Rock, concealing her attraction for him because of his reputation, giving in to it by focusing on him when she danced, being touched by his professional help and his gentlemanly demeanor as he worked with her before her dissertation defense, how she'd learned about his failed seduction of The Contessa and the test she'd devised for him. She confided everything about her quest. She told him about the animal-skin bag with the figures inside and her vision with her mother. She walked him through the years of research she'd done into the tribal legends that had convinced her that the existence of the tribe wasn't a myth.

She expected that, at best, he'd explain diplomatically how visions and legends didn't belong in a scientific approach to archaeology. He surprised her when his reaction was, "Wow! I am so envious. I've never had any experiences like that."

"Then you don't think I'm crazy?"

"Are you kidding? If you were 'sane', you'd never have gotten this far."

Cat was so pleased with his reaction. She wondered whether he was right that they were more alike than she'd realized. She'd seen him as a 'bad boy' who loved seducing women and breaking rules—while *she* was just a nice girl who had a 'fun' attitude toward sex. Was there more to her than that? Did she also have an edgy, rebellious side?

I'll brood about that another day.

By the time they'd finished talking, the clouds had gone from gold to scarlet and finally a faint rose. As the stars came out, the air took on a slight chill. Colin was able to find enough wood to start a fire. He put his arm around her. She hadn't felt such peace in months, and it seemed that neither had he.

As the moon peeked over the horizon, he asked, "How do you feel about making love under the stars?"

She responded with a naughty smile. "I suppose if we're serious about understanding what the Lost Tribe was like, we should study every aspect of their lives." She swept her hand in an arc. "And since this is such a glorious location—"

"We should conduct field research," Colin smiled, finishing the thought. "It's spooky that we're thinking the same thing and completing each other's sentences already. What do you think that means? That this is a magical spot that connects us in a special way?"

Cat laughed. "No, I think it means we're both horny. And if you take your clothes off, I'll show you the *real* magical spot that connects us in a special way."

They stood up and quickly stripped. Colin sat down, put on a condom and Cat mounted him. She sighed as she slid her wet pussy down and engulfed his hard, wide cock. She delighted in the feeling fullness— possessed by Colin and possessing him at the same time. It was a beautiful sense of being fused and completed that she'd never felt with any other man.

They wrapped their arms and legs around each other and kissed.

Colin broke it, held her face in her hands and stared longingly.

Cat was transfixed by his piercing blue eyes and his gaze of pure adoration. It sparked a sexual hunger inside her so strong that she found it unnerving. It was as though her body was responding to him with a mind all its own. The strength of her attraction for this man and the power of her body's ache made her feel as if a part of her that had been asleep her whole life was now stirring. His rich, musky scent caused her to draw in a sharp breath and become even more aroused.

The passion climbed, and she exploded with him following. Sated and blissfully content, Cat sighed, and they kissed again.

* * * *

Colin's only major disappointment in his and Cat's first few months together was that they had been apart on Valentine's Day. Colin had been asked to give a lecture at a prestigious week-long conference at Columbia University. It had been too big a deal for him to turn down. And since Cat couldn't take the time off to make the trip, he'd promised that he'd make it up to her. The morning after his return, however, their life was complicated by a phone call.

"Colin Tucker here."

Thirty seconds later, his eyes went wide. During the long silence as he listened, Cat tried to figure out from his shifting expressions what was going on. It definitely wasn't *bad* news. But his face said 'I'm mystified' more than 'this is great news'.

He set this phone on the table and got up. He shook his head and ran his fingers through his hair. "I've just been offered a job," he said in disbelief. "No. Not *a* job. *The* job. The Williamson Chair of Archaeology *and* Director of the Williamson Institute at Columbia University." He began walking around the patio. "The invitation to the conference last week was a pretext so the committee could meet me in person. I wondered why there were so many small chats at different receptions. *The* job. I've been offered *the* job in our field. They've even talked to Aunt Clarissa and gotten her to allow me to travel to England if I need to. Cat, I don't know what to say."

She got up and hugged him. "Are you kidding? This is a once-in-a-lifetime opportunity. There's only one answer. Yes!"

He hugged her tight then let go abruptly. "No! Columbia's in New York. You're here! I don't want to do a long-distance relationship—not when things are going so well with us."

"Colin! Don't be an idiot. We'll figure it out."

"No! Your research is here. The Lost Tribe. I'm not going to take you from that. I'm calling them back and declining."

Cat grabbed the phone off the table. She put her hand up as he headed toward her. "When do they want an answer?"

"A week."

"Here's what I think we should do. You and I are in a relationship. That means big decisions get made jointly. We're going to approach this like professionals. We'll gather data. Analyze. Consider options. We work the problem systematically and patiently to find a solution we can both agree on, okay?"

"But—" he objected.

"And there are no 'buts.' Now get over here and give me a proper kiss. I've never been kissed by a Chair before. I want to see what I've been missing. I may never go back to regular professors."

Chapter Twenty

"Blue wire...yellow wire...junction from A to F...then G to Q." The masked figure spoke quietly, but distinctly.

"Done."

"Once you hit reset, we'll have sixty seconds. It's a fifteen-digit code." Frank handed his partner Vincent a piece of paper. "Remember... Type in the two wrong ones first, then the right one. It'll make it look like we didn't have all of it and were lucky."

Vincent worked the keypad as instructed. The alarm screen went completely blank. The door clicked. "Bingo! Who'd have thought the director had a private entrance in the adjoining building disguised as a utility entrance, the weakest point of entry. He's so cocky that he refuses to let them change the code. *There's* someone who's going to be taken down a peg or two tomorrow."

"Unclip everything and let's get on with it," Frank ordered impatiently. "Are we here to chat or rob?"

They moved silently throughout the museum, easily bypassing the keypad on the door marked 'Cleaning and Restoration'. The object was sitting on the bench.

"Perfect. It's still wrapped from having been shipped. Put it in the backpack."

The pair retraced their steps. Safely back in the car, they admired their prize.

"Two hundred K. Not bad for a night's work. What's the deal with this? Why all the mystery? Why is the buyer so closed-mouthed?" asked Vincent.

"I'm not sure yet, but I'm working on it. I have a feeling that whatever he's up to involves a lot more money than he's telling us. Given the risk we're taking, I'm going to make sure we don't get stiffed. For now, we make nice."

The pair headed off.

* * * *

Colin sat at the breakfast table mindlessly stirring his cup of tea while reading on his iPad. He frowned and stopped mid-stir.

"Cat! There's been another one! And this one's *really* bad news."

She stepped out of the bathroom with a yellow towel wrapped around her. When Colin tried to remove it, she scowled. "Business first!"

"Yes, Ma'am." He pointed to the story. "This is the fourth theft of a Native American artifact in the last few months. But this is the worst. Recognize it?"

She picked up the tablet, increased the size of the picture and studied the image carefully. "No! The one you saw in London. Damn!"

"I'm sure the museum has pictures of it from all angles. And there are the notes of what people have concluded already. It's not a total disaster—but it still sucks."

She sat down and read the news article carefully. "All these thefts all of a sudden… What's going on?"

Determining how to respond to Columbia's offer had made it a difficult week for Colin. But after he and Cat discussed it, he finally settled on a plan they both could live with. Colin would accept the job—*if* Cat would be hired as well somewhere in the university.

When Colin communicated the condition to Columbia, there was much hemming and hawing on the other end, but they finally agreed. "It may take a semester for us to find an appropriate spot for Doctor White Eagle. As long as she can be patient, we promise we ultimately will." The counter-condition, however, was that Colin had to start immediately.

Because the spring trimester at Red Rock hadn't begun yet, the university reluctantly agreed. They were pleased for Colin but unhappy to see him go. He flew to New York a few days later.

The most difficult thing connected with their decision was Cat's resigning from the museum so soon after she'd started so she could move to New York with Colin. Everyone was gracious, however. The other drawback was that Cat's search for the Lost Tribe would have to slow. But the plan was that she'd return to Arizona during the summers until she found what she was looking for.

Following teary farewells and a good-bye cake, she packed her life into a rented U-Haul, drove across the country and squeezed everything into the apartment

Colin had found for them on the Upper West Side. It was small but had lots of character. It was in a building directly across from Riverside Park and had a view of the Hudson River, which gave her at least some connection with nature.

Cat ran into bad weather as she drove through the Mid-West, so she arrived in the Big Apple a couple of days later than planned. That gave her only one day with Colin before he had to go on a trip to London for the Institute. But it was a wonderful day. Despite the late February cold, they took a Circle Line cruise around Manhattan. Colin told her about the history of the tribes who had lived there. He even described the geology of the island and explained how the placement of the skyscrapers revealed where the bedrock was. Any other girl would have been bored to tears, but Cat was fascinated.

Next, they went to the Institute, where Colin introduced Cat to his colleagues — and he took Cat to the Institute's storage area to show her their priceless collection of ancient Native American jewelry. Breaking about a million rules, he even let her try on some of the pieces. But best of all, he told her about his initial contacts with the various Native American nations and tribes the jewelry had come from. He wanted to work out an arrangement that recognized their ownership but still let the Institute display them. Cat was moved to tears.

After going back to the apartment to dress for dinner, they ended up at a small, intimate, romantic Italian restaurant on 110th Street where the owner flirted shamelessly with Cat. Having him take her hand, peer into her eyes and tell her that he was helpless to resist her because she had the face of a goddess was enough to get Cat's juices flowing. But what really started making her hot was what Colin did with his foot.

Because the lighting in the restaurant was dim and the tablecloth went all the way to the floor, no one could see Colin take his foot out of his burgundy loafers and very slowly inch it up Cat's leg. Up and down, up just a shade higher and down, up another quarter inch higher and down. First, it was up and down her calf. Then he turned the corner at her knee and slid his foot under her black pencil skirt. The fabric was tight enough that the sensitive patch of skin on the inside of her thighs — just above where her stockings ended — felt the delightful scratching of Colin's wool socks. But her skirt wasn't so tight that it prevented Colin from running his foot all the way up and down her leg.

And just when Cat felt Colin couldn't make the erotic torture any worse, he gave his foot a final nudge and let the ball of his foot settle against the tiny piece of silk covering her sex. He spent the remainder of dinner rhythmically massaging her clitoris. By the time the check came, Cat couldn't take the teasing a minute longer. They raced back to their building, kissed and ran their hands all over each other while the slow elevator crept to the sixteenth floor.

As soon as they stepped inside, Cat gasped and her heart leaped. The apartment was filled with tiny candles, roses were everywhere and romantic music playing softly. Colin had obviously arranged for someone to let the florist in while they were at dinner and to position the dozens of brilliant red and white roses. It was the most romantic sight Cat had ever seen. "Happy Second Valentine's Day, luv. I told you I'd make it up to you, since we were apart on the actual day. I love you more than you can imagine." There was so much love in his face that tears welled up in her eyes.

She threw her arms around him and gave him the most loving kiss possible. "I love you, too."

"For the rest of the night, I am your servant, m'lady. What is your command?"

A naughty glint showed in her eyes. "All these candles are making the apartment very warm." She struggled with the buttons on her blouse. "But I can't get anything off. I could use a hand, kind sir."

"But of course. A gentleman never abandons a damsel in distress. Follow me."

He tossed her white knit hat and scarf, tan leather gloves and navy-blue coat onto the chair in the hallway. Her red satin blouse and matching bra ended up on the small dining room table. He had her stop at the doorway to the bedroom so she could shimmy out of her black skirt and kick off her black heels. Tossing her onto the bed, he peeled off her black patterned stockings and red thong.

Colin climbed onto the bed and kissed her passionately. Working his way down her body, he spread her legs and dove into her wet, swollen pussy, and he brought her to orgasm within thirty seconds.

But he didn't stop there. Not even allowing enough time for her breathing to slow down, he inserted a finger and pressed against her G-spot. She squirmed, her pulse shot up, her breathing deepened and — despite the fact that she didn't want all the neighbors to know that she and Colin were having sex — she couldn't stop herself from moaning loudly. But this time he kept her on the edge of her orgasm for what seemed like forever — which only increased the volume of her moans and her desperate begging for him to let her come. Finally taking pity on her, he teased her clit with his tongue and brought her to a second, even stronger release. She arched her back, raised her behind off the bed and bucked against his face as the pleasure washed over her.

Obviously deciding he'd waited long enough, he slid on a condom and said, "And now, my turn." In a flash, he was on top of her, penetrating her deeply and grinding against her clitoris. He continued until they were both satisfied and exhausted. But instead of rolling over and going to sleep, he said, "So, would you like your present now?"

"I can't think of anything that would make this a better Second Valentine's Day, but I'm not about to turn down a—"

While she had been talking, Colin had gotten out of bed, picked up his black silk robe from the floor and fished around in its pocket for something. Then he was down on one knee and holding out a beautiful diamond ring. "Cat," he said, "you know that words aren't my strong suit. But you know I love you, and I want us to be together forever. Will you marry me?"

Cat was speechless as she sat up naked in bed. It was exactly what she'd dreamed of—although she hadn't thought it would happen the very day she'd arrived.

"Colin, are you sure?" she asked. "There's no reason to rush any of this. I'm here. I've moved. And you don't have to propose because I did that. You don't owe me anything—especially a proposal and a ring. I'm fine with letting things unfold at their own pace."

"Cat, I'm sure," Colin said, looking straight into her eyes. "This is absolutely what I want. I just hope it's what *you* want as well."

And it was so much what she wanted that she dragged him back into bed, kissed him deeply — then decided that this was the time to teach him the joy of long, slow, languid, spiritual lovemaking. As much as she enjoyed his animalistic, high energy approach to sex, she much preferred the feeling of lying on their sides face to face, barely moving, with her lover's warm, hard cock inside her. She'd squeeze his shaft and push her pussy against him just enough to keep his penis rigid, but not so much that Colin would climax again. For Cat, being fused like this what made her feel fully connected to him. That was what making love was all about for her.

She had never felt more bonded with Colin. She loved the feeling. She was now his forever. A license? A church? None of that mattered. The deep, soulful look they shared when their bodies were joined in the middle of the night affirmed that they were married — body, heart and soul, now and forever.

When Cat awoke in the morning, Colin had already left for the Newark airport. He'd left a note.

Didn't want to wake you. Will call when I reach London. Love you forever. Cheers.

She looked out of the window. It was a beautiful winter day with a brilliant blue sky. Bright sunlight reflected off the icy Hudson River. This was so different from the desert, and it felt like a genuine adventure.

She held her ring in the sunlight streaming in and played with the brilliant sparkling around the room. "I *love* having a fiancé, rather than just a boyfriend," she confessed to the window. Breathing on the glass so that it fogged up, she drew a heart and giggled. Sighing, she marked it as the happiest day of her life.

Colin didn't call when he got to London, but she figured that it had something to do with the time difference and trouble getting his US phone to work in England. He didn't call the next day as well, although at least her call went to voicemail.

On day three, she started getting worried. It didn't help that she came home to find their apartment door unlocked. She was sure she'd locked both the door and the deadbolt. The super's explanation—"Old locks. It happens."—didn't help. Her call to Colin went to voicemail again, so she phoned Ian, his brother. He assured her Colin was fine, and, yes, he was having trouble with his phone. But something in Ian's voice made her uncomfortable. She knew perfectly well there were bright red telephone booths all over London, and that it was simple to call the US from one of them.

When she looked at her diamond ring, she decided Colin was just being Colin. When he was very excited about something, he'd get so wrapped up in it that nothing else mattered. Since this was his first return to London since his 'exile', he was surely binging on being back. She decided she was overreacting because she was by herself in a strange city, feeling lonely. She focused on unpacking and making the apartment feel as much like a home as possible for his return, which would be in only a few days.

Looking back on the evening of day five, she could see the signs. She was restless and in a bad mood. At the time, she thought it must be because a major snowstorm was causing the wind to howl and the windows to rattle. She'd never experienced a winter storm like this in Arizona. When she went to bed, she had trouble falling asleep.

It was three a.m. when the phone rang. She was sure it meant someone had died. Her heart raced with worry.

"Hey, Cat. How's my honey?"

She was relieved to hear his voice, but her chest tightened. It was the voice he used when he'd done something that was going to upset her. She knew in an instant that this call was not going to end well.

"What's going on, Colin? I didn't hear from you for almost a week then you call me in the middle of the night?" She was angry and apprehensive, but she wanted to hear what he'd called to say.

"Yeah, I'm sorry about the time difference. I really needed to talk to you about something, and I couldn't wait any longer. I knew you wouldn't mind."

She turned on her nightstand light and sat back against the headboard. "What is it, Colin?"

"I'm really sorry about this, Cat. This just isn't me — the job at Columbia, living in the States, us settling down. I thought it was me, but it isn't. It's not fair to you for me to pretend it can work out. I've quit my job in New York. I'm staying in England. As long as I keep a low profile, Aunt Clarissa says it's okay. I've missed London terribly. It's where I grew up. It's home. I'll do freelance work over here until things blow over enough that I can get my old job back. There are digs all over Europe looking for archaeologists who are willing to push the envelope. It'll be great, exciting. I now realize we're just too different. We're lucky to see that now. Otherwise, it would have been an unhappy marriage and nasty divorce. I'm sure you're disappointed, and I feel terrible about doing this to you. But you have to believe me when I say I'm truly sorry. I really did try my best. If I thought — "

It felt like being hit by something so hard that it paralyzed her and made her go deaf and blind. The room looked fuzzy. All she could hear from the phone was a faint, muffled voice. Her head started to spin. She was lucky she was in bed.

The worst wound was to her heart. The part that loved Colin went into spasm and…just died. She didn't feel angry. She wasn't going to try to convince him to change his mind. This was her fault. She'd ignored those moments of doubt. She felt numb. She ended the call while he was still talking and dropped the phone on the bed.

It rang. She didn't even look at it. Eventually, it went to voicemail. It did that again, and then again.

Stunned, she sat looking into space for…she didn't know how long. Her senses gradually came back. She grabbed a pillow, hugged it and sobbed uncontrollably. It felt like she was falling down a bottomless black hole. The longer she fell, the more she felt the life being sucked out of her. She felt so dizzy that she tipped over and lay on her side. She cried herself to sleep, but heartache woke her up in an hour.

Cat had been dumped before, but never like this — by a narcissist who didn't even seem to recognize, never mind appreciate, that she'd not only fallen helplessly in love but that she'd also upended her life for him. And to add insult to injury, someone who didn't have the decency to wait until morning to phone her.

What does a person do when she's just been dumped, is in a strange city, it's four a.m., and there's a major storm unloading a foot of snow? For Cat, the only thing that would make her feel better was to go outside, despite the weather and the darkness. She bundled up and walked over to Riverside Park. She sat on one of the benches as a fierce, frigid wind whipped droplets off the river. The icy snow pelting her felt like tiny nails. Her face hurt like hell. She didn't care.

She recalled the tradition of an ancient Native American tribe she'd studied. After a particularly dishonorable failure, a chief would end his life by sitting outside on a deadly cold night. It would be a peaceful death, because the medicine man would prepare a drink that made him feel warm enough until he fell asleep — and froze to death.

Cat felt like a failure. She took all the blame. She'd stupidly believed that Colin had changed. The thought of ending her pain by sitting on the cold bench and letting the snow cover her had a momentary appeal. The pain inside was beginning to spread. She knew it would only grow. It would be her constant companion for months. When she thought of the future, all she could feel was dread.

But she refused to do anything that could make Colin think he had any kind of power over her. "I will not die because of that selfish prick," she resolved as she got up. She brushed off the snow that had fallen on her and trudged down to the Starbucks on 115th street, hoping it was open. As she turned onto Broadway, she spotted a homeless woman huddled in a doorway who was struggling to protect himself from the storm. Walking up to the woman, Cat took off her gloves, removed her engagement ring and gave the woman her gloves, scarf — and the ring. "There's no reason today should suck for both of us. Trust me. It's real."

After warming up at Starbucks, she made her way back to the apartment. She packed up her things until it wasn't too early to telephone Sedona. She humiliated herself by calling her former boss, telling him what happened and begging for her job back. Then, despite all the traffic advisories, she got into her car and headed through the snow for Arizona.

As she crossed the Hudson River over the George Washington Bridge, the wind buffeted her car mercilessly. She fought back the tears. "Just how did my life end up here?"

Chapter Twenty-One

The previous week

The officer in the immigration booth smiled politely when Colin handed his passport over. Studying the computer screen facing him, he typed something on his keyboard. "I'm just waiting for the system to clear you, sir. It's been slow all day."

There was a tap on Colin's shoulder. "Will you please come with me, Professor Tucker?" He turned to see a muscular man in a black suit. There was a visible bulge where a shoulder holster would be. "Of course." *Word of Aunt Clarissa's permission apparently hasn't made it all the way down the chain of command.*

He was escorted into a sterile interrogation room with a mirror on one wall. Five minutes later, he was joined by three individuals—a striking dark-haired woman, a tall Black man and a shorter man with distinct Native American features. The combination puzzled him.

"May we get you something?" the Black man asked.

"No, thank you." Colin tensed up at how serious they all seemed. "I don't mean to be rude, but am I under arrest?"

"I'm sorry. That was thoughtless of me. I should have begun with introductions, Professor. I am Agent Stanley Granville, from Scotland Yard. This is Agent Magda Kyriakou, from Interpol. And this is Agent Cha'Tima Loloma, from the U.S. Bureau of Indian Affairs. We apologize for the cloak and dagger greeting at Immigration. You're in no trouble. We just want to keep this meeting secret."

Colin frowned. "Forgive me if I appear skeptical. A secret meeting with three law enforcement officials from different parts of the world before I'm allowed to enter my country? Even if you say I'm not in any trouble, should I be calling my solicitor?"

The three of them sat down around the table with him. Granville turned to Loloma. "I think it best if you explain."

"We want to ask for your help. Actually, we want not only your help but also Doctor White Eagle's as well. I assume you're aware of the theft and destruction of Native American artifacts?"

"Sadly, yes. I seem to be reading about such incidents more frequently of late."

"There's been a definite uptick. And we've received intelligence that a particularly serious one—one that will affect Doctor White Eagle—is being planned."

"Cat? How?"

"Her work on the Lost Tribe myth. We've learned of a band of treasure hunters who are convinced the supposed map exists. They've embarked on a campaign to find it. They're after anything that will give them a clue—then they'll destroy what they've found. We hope the two of you can work with us to figure out their strategy and catch them."

Colin rubbed his chin. "What makes them think the treasure's real? You said it yourself. Cat's work is on the *myth*." He saw no reason to throw fuel on the fire by telling them Cat was after the same thing.

"True…false…it doesn't matter. All that counts is that the thieves think it's true." Agent Granville joined the conversation. "We know that at least one player in the conspiracy is here in Britain. We expect some artifacts to be smuggled here."

Colin looked over to Agent Kyriakou. "You're from Interpol's office in *Athens*, correct? There's a Greek connection too?"

"Not exactly. I'm here because of the items that got, shall we say, 'miscatalogued' from your last dig. We overlooked that as a courtesy to your aunt."

Colin shifted in his seat. "You have me at a disadvantage. I'm not seeing the big picture here. You say you want our help, but you're not telling me exactly what that would entail—and why this meeting is so secret."

Granville and Kyriakou turned to Loloma.

He nodded back at them and leaned forward with his arms on the table. "We have reason to believe that two of the Bureau's undercover agents specifically charged with stopping such theft are, in fact, among the worst offenders. It's the perfect cover, because otherwise they have a stellar reputation in the BIA. They've been *very* careful, however. We have no hard evidence—only rumor—but we're sure it's them. Worse still, they're getting more aggressive. A member of one of the tribes whose burial site was pilfered has disappeared. We fear the worst." He paused and shook his head sadly. "In light of that, our agencies have put together this joint task force. But we need someone inside their operation, so we can stop them." He nodded at Colin.

"Inside…the theft. Someone undercover? Me?" He laughed. "I mean no disrespect, but that's crazy."

"Not really—given your reputation," Agent Kyriakou interjected. "The plan is that I arrest you for stealing those Greek items and throw you in jail—very publicly. We also let word leak that we suspect you were involved in the most recent theft of a very important Native American artifact. People in your field will be disappointed to hear that. But, frankly, Professor, given your reputation, no one will think it's 'unbelievable'."

Colin sat feeling grim. His past was coming back to haunt him. "The piece I saw at the London exhibition? You're pinning that on me?"

Granville slid a large envelope across the table. It contained pictures from security cameras at the National Gallery of him studying and taking photos of the piece. "We have video of you spending an inordinate amount of time examining the pottery. Then it was stolen shortly after you arrived in the States. Combined with the other robberies, you look like an ideal suspect. That will let the real thieves—Richard and Wilkins, the two corrupt BIA agents—think they got away with it.

"We're confident they'll ask that you be released into their custody. They'll claim you can help them solve some of their cases. It's a common practice. But they'll actually want you as a resource for their Lost Tribe operation. We know they're under pressure from their buyer to wrap things up quickly, so they'll jump at the chance to have you helping them. You'll be *our* undercover person. You'll keep us informed. At the right moment, we'll arrest them and break up the ring... *And*, of course, we'll then publicly exonerate you, describe how you helped us and thank the two of you. Don't worry. We won't hang you out to dry."

"The two of us. You haven't described Cat's role."

"Because she knows more about the myth than anyone," Loloma responded, "we desperately need her expertise. Publicly, of course, she'll be furious about this and break up with you. Then we'll set up a way that you can secretly communicate with her. This will let her tell you how to conduct the search, but Richards and Wilkins will think it's coming from you. The faster we can shut this down, the better for everyone."

Colin sat quietly, staring at the table. He tapped his finger on the gray metal surface every few seconds, while his companions around the table waited patiently. After a couple of minutes, he looked up. "I will help you, but Cat can't be involved. It's too dangerous. You think these guys already killed someone. I'm not letting Cat be put in the crosshairs. If I need help, I'll ask my brother Ian. As far as communicating with you goes, I'll decide how I do that."

"With all due respect," Loloma said, "Dr. White Eagle knows much more about the myth than you do. She'll be in no danger. You're the one who'll be with Richards and Wilkins."

Colin stood and walked around the room. "Forgive me. I was just on a seven-hour flight. I need to stretch my legs." He held up one finger, as though he were teaching a class. "First, if I were Richards or Wilkins, I'd be on the lookout for anything *even* remotely suspicious in my behavior. Having regular conversations with Cat would be impossible."

A second finger. "If I don't deliver the way they want me to, they'll kill me and kidnap Cat. They have to be convinced that I know everything she does, which brings me to number three.

"As long as this is a cloak-and-dagger operation, someone needs to enter our apartment in New York when she's not in and copy everything on her hard drive. That's where she keeps her notes. I'll give you the key so she never realizes anyone was there. That will let me convince Richards and Wilkins we don't need her at all."

Kyriakou objected, "No, I think it's essential for her to be part of this. Her expertise is essential. She'll be able to figure out the pattern in their thefts, so we can get one step ahead of them."

Colin pulled out a chair and sat beside her. "Humor me for a moment, Agent Kyriakou. Imagine that the archaeologist you just agreed to marry dumps you over the phone from miles away. He announces he's not returning to the country, then he gets arrested for stealing and smuggling artifacts. How would you feel?"

She shook her head. "So many emotions. Devastated. Hurt. Furious. *Especially* furious. He not only turned his back on me, but he betrayed our field. He went from scholar to scoundrel in a heartbeat. I'd want to cut off his ba —" She blushed and laughed. "I'd be very upset. I wouldn't have a thing to do with him ever again. I wouldn't care what happened to him."

"Excellent. Now tell me if you would be able to *pretend* to be that hurt and angry, if you knew he was *in fact* an undercover agent in a risky operation trying to protect everything important to you. Could you fool someone who might be watching you, looking for clues that your fiancé was not the scoundrel he claimed to be?"

She looked straight at him. "Of course not."

"Cat's pain and fury at me will be her best protection."

Her face turned somber. "You may be protecting her, but you'll do so by breaking her heart. When she learns the truth, the hurt may be too deep. She may be unable to forgive you."

He stared back at the table. "I know. And I'll have to live with whatever she decides. But I'd never forgive myself if I dragged her into something that got her hurt." He looked back up. "We have an agreement, then?"

The three agents looked at each other and nodded.

"Yes, Professor," Agent Granville said, "everyone who is part of this operation will support the false story. We will not tell your fiancée the truth."

He smiled grimly. "Fine. In that case, you should probably stop referring to her as my fiancée. I doubt Cat will think of herself that way anymore."

Agent Kyriakou leaned back in her chair, crossed her arms and studied him. "You are an unusual man, Professor. You love this woman so much that you will champion a cause deep to her heart — even at your own peril. Yet, to protect her, you are willing for her to hate you. That is sad, tragic — but romantic. It feels very Greek."

"No, Madam." He laughed. "I am an idiot. I find the woman of my dreams, and I am willing to throw her away. Let's hope that Fortune favors the foolish."

"One never knows. Perhaps things will work out for the two of you."

"A pleasant pipe dream... Some things are unforgiveable. Not giving Cat a choice in this situation about something so important to her is crossing that line."

"How can you be so sure?"

"I would feel the same way."

* * * *

Present day

The drive from New York to Sedona took five days. It was long enough for Cat to go through repeated cycles of sobbing, screaming at Colin, blaming herself, thinking, hoping and despairing. At the end of each day's driving, she was emotionally exhausted. By the time she arrived home, however, she was as much at peace with the situation as was possible.

The most difficult moment was when she pulled into the parking lot and sat looking at her condo. She hadn't rented it out because a voice in the back of her had said she couldn't completely trust Colin. She'd felt guilty she'd done so and not told him. Now she hated that the voice had been right. *Why couldn't I have seen it earlier? We could have had one night of great sex and left it at that. Why did I believe him when he said he truly wanted more?* She banged her hands against the steering wheel.

She took a deep breath, ran her hands through her hair and closed her eyes as she exhaled. She sat still and silent. "No more," she resolved out loud. "I'm done!"

Even though she was exhausted, emotionally and physically, Cat couldn't calm her mind or relax her body.

After a fitful night's sleep, Cat forced herself to show up at the museum. Her colleagues recognized what a tough situation she was in — unceremoniously dumped by her freshly minted fiancé, having to beg for her job back. When the reports that Colin had been arrested as a thief and smuggler came out and the FBI showed up at her office, some people eyed her suspiciously. She had to get away, so she told the Director that she needed to do field work for a few weeks. He didn't argue. "We're here for you, Cat. Bad stuff happens to all of us. You didn't deserve this. Handle your job however you see fit."

She knew her best therapy was climbing in the canyons looking for artifacts for the museum and searching for clues about the Lost Tribe. She put in long, hard days, but they were productive.

Climbing hundreds of feet off the ground forced her to concentrate on the present moment. Focusing on not plummeting to her death meant there was no room to fret about a failed romance or a felonious ex-fiancé.

Spending so much time in and around the cave dwellings gave her a much stronger identity as a Native American. When she meditated surrounded by the red rocks, it was as though she could picture how the tribe had lived. She finally felt at peace about who she was. She kept hoping that her mother would appear so she could tell her she no longer felt like 'a stranger'. That was the first step in retrieving the forgotten story of her tribe.

She, the mountains and her ancestors who had lived here thousands of years ago belonged to each other. It was why she was getting more comfortable climbing. It was as though the skills her ancestors had perfected to survive in such harsh conditions were stored in her DNA.

"Five hundred feet." Cat shook her head. Her stomach tied into knots. She closed her eyes and mumbled as she did the math in her head. "One hundred seventy miles an hour." She shuddered. "I should be travelling at least a hundred seventy miles an hour when I hit the ground. It's a good thing I parked my Jeep out of the way. That would really put a dent in the hood."

She took a deep breath and chuckled, chiding herself aloud. "Okay…it's only the first 50 feet that bothers you. But still…you're pathetic, Cat. And since you're talking to yourself again, you've definitely been in the field too long"

She squinted as she looked up and examined the jagged, rust-colored rock wall. Sighing, she took out her notebook.

Week five. Site B23. Plateau at five hundred feet.

"Longitude and latitude?" She glanced at the GPS on her wrist and wrote down the numbers. "Date and time?" She punched the buttons that changed the display. "Ten a.m. March thirty-first." She wrote down the information. "No matter what everyone else says, we know it's on one of these plateaus," she said confidently.

She put her notebook away and wagged her finger at her shadow on the ground. "Talking to yourself again, Cat."

Knotting her long black hair, she fastened it so it would stay out of her face and cinched her helmet.

She stepped back and carefully examined the rock face to plan her ascent. Noticing something, she shielded her eyes to get a better look and she widened her eyes in surprise. *Can't be.* She grabbed her binoculars and studied the rock face more closely. *Someone else climbed here? No. People who climb for fun wouldn't find this an interesting spot. Must be an optical illusion – the minerals in the rock reflecting the sun.*

Squatting, she double-checked everything. "Harness. Rope. Hardware. Chalk. Water."

As she neared the end of her checklist, she began getting nervous.

Positioning herself at the base of her climb, she arrived at the final two items.

First, she closed her eyes and reverently fingered the black obsidian attached to the thick leather thong tied around her neck. She moved her lips silently.

Then, as her mouth went dry, she said out loud, "Stupid archaeologist... *Still* afraid of heights!"

After the first fifty feet, she relaxed. Two hundred more and she paused to take a break. When she had been a scared novice, she'd discovered that if she forced herself to appreciate the beauty around her, she remained calm. Now that she was more experienced, she stopped frequently just to drink in the wonders of nature around her.

Today was perfect — warm with a light breeze, blue sky, gorgeous colors in the stones as the sunlight danced on the red rocks on the opposite side of the canyon. *This is why I climb. I can't see this from the ground.* As she looked toward the valley, she took in the vibrant hues of the flowers on the hillsides. Poppies sprouted everywhere. They looked like a huge, golden quilt covering the landscape. She closed her eyes and took a deep breath. The purity of the air was invigorating.

She also paused to re-check her strategy. The first part of her ascent had been relatively easy because there were plenty of cracks and ledges to use as hand and foot holds. But the next stretch of rock presented her with two mysteries that she needed to think about.

First, the wall above her looked like it had actually been smoothed out by someone. The marks on the stone told her that maybe as far back as ten thousand years ago, someone had used tools to make it difficult to climb past this point. This was supposed to be impossible. The prevailing wisdom held that no one had lived in this area then. Even if they had, their tools wouldn't have been advanced enough to do this.

Cat's heart started racing. *This might be it!*

The other mystery was more troubling — fresh residue of the chalk that climbers used. Not only had someone else gone up the rock face, but they'd also done it very recently – so recently it was possible that when she reached the plateau, they might still be there. Her stomach tightened. The only reason anyone would make this climb would be if they were after the same thing she was. But that made no sense, because she'd told only one person about her theory in enough detail that he might also develop the same hunch.

But it can't be him because that worthless piece of trash is in prison – where he belongs.

Not wanting to be distracted by bad memories, she pushed on. Having small hands and feet was an advantage, because she could work with the tiniest cracks, crevices and bumps on the wall. Climbing carefully, she moved up the challenging rock face.

The closer she got to the plateau, the more signs she saw that whoever had gone before her had experienced a difficult ascent. "*Two* guys," she confided to the rocks. "Without a doubt. Two *guys* trying to bull their way to the top. No finesse. Just like ole' stuck-in-prison Co—" She froze at the sight of a discarded blue granola wrapper stuffed into a crevice. Not only was it Colin's favorite brand but leaving trash on a climb was also one of his stranger habits. "*I'll pick it up on the way down,*" he'd always say.

As she put the wrapper into the pocket of her tan shorts, a thought crossed her mind. *No. It can't be.*

Finally, she decided her imagination had gotten the best of her again. After all, try as she might, she couldn't get her heart-breaking ex-fiancé completely out of her system. Her memories of their time together were still powerful—the animal magnetism that had first drawn her to him, the love it had bloomed into, the agonizing hurt and overpowering fury when everything had collapsed.

She took a deep breath to center herself.

It's just my imagination. That's all that's happening. Some idiot with the same taste in granola has the same weird habit. It's natural he'd come to mind.

Hearing a high-pitched whistle, she looked up to see an eagle fly over. She waved and smiled. "You're right, my sister. It's all in the past," she lied and pressed on.

As she reached the plateau and pulled herself onto the hard, dusty surface, she froze. Stunned at what she saw, she gasped. *Impossible!* Forty yards ahead, two men were on their knees examining something in the stone. The one in the red nylon parka and blue jeans was Colin!

Anger and heartache ripped through her. *That bastard is absolutely the last person I want to see! What's he doing here? Poaching my research?* Questions flew through her head. *When did he get out of prison? How could he have been let back into the US? How did he know to climb here?* She ground her jaw. *How do I keep from pushing him off the edge?*

She'd worked hard to put everything behind her. She hated that despite all her early misgivings that Colin wasn't made for relationships, she'd let him break her heart. There had to be more to the story.

Ever since that devastating winter night during which their relationship had died, she'd wondered how she'd feel the next time she saw him. She had such conflicting feelings that she had no idea which would win out. As she stood up and removed her climbing gear, the answer came surprisingly quickly.

Colin apparently didn't hear her walk up behind him because music was likely blasting through the white ear buds he always wore. When she put her hands over his eyes, he spun around, probably ready to take a swing at whoever had snuck up on him. As soon as he saw it was Cat, he exchanged a quick, panicked look with the other climber — who, recognizing her, took a step back.

Her ex stood — his athletic six-foot four-inch frame towering over her. He gave her a guilty smile. His brilliant blue eyes, handsome face, tousled sandy hair and masculine scent were every bit as seductive as before.

Her breathing instinctively deepened. Heartbreak and prison hadn't dulled the magnetic pull he had on her.

He shuffled uncomfortably then smiled warmly. "Well, isn't this a surprise? You tracked me down, Cat. Well done, you. I knew you couldn't get enough of me." Despite his air of seductive self-assurance, she knew him well enough to know he was *very* nervous.

She flashed him the smile that always made him melt and looked up at him sweetly. "I guess I can't hold a grudge. Don't take this wrong, but why aren't you behind bars?"

"You know me, Cat — free spirit and all that. I never did like handcuffs. You, on the other hand..." He added a sexy chuckle. She could tell he was scrambling to keep their unexpected reunion light.

She stepped closer and put her right hand softly on his waist. Giving him her best lingering gaze, she moistened her lips. "After all this time, don't I get a kiss 'hello'?"

He relaxed. "I'd say that's the least I owe you." He bent down—which put him in the perfect position.

She grunted as her fury drove her left fist hard into his jaw. "You bastard!" she screamed. He was caught completely by surprise. His eyes glazed over as he blacked out from the force of the blow. He stood motionless for a second, swayed and toppled to the ground with a thud. A small cloud of dust puffed up when his body hit.

Cat was stunned as she looked down at the crumpled heap at her feet. *Oh my God, I've knocked him out! I never imagined I could hit him so hard. I hope I didn't hurt him.* She flexed her sore hand to reassure herself she hadn't broken anything.

Colin's climbing partner stepped closer and nodded approvingly. "Brilliant shot, luv. One punch. *Very* impressive. He deserved it. You been working out?"

"Boxing lessons, Ian—cheaper and more fun than therapy—just in case I ever ran into His Royal Highness again." She nodded toward her unconscious ex. "This worthless piece of shit can rot in Hell for all I care. But I'm glad to see *you*."

"You too, Cat." The burly Brit gave her a big hug. "I can't tell you how excited I am. You were right all along. What you're looking for is over here. Come on." She looked with concern at the still-unmoving lump of red and blue. "Don't worry about him. He never could take a punch. He'll be fine."

Ian led her to the spot the two men had just been studying. It contained an exceptionally complex set of carvings. Her heart soared. She'd been searching for this for years. It was a huge step in proving the existence of the Lost Tribe. She closed her eyes and offered a word of thanks to her mother, whom she knew had been with her throughout her search.

He looked at her with admiration and respect. "If you translate this, it will make you famous — the 'Rosetta Stone' for all the Native American languages in this area. Do you think that's really it? And discovered by a 'bird' — excuse me, *woman* — in her twenties no less. The old geezers are going to piss in their pants. This is fucking brilliant. You're going to make history."

Cat beamed. "It's too soon to say. But thanks for the vote of confidence."

Then she turned serious. "Let's have the truth. How did Colin get out of prison? And what are the two of you doing *here*? It can't be a coincidence. He was the only person I discussed my ideas with in any detail. Is there anything you want to tell me? He'd better not be pulling something shady, because I'll turn him in. And if he's using my research, I'll cut off his balls."

Ian answered, not quite looking her in the eye.

"I honestly don't know the whole story about how he got sprung. One night I got a call from him asking me to pick him up the next day. He said something about 'prison overcrowding'. You know Colin — maybe it's true, maybe it isn't. But I have a feeling that being arrested and disgraced was a real eye opener about how selfish and stupid he'd been. He'll never admit it — you know what an arrogant horse's arse he is — but he actually does seem different. He's more serious. He told me he wanted to climb here because of some research he'd done on his own. Maybe I'm an idiot, but I believe him. This really is a coincidence."

She studied Ian's face. He was hiding something. She gave him a glare worthy of Medusa. "If you're lying to me, Ian, I've got enough wrath for two."

He put up his hands and took a step back. "I promise, Cat. I'm telling the truth."

She photographed the drawings, collected rock samples and made some notes. Ready to climb back down, she gestured toward her still-unconscious ex. "So, what do we do with Prince I'm-too-sexy-for-my-underpants here?"

"Don't worry about it. He'll be fine." Ian gave her a goodbye hug. "By the way, still afraid of heights?"

She smiled proudly. "Only the first fifty feet. It's nothing like before. I found a way to work through it."

He gave her a flirtatious wink. "I'll say. You came up with the most ingenious method I ever heard of."

She couldn't suppress a surprised but naughty smile. "You know about that?"

"Cat, that's the stuff legends are made of." There was awe in his voice. "Colin told me a little about it. Someday I'd love to hear the whole story."

"Okay, someday I'll tell you. Another time. I promise."

"Understood. Over a pint, then." He tilted his head in Colin's direction. "Any message I should deliver when His Lordship wakes up?"

"Let's see." She paused to tighten her harness. "Tell him, 'I'd put some ice on that.'"

"And?" prodded Ian.

"Oh, you want *honesty*? Fine. Tell him to stay away from me. He shouldn't even think of taking any credit for this find. This is my discovery, and he knows it. *And* he can go fuck himself."

"That's my girl!" Ian responded with a big grin.

Cat was so excited that it felt like forever before she made her way back down. Within minutes, she'd stowed her gear in her Jeep and headed for her camp.

She couldn't wait to start untangling the mysteries connected with her momentous discovery. But just as important, she needed to process everything racing through her head.

Colin's out of prison? Released because of 'overcrowding,' my ass. No. He lied, bribed or conned his way out.

How did he turn up at a site only I could locate?

Did getting arrested really have the impact on him that Ian thinks? Is it possible that he and I...?

She slammed on the brakes, gripped the steering wheel and gently banged her head against it a few times.

Am I crazy? After how deeply he hurt me, why does part of me even imagine getting back together? I'm done with him. Done! Don't I believe that?

Then the part of her that had launched the punch weighed in. *Why are you even thinking about this? This is Colin, not some regular, decent guy. The only person he'll ever love is himself. He broke your heart once. Broke it? Hell, he stomped on it, tore it into millions of pieces and pissed on it for good measure. You'd be a world-class idiot even to consider giving him another chance!*

Chapter Twenty-Two

As the black Hummer lurched to a stop at the base of the rock face, Ian was handing Colin an ice pack for his jaw.

"What's the problem with little Lord Fauntleroy there, Ian? Does Prince Colin have a boo-boo? Here... Let me help." The tall, athletic-looking man with mirrored sunglasses fished a breath mint out of his jeans and threw it on the ground in front of Colin. "How'd the reunion go, sport? From the look of that eye, I'd say it was a lovers' quarrel that you lost. Decked by a squaw! Wow, you Brits really are pussies, aren't you?"

Colin and Ian glared back, clearly unhappy that they had company — *this* company in particular. Ian gestured toward the huge Hummer. "Interesting ride. This is the American idea of keeping a low profile?"

Frank shot the spit from his chewing tobacco in Ian's direction. "We need to move quickly. This is great for driving in the desert. We wanted to slow her down by shooting out a tire, but we lost track of her because she was checking out so many different sites. She rarely uses her satellite phone, so we couldn't peg her location that way. And if we got too close, she'd suspect something. We looked in her apartment the other day to see if she'd mapped out her search pattern on her computer ahead of time, but we came up dry."

Colin's face burned. He grabbed his small pick and marched straight at Frank until they were nose to nose. "You were going to *shoot* at her? You searched her apartment? I told you to leave her out of it! I have all her data. I said I'd find it."

Frank just sneered. "We both know you can't tell anyone anything, Your Lordship. One word from me and you're back in prison, so put that toothpick down. Vincent here's an excellent shot. Hitting the tire of a slow-moving Jeep at a few hundred yards is a piece of cake for him. She wouldn't have gotten hurt. And she'll never suspect we were at her place. We know how to cover our tracks. So, did you find it?"

Colin stood unblinking with his jaw clenched, flexing and unflexing his hand around the pick handle. He finally stepped back from the confrontation.

"Yes, I found it."

"And did you destroy it before she got here?"

"No."

"She saw it too?" Frank slowly shook his head back and forth. "That's going to be a problem, my friend... for *everyone*."

Colin tapped the pick against Frank's shoulder.

He just grinned and spat on Colin's boots. "Do that again and you'll discover that you were behind one of our unsolved cases."

Ian grabbed his and pulled him away, probably before he did something stupid. "If you felines are through hissing, let's get down to business. I'm sure you charmers have other people to harass. Just fill them in, Colin."

He nodded, ran his hand through his sandy hair and adopted his 'archaeology professor' demeanor.

"This is the site. Those are the petroglyphs. But there weren't enough clues to tell me how to decode them — and it's too soon to destroy anything in case I need to come back. I have pictures and notes of everything so I can work on it. Cat does too. The only problem is she has the advantage in deciphering them."

"In which case, Vincent and I suggest you find a way to change that and beat her to the punch. Quickly." Frank turned and shouted toward the Hummer. "Don't we, Vincent?" His companion — his feet propped up on the dashboard — just waved his sniper rifle at them. Frank walked back to the black monstrosity, climbed back in and the pair left.

Ian nodded in the direction of the departing Hummer. "Lovely chaps. It's a shame they couldn't stay for tea. We could have poisoned them." He eyed the small green shrubs at his feet. "Surely one of these plants is deadly." He looked back at Colin. "Do you think you can figure this out before Cat does?"

He rubbed his swollen face. "How honest do you want me to be?"

"That's what I was afraid of."

"Let's go. Things weren't supposed to go this way. I've got to keep everything from spinning out of control. This mess has already done enough damage to Cat's life. I need to protect her and keep her from ending up in the middle of things."

"In case you hadn't noticed it, little brother, all of us are *already* in the middle of things. At least you and I know what's happening. Do you honestly think leaving her in the dark is the best way to keep her safe?"

He tossed his backpack into the truck.

"I know Cat, Ian. She's going to be hard enough to protect knowing *nothing*. If she knew everything, it would be impossible."

His brother shook his head.

"You're the boss. But if I were you, I'd get ready for that left cross of hers again. Cat's too smart to fool. You know that even better than I do. She'll find out. And since the only reason I lied to her was because you asked me to, *you're* going to take the punch she'll want to throw at me."

* * * *

By the time Cat arrived at her campsite, it was too late to head back to Sedona. She'd leave at dawn. She made a campfire and cooked dinner. When she was done, she unrolled her sleeping bag and climbed in. The fire's warmth was a cozy embrace on a cool night. She studied the photographs she'd taken of the symbols and shivered with excitement.

She looked straight up and loved how beautiful the night sky was in the crystalline desert air. The stars sparkled like diamonds against black velvet.

Normally, staring at the heavens calmed her so much that her mind would go blank. But after her encounter with Colin, she couldn't think of anything else but their history together.

Despite the hurt she still felt from his cowardly way of dumping her right after proposing to her, the first memory that surfaced was how intoxicating it felt to be the object of his unbridled love and desire. She had never before felt so worshipped and wanted.

As she cradled her sore hand, all she could think of was how complicated her life had gotten.

How did an orphan left on someone's doorstep in the middle of nowhere end up in love with a brilliant British bad boy aristocrat whose main talent seems to be breaking my heart?

Staring at the star-filled Arizona sky, she sighed. Her eyes began to tear as the memories — good and bad — flooded her brain.

Damn! I am not going to cry on the day I made this discovery! Damn you, Colin Tucker! I thought this was all behind me.

But it wasn't. And given how strongly she'd loved him, part of her feared it never would be.

All Cat wanted to do was enjoy her triumph. But like an annoying song that stuck in her head and wouldn't stop, the same questions played over and over.

Why is Colin out of prison? What's he up to? How did he find the site – and find it ahead of me? Why does he still affect me like that when all I really want to do is kill him? Has he really changed? Would it make any difference?

She sighed deeply. Emotionally exhausted, she turned over and fell asleep.

* * * *

As soon as Cat entered her apartment, she headed to her desk to check her email. Something didn't look right. *That's odd. Why is that pen there?*

As she sat down and examined her desk more carefully, puzzlement turned to apprehension. *Someone's been here!* She got up with a start, grabbed the baseball bat she kept beside her bed and cautiously inspected the rest of her condo. She didn't think the intruder would still be there, but she just wanted to be sure. She slowly surveyed everywhere to see if anything else was out of place.

Nothing is missing. Nothing else looks like it was disturbed — just what's on my desk. The pen... My laptop. It's off a smidge. Someone went to a lot of trouble to cover their tracks but got sloppy. Why? Who?

Something clicked in her head. "*Colin!* You son of a bitch! That's just like you. Get most of it right then make a stupid mistake... Pick my lock. Copy the hard drive of a computer that doesn't have what you want. Then forget I'm left-handed when you try to put everything back the way it was. Damn you! Trying to steal my notes!" She banged her hand against the desk in anger. "Owww!" she shouted, being reminded it was still tender from her knockout blow.

She turned on the computer to see if she could see any signs of what Colin had tried to do. Not surprisingly, there weren't any. She knew his tricks. He would have just copied everything onto a flash drive. Getting up and walking over to her dusty blue backpack, she fished out a ragged, water-stained book with *Shakespeare's The Tempest* engraved on the burgundy leather cover. Opening the book, she removed a portable hard drive from a hole she'd cut in the pages.

Feeling victorious at having thwarted Colin, she headed for the bathroom, filled the whirlpool tub and undressed. As she sank into the warm water and fragrant bubbles, the enormity of what she was about to accomplish sank in. *I may finally have proof!* She fingered the stone around her neck. *I hope my mother would be proud.* A tear ran down her cheek.

Caressed by the warm water and soothed by the crisp citrusy aroma, she relaxed. But her mind couldn't help but go to the last thing she actually wanted to think about — Colin. And against her will, that familiar yearning stirred deep inside. The fact that her body responded to him so strongly, even as furious as she was at him, made her wonder whether she'd lost ground.

Cat spent the next week poring over the symbols. She made enough progress to realize they constituted only half of the Rosetta Stone. But when she added data from her earlier research—which had been hidden in the portable hard drive—she hit the jackpot. She now knew where to find the second half and she needed to get there before Colin. She would head back into the mountains the following morning.

* * * *

Standing in front of the wall filled with symbols, Colin was torn. He'd found the rest of the key to translating the language used by the Lost Tribe. Cat had been right all along. This was a historic moment, but Cat's not being there was simply wrong. The discovery was possible only because of her research. But he was about to hand that information over to a pair of thieves—and probably killers—who were selling it to some rich bastard. Then they'd go on to more plundering. He felt sick to his stomach. His only hope was that the team he was working for would be able to catch the criminals and put them in jail.

"Well?" Frank prodded. "Is that it?"

"Yes. That's it," he said glumly.

"Smile, King Arthur. You and your brother won't rot in prison." Frank examined the carvings closely. "And you can figure out what all this crap means?"

"Yes. It may take a few days. But when I combine these symbols with the last ones we found, I'll be able to."

"You're sure? I don't want to set up something with the buyer and not deliver."

"I'm sure, Frank."

"And you're confident your girlfriend won't find these and fuck things up for us?"

"We don't have to worry. She could never do a climb this high. This is way past her limit."

"You'd better be right. I'm leaving her out of this because you say we don't need her."

"We *don't* need her. I've got this covered."

"Okay." Frank clapped his gloved hands together, and a small dust cloud appeared. He pointed to Colin and Ian. "You two go down the way we came. Get rid of as much evidence as you can that says we were here. Vincent and I will rappel down this wall. It's faster. I want to set up a meet with the buyer ASAP. We need some supplies. We'll see you at camp later."

* * * *

Cat squinted as she looked up the sheer wall of stone facing her. Her heart pounded when it hit her. "Nine hundred feet! I can't climb nine hundred feet. That's twice my highest climb so far and I'm alone. One mistake and I'm dead." She sat down on a rock and took deep breaths until she was calm again.

She stood up and examined the rock face. Her pulse started racing again. *No! I have to do this. Just handle it one piece at a time. You know what's up there. You can do this.*

She went through her pre-climb ritual. When she got to the part where she fingered the black obsidian on her necklace, she thought a prayer to her mother was appropriate. *Mother, I climb for our people. Please give me the courage to master my fears and the wisdom to… to…* She laughed. *I guess there's no way to put this but the wisdom not to make a stupid mistake and end up as roadkill.*

It was the most dangerous climb she'd ever done. She took extra care with anchors and cams. If anything went wrong — she slipped, a piece of rock she was holding on to broke off, a serious gust of wind hit her when she was off balance — her gear would the only thing that could save her life.

It was a long, tough climb. Every move she made was deliberate. Every part of her body was sore from the exertion. Having been intensely focused every second, she was mentally exhausted. She was relieved when she finally saw the top edge. When she was fifty feet from the plateau, however, she saw the oddest thing. A large drone carrying a package flew overhead. She could swear it looked like it was landing where she was heading. Being so close to the top, she quickened her pace. The rock was easier to climb at this point. She decided she could skip the last couple of cams.

As she began pulling herself over the ledge on to the top of the mountain, there was a loud explosion. The shock wave threw her back. She instinctively grabbed hold of her rope, but found herself in mid-air, falling upside down. She smashed against the side of the mountain as she plummeted — then everything went black.

* * * *

As the mountain shook, Colin grabbed hold of the rock face. Looking below him, he yelled to his brother, "Are you all right?"

Ian gave him a thumbs-up. "What the fuck was that?"

Colin shook his head. "Frank and Vincent!" he yelled. "I was afraid of something like this but I didn't think they were *that* stupid. I bet they planted a bomb to destroy the site. We need to go back up and see how bad the damage is."

"Colin! Look!" Ian shouted. "We've got to help."

It was a terrifying sight. A hundred yards above them and to the right, a climber was suspended in mid-air, not moving. He'd obviously been thrown off by the explosion. His rope had saved him. But the wind was blowing strongly enough that the climber would soon be swinging like a pendulum. It was only a matter of time before the sharp rocks cut through the rope and the climber would plummet to his death.

"He's unconscious. That rope's not going to hold. I'll go up and help," shouted Ian.

"No! The explosion made things unstable. The stuff between you and me is ready to go. He looks sort of small, so that's a plus. That ledge above him is stable, so I'll have solid footing. I can grab his rope and pull him up." He got out his small binoculars and studied the situation more. "I think that's a woman!" As the wind picked up, the dangling climber was turned around. Staring intently, he studied a decal on the helmet. "Jesus Christ, Ian. That's Cat!" His heart sank with worry, then exploded with anger. "That son of a bitch! I'm going to kill him!"

"It's Cat? Then I'm definitely helping."

"No. It's too risky. But go down and find her car. I'm sure she's got a satellite phone at her camp. We'll need to call for help. You do that and I'll get her."

"Just promise me you won't take any crazy risks. You'll be no help to her if you fall trying to rescue her."

Colin frowned. "You know, sometimes it's a real pain in the ass that you know me so well. I promise."

As Ian hurried down, Colin quickly plotted his strategy and headed for Cat. The hardest thing was keeping his fury under control. Fortunately, the difficulty of getting to her forced him to focus on the task at hand and shoved to the back of his brain everything battling for his attention—his fear that she might already be dead, his concern that even if she were alive, her injuries would be too serious, his rage at Frank and Vincent, his guilt for ever having agreed to this scheme, his shame at not being honest with Cat and telling her what he was up to. Worst of all, the fact that—in so many ways—this was his fault. He'd never be able to forgive himself. It was inconceivable that Cat would. If he could at least save her, he might be able to live with himself.

Despite his promise to Ian, he did take risks. He knew every second counted, so he pulled all his rock-climbing skills out of the bag and reached her in record time. Lifting her to safety, he examined her quickly. Her helmet had cracked wide open from the impact. She was seriously injured. Her breathing was ragged, but she was alive. He was relieved but heartbroken. "I am *so* sorry, Cat." His voice broke. "If we get through this, I will spend the rest of my life making it up to you, if you let me." Wiping away the tears, he strapped her to him, refocused and rappelled down.

When he got her to the ground, Ian helped carry her to the back of the Jeep. He shuddered at how seriously injured she was. "Fuck, Colin," he said gravely, "this is bad."

Colin dressed her wounds. "Frank and Vincent *cannot* know she was here, Ian."

"I agree. But what do we do?"

Colin examined some maps on the front seat. "I know where she camped. We take her there, call a search-and-rescue team and tell them she needs help. Then we hope we make it back to our camp before Frank and Vincent. I'll drive her Jeep. You follow. And I need you to do one other thing."

"Okay."

Colin was filled with rage. "Keep me from killing the two of them."

Ian's expression mirrored his. "I'll think about it."

Colin did as much as he could to make Cat comfortable. She was still unconscious, and her breathing was becoming increasingly labored.

"I can't leave her, Ian." His voice was dark with worry.

"You have to. You know as well as I do that if Frank finds out what happened, he'll kill all of us—including Cat. Her only chance is for us to leave...now. I called search and rescue and gave them the coordinates. They're on their way."

Colin leaned over and kissed her forehead. "I'm sorry, Cat, for everything. I love you." As he stood up, he wiped the tears from his face.

The sound of the Jeep roaring off penetrated the agony that had taken over Cat's body, and she just barely came to. The first thing she was aware of was searing pain in her head, her right arm and around her torso. She forced herself to focus. *I was at the top. I was thrown off by...something. An earthquake? An explosion?* The pain was so intense, even thinking made it worse. She lay as still as she could. She forced herself to open one eye. She was at her campsite. *How did I get here?* She was in such agony that she closed her eye. She tried to relax and breathe. But with every inhale, the pain got worse. She tried to fight through the torture. *Air! I need air!* It felt like a boulder was crushing her chest. *Why can't I breathe? Fight! Fight! Fight!* She threw every bit of energy into a desperate gasp but lacked the strength even for that. Her head spun. *Dizzy. I'm freezing. Need help.* Cold spread through her body. She lost feeling in her legs. In her arms. Then everything went black.

"Cocheta. It's time to wake up." The female voice roused her from sleep.

Leaving her eyes closed, she assessed her injuries. There was no pain. Moving her arm was effortless. Her entire body felt healed.

She opened her eyes. She was inside a cave beside a warm fire. She looked around and saw beautiful paintings on the walls. A woman stepped out of the shadows and came toward her.

"Mother!"

She leaped up, ran to her and wrapped her arms around her. Cat and her mother embraced.

"I was in pain. It was agony." She looked at her body. She was dressed in a ceremonial robe of her people. She felt light and happy. "How is this possible?"

Her mother smiled. "You're a scholar, Doctor White Eagle. You tell me."

Cat stood quietly for a moment. "Is this another vision?"

"Not exactly."

"Not exactly?"

"This time it's different. I'm here as long as you want me to be. You're here as long as you want to be."

Cat frowned then looked at the ceremonial robe. Her face froze. "This robe. If this isn't a vision, that means...I'm dead."

"Yes," her mother said sadly.

"What happened?"

Her mother put her hand on Cat's forehead. "Close your eyes."

It was as though she were watching a movie. Colin, Ian and two other men were on the plateau as she climbed toward it. The two brothers and the other two men left in different directions. Just as she reached the top, a drone flew in and exploded. She was thrown off and crashed into the side of the mountain. Taking insane risks, Colin reached her and carried her to the ground. He and Ian took her to her campsite and left. Her tortured body lay at her campsite. She was obviously in an enormous amount of pain. All at once, her body shuddered, then there was no movement. Her face was that of a woman who had died in agony.

She opened her eyes and looked at her mother. "He just left me there to die?" She felt crushed and confused. "How could he?" She walked back to the fire, sat down and just stared into the flames. "So, that was the end of my path. Failure? Failure as a researcher. Failure in love. So worthless as a person that Colin left me to die?"

She began to weep. Her mother sat beside her and put her arm around her. "You have always been too harsh on yourself, my daughter. Even if this is the end of your path, it is not a failure. You have achieved much for our people, Cocheta. Your research may let someone else reveal our past at some point in the future. And perhaps parts of your story are still hidden from you. But if you choose, this will be the end of this path."

"What do you mean, 'if I choose'? What choice do I have now that I'm dead?"

"Wakan Tanka always gives us choices, little one," her mother smiled. "You can go back. But you must decide now."

Cat opened her eyes wide, then she laughed. "Go back to a lying, worthless ex-boyfriend who not only broke my heart, but he also left me for dead? Continue searching for a secret in mountains that has killed me once already? And let's not forget being surrounded by colleagues who mock my work incessantly. Why would I want to go back? To experience more pain and failure?"

Her mother pointed at a series of paintings on the wall. "Let me show you something, my daughter."

Her chest exploded from what felt like a bolt of lightning. No! The lightning hit her again. It was agony. *Please! Stop it! I just want to sleep!*

"No!" the voice screamed, "I refuse to let you die! Live, Cat! Live!"

The lightning struck yet again. Cat screamed inside, begging for it to stop. All at once, her body shook. She gasped and frantically pulled in the cold mountain air. Her body was still racked with pain, but at least she could breathe.

"You are safe. But you must rest." She pulled Cat's hair from her face and stroked it gently.

"Mother?" Cat murmured weakly. The effort made her head throb.

"Shh, child. Sleep." Cat could barely hear her as she was fading into sleep once more.

The figure in camouflage sat quietly beside her and sobbed in relief. She put a blanket over Cat and changed the dressing on her wounds. She picked up the satellite phone. "It was worse than I expected. Her heart had stopped. But I was finally able to revive her... No, I don't know how long... Yes, I understand... All we can do is wait and see." She sat beside Cat and lovingly stroked her hair.

* * * *

"You blew it up! Are you crazy? That was a priceless artifact in a location with so treacherous a climb that no climber would ever just stumble on it." Colin grabbed Frank by the shirt. "Why, for fuck's sake, would you do something like that?"

Frank glared at him. "Calm down, Princey, and take your hands off me. I don't like loose ends. And if you don't stop bitching at me so much, you're going to find *yourself* a loose end. You took photos, made the charcoal rubbing and we have the info. That's what the buyer wants. Besides, it gives us leverage. I think it's time we *renegotiate* with him. With nothing but rubble on the top of that mountain, we're the only ones with the clues. He can't say no."

Colin was filled with fury. He was having trouble containing himself.

"But don't feel bad. We couldn't have found those carvings so fast without you. I was afraid it was going to take months. We're lucky you pilfered your girlfriend's research before you dumped her. But why wouldn't you? You're a thief. If you weren't such a pain in the ass, I might ask you to work with us some more."

Probably having seen Colin clench his fists, Ian grabbed him before he lunged at Frank.

Their captor pointed his gun at them. "Ian, we leave in thirty minutes. Make sure his head is where it's supposed to be. I don't want him to screw things up at the final exchange. Remind him we have a deal. He helps us with this, and I make sure all the charges are dropped. If he fucks around, the two of you get forgotten in a Greek prison that stinks of piss so bad you'll think it's been cooking since Agamemnon. Or maybe your bodies get picked clean in the desert by vultures."

Ian gave him the finger and followed Colin as they walked away.

"Hey! You teach classics. I thought you'd appreciate that," he shouted. "Just get your asses into the Jeep."

When they pulled into the gas station, Colin headed for the restroom. Knowing that Frank would send Vincent in after him, he acted quickly. He slid a small slip of paper behind the urinal he was using. He'd written a warning with the longitude, latitude and time of the exchange on it.

As expected, Vincent stepped in. "Let's go, Your Highness."

As Colin left, he could only hope that the right person found his clue.

Chapter Twenty-Three

Frank, Vincent, Colin and Ian stepped out of the Hummer and grabbed their climbing gear.

Frank looked up and squinted against the sun. "Our friggin' crazy buyer insisted the exchange be face to face—on top, at dusk. I'm not taking any chances. We climb now and wait. Make sure you have the stuff, King Henry."

The four of them ascended. Once they got to the top, Colin and Ian sat by themselves.

"The message?" Ian asked quietly.

Colin simply nodded.

"How much do you trust this pair?"

He cocked one eyebrow.

"Me, neither."

"What do we do if things go south?"

"Whatever we need to. Just make sure there's always someone between you and the edge."

Ian nodded.

Colin looked into the distance. "Do you think search and rescue reached Cat in time?"

"I told them it was life and death and gave them the longitude and latitude. They said they'd send a chopper. They weren't happy I wouldn't give my name. I hung up when they pressed me. I'm sure they sent someone right out."

Colin squinted as he stared into the distance, trying not to be obvious about it.

"Do you see something?" Ian asked quietly.

"That flock of ravens. It's unnerving. I've never seen such a large number of them flying together. And they just keep flying in a big circle." His shoulders slumped. "It's an omen." He shivered. "It means Cat's not doing well. This was my fault."

"How many times have you told me you don't believe in omens? You're worried. You're panicked. Take a breath. You didn't know it was going to turn out like this. You were trying to protect her."

"It doesn't change that she got hurt and may die. I can't stop thinking of her lying on the ground at her campsite in agony. I want to kill those guys." His face tightened and he clenched his fists.

"Chill out, dude. If those two bastards even imagine Cat's out there, they'll kill us in an instant then go after her. As soon as we're done here, I promise we'll make sure she's all right."

Colin closed his eyes as he was filled with sadness. "Something terrible has happened. I just know it."

The blue sky lost its sparkle and turned gray. The clouds morphed from white to gold then rose. Colin heard the distinctive sounds of a climber setting an anchor. They all looked over the edge to see a figure clothed completely in black, moving with surprising speed on such a difficult terrain.

When the climber reached the top, Frank stuck out his hand to help.

"Do I look that stupid?" came a voice muffled by a black balaclava. "Move back and give me some room."

Ian turned to Colin. "Is there something familiar about that voice?"

"Must be a coincidence."

They all stepped back. "What is it about you Brits that makes you all so fucking annoying?" Frank spat out.

The climber pulled themselves over the edge, stood and took off the balaclava.

Visibly flabbergasted, Ian instinctively took a step back. "Holy crap! Aunt Clarissa?"

"Nephew," she said calmly. She turned toward Colin, whose mouth was hanging open. "Nephew."

Frank strode up to her. "What the fuck! You all know each other? Are you people playing us?"

Vincent took two steps back and let his hand rest on the handle of the gun on his waist.

Clarissa shoved Frank back as he got too close. "You have no manners, young man. Of course, I'm not playing you. Who do you think provided you with all the resources for us to do this? The plans? The targeted objects? The security code? And especially my brilliant nephew. Speaking of whom, you'll excuse me for a minute."

She walked over to Colin and Ian, who still appeared dumbfounded.

Colin ran his hand through his hair in disbelief. "You're the buyer? You're a thief and a smuggler?"

"Yes, Colin, but not entirely by choice. I owe the two of you an explanation. When your worthless sot of a father burned through all the family money, the accountants said we had to sell the estate. Since it's been in the family for hundreds of years, I wasn't prepared for that to happen. I found...let's call it an alternative revenue stream that lets me pay off the debts.

"I've done small amounts of smuggling and selling over the years — never enough to attract the authorities' attention. When I heard about the Lost Tribe treasure map, I knew I could make enough on that to protect the estate permanently and to retire from my sideline. So, Colin, you are not the only member of the family who bends the rules.

"And let me compliment you on the excellent job of helping Cat White Eagle move her research along so quickly. It's why we've been so successful. Very impressive, nephew. It's a shame that relationship blew up. I'd been hoping the two of you could take over the family business." She looked back and forth at them. "Have either of you anything you'd like to say at this point?"

"You *climb*?" Ian blurted out. "*Really* well! But you're sixt — "

She poked his chest with a sharp finger. "Continue that sentence at your own peril, nephew. I'm an archaeologist. I've climbed for years. Your uncle thought it was 'unladylike,' however. Our compromise was that I'd do it in secret."

She turned to Colin. "And you? Anything else?"

The sequence of events that had brought him to this moment flashed through his head. The Greek dig. Danielle. The job at Red Rock. Cat. Her research. Recruited by Interpol. Being used by his Aunt, Frank, and Vincent to steal — and demolish — priceless artifacts. Then there was the loss of his relationship with Cat and how much jeopardy she'd been put in. He didn't even know if she'd survived the blast.

"I've been your puppet this past year." He didn't even try to hide the disgust in his voice. "How many strings have you pulled to make me dance?"

"More than you can imagine, nephew. But it was just business." She lowered her voice. "There is one thing I do need to apologize to you for." She turned to make sure Frank and Vincent couldn't see. She handed him the slip of paper he'd left in the rest room. "I couldn't allow you to involve anyone else. Just know that I always have your best interests at heart."

Ian gulped. "We're fucked, Colin."

Colin gritted his teeth and stared his aunt down. "You and I have a score to settle, Aunt Clarissa."

She took his hand gently and patted it. "The night is young, nephew. The night is young. A good scholar waits until all the data is in."

As she turned away, Ian mouthed, "What the fuck?"

Colin mouthed, "Bitch!"

"Okay," shouted Frank. "You can continue your family reunion later. I want to get this over with." He pointed at a backpack that was about five yards from the edge. "There's the package. Confirm it has what we agreed."

Clarissa walked over, examined the photos and the rubbing. "Very well." She took out her phone and tapped in the numbers. "The money has been transferred."

Frank looked at his phone to confirm it. "Excellent. There's just one thing. The price has now doubled."

Clarissa scowled. "That wasn't our agreement."

"It's our *new* agreement," Frank smiled broadly.

"Forget it. I can just go to the site myself." She held up the backpack. "I don't need this."

Frank turned to his partner. "Vincent, did you forget to tell the Lady of the Manor that we blew up those symbols for this very reason?"

He clapped both hands against his face in mock surprise. "Oh my goodness, Frank. I got so caught up in the excitement that I overlooked that." He turned to Clarissa with a self-satisfied grin. "My bad, your Ladyship. Does that matter?"

"You blew up the site?"

"Yes," Frank smiled proudly.

Clarissa studied him and frowned. "It's possible I have underestimated you. Come over here and look at these materials. If they're clear and detailed enough for us to decode, I'll accept your terms." She scowled. "It's only money. I'll just pass the extra cost along."

As they walked to where their aunt was standing, Frank and Vincent looked at each other. Their eyes were bright with seeming delight. Frank took out his phone again.

As Colin and Ian reached her, Clarissa said quietly, but with intent, "Listen carefully. You will do exactly as I say. I will explain later." Everything about her — the strength in her voice, the determination in her eyes, the power in how she carried herself — said there was only one response. "Colin," — she spoke softly — "you will pick up the backpack and say you don't need to examine it. Then, when we're concluding business, Ian, you'll slowly move ten yards to your left, Colin, ten yards to your right. Your lives depend on it."

Colin looked toward the thieves. "It's everything she needs, Frank. Pay the man, Aunt Clarissa."

As Colin watched his Aunt Clarissa enter the transaction into her phone, he and Ian slowly moved away.

"There," she yelled. "Satisfied?"

Looking at the phone, Frank beamed. "Almost. There's just one more thing." He held his phone in front of him and Vincent aimed his gun at them. "Normally, I'd just send the pack of you to your maker without any conversation. But since you all think you're so much smarter than us, I want your last feeling to be recognizing how stupid and gullible you were." He held up his phone and hit one-one-one. "When I hit 'pound', that ledge you're standing on will collapse. Vincent put some charges in there. The three of you will be out of my hair forever. If you move, Vincent will shoot you. Either way, you're dead."

Clarissa crossed her arms and frowned. She narrowed her eyes and tapped her foot impatiently. "Fine, Frank. You're smarter than us. We're a bunch of stupid, snotty Brits. How much more do you want? This is getting tedious."

Mocking her, he put his finger to his cheek and looked up. "Let's see, we have twice what we originally asked for. We've got copies of everything in that backpack that we can sell for ten times what you'd give us. Do we want anything else?"

He looked at Vincent, who shrugged.

"I guess admitting how stupid you are is enough. Sayonara, Grannie." He punched the keypad.

Nothing happened.

He looked at the phone, scrunched up his face and tried again.

Nothing.

"Problems, Frank?" Clarissa asked seriously. "I'd be careful with charges that didn't go off. Someone could get hurt."

"Smug and bitchy right up to the end, eh?" He sneered as he pulled out his weapon. "Put yours away, Vincent. I'm going to do the old witch myself."

"If you insist," she said, "but I'd worry about the fireflies."

"Fireflies?"

"Right. All those red dots on you and Vincent."

The two looked at themselves and at each other. Their heads and chests were covered with red dots.

"Oh, silly me. Those aren't fireflies. Those are lasers from sharpshooters aiming at you." She turned to her right and pointed. "There are three up there." She pointed higher. "There's another four." She turned to her right. "There's... I'm sure you get the point. You know how this sort of thing works, Frank. Whoever has the high ground wins. So, I guess I *didn't* underestimate you. I knew you'd try to double-cross and kill us. And if you don't drop to the ground face down *now*, I'll give the order to shoot."

The pair stood frozen in place.

"*Now*, gentlemen."

Frank spat, tossed his gun away and lay down. Vincent followed suit.

"Nephews, you'll find handcuffs in my backpack. Please use them to restrain our guests."

While Colin grabbed a pair and began doing that, Clarissa pulled a strobe out of her backpack. She placed it in the middle of the plateau and turned it on. Thirty seconds later, a distinctive *whup whup whup* announced the arrival of a black, unmarked helicopter. A team of similarly dressed armed individuals slid down ropes. One walked over to Clarissa and saluted sharply, "Orders, Ma'am."

"Please remove this filth, Captain."

"Done, Ma'am."

Frank and Vincent were each put in a harness and hoisted into the helicopter. The ground team followed up the ropes. The chopper quickly disappeared into the night.

Clarissa turned to him and Ian. "I imagine you boys have some questions." She scanned the plateau. "There's enough wood here for a small fire. Please get that going and I'll explain everything."

"No." Colin was frantic. "We have to make sure Cat's all right. She was in terrible shape when we left her. You've got to radio for another helicopter—or contact search and rescue and see if they have her."

"Of course. But first we need the final member of our team." She nodded toward the cliff edge as a climber's headlight popped up at the edge. "Quickly, Colin. Go help that climber."

Running over to the edge, he expected to find one of his aunt's minions. He reached out to help. When the climber's delicate hand slipped into his, he felt a familiar electric jolt. He was astonished but ecstatic. He pulled Cat up and crushed her against him.

"Oww! Broken ribs! Wrenched shoulder! Hurt everywhere!" she yelled as she pulled back. "If that's your way of saying 'I love you and please forgive me for being a selfish jerk', forget it." She scowled and made a fist. He instantly stepped back and put his hands up. She winked playfully and gently hugged him.

Tears streamed down his face as he wrapped her in his arms and sobbed. "I was afraid you were dead."

"Well," she said, smirking, "actually I was. But I'll explain."

His mouth dropped open. "You were *what*?"

"Colin!" Clarissa yelled. "Please escort your young lady over here. We have much to discuss."

Clarissa stood as they approached and gave Cat a warm, soft hug. "How are you doing, my dear? The climb wasn't too much, I hope. We could have brought you in by the helicopter."

"As I told you, my mother showed me how to handle the pain. I'm just a little sore." She spread her arms but winced. "Okay, a lot sore. But these mountains were my people's home. It's a matter of principle. We *climb*."

Colin felt disbelief, confusion, relief, gratitude — but especially love. As they sat down, he wrapped his arm gently around her. Clarissa smiled warmly at the two of them and sighed.

Ian cleared his throat. "I hate to ruin this Hallmark moment, but I'd love to know what's going on." He turned to his aunt. "You're not a thief after all. You're a *spy* or something?"

"Hardly," she laughed. "Someone simply asked me for help. And you know how it is in our world. One does favors. People feel indebted. They say, 'Never hesitate to ask.' I take them up on it. One thing leads to another and the matter gets addressed." She brushed the air with her hand dismissively.

"You can be annoyingly opaque, Aunt Clarissa. Let's take this one question at a time. Who was the *someone* who asked you for help?"

"Why, *Cat*, of course."

Colin turned to Cat, deeply puzzled.

Her expression mirrored his. "*Me*? *No*! I never asked you to help me break up a ring of thieves."

"Of course you didn't, dear. A few years ago, you wrote to me asking for help. You said you were a graduate student in archaeology just starting your dissertation. You explained you were working on the myth of the Lost Tribe. Your adviser wasn't keen on your topic and had reservations about your methodology. You asked if I had any advice about the most professionally acceptable way to research a *myth*."

Cat shrugged her shoulders. "I guess I did. I was so panicked that I wrote to *every* archaeology department I could find. You didn't write back, though. I would have remembered."

"I would have, if the matter hadn't gotten so complicated. I consulted a colleague of mine in the States. She said rumors about the legendary Lost Tribe treasure map had begun circulating again. Thieves and smugglers were coming out of the woodwork and were decimating Native American sites. She feared that any artifacts that could have even the slightest clue about the Lost Tribe were in danger. She was actually aware of your research and thought you were on to something big. I told her to leave things in my hands and I'd talk to some friends to see how the artifacts in question could be protected."

Colin shook his head. "Scotland Yard, Interpol, the Bureau of Indian Affairs," he ticked off. "Friends?"

"In truth, I've worked with them for years. That 'sideline' I told you about is real—only, like this operation, it's for the purpose of ferreting out and catching thieves."

He shook his head in disbelief. "Danielle? Did you set that up?"

"No. But that particular episode and your 'borrowing' objects from your last dig were of enormous help. Your vices were handy this time, nephew. But I must insist you give them up," she said sternly.

"There's no worry about that," joked Cat.

"Oh, really?" Colin hugged her playfully.

"Oww! Broken ribs, remember?"

"Sorry," he apologized, kissing her on the top of her head.

"Once we set the plan in motion, the task was to keep all of you safe, while fooling Richards and Wilkins. It was important for the world to believe that your breakup was real and that Colin had been arrested. I'm very sorry, Cat, that you had to endure such heartbreak." Clarissa got somber. "Unfortunately, we had complications. The drone surprised us. Fortunately, one of our snipers was able to hit it and detonate it before it could land — otherwise the debris from the blast would probably have killed Cat. The carvings are still intact."

"That's a relief," Cat said.

Clarissa turned to her. "I'm truly sorry, Cat. I'd been watching you to keep you safe, but I had no idea you could climb so quickly. That was the only time I lost track of you. We didn't realize how much danger you were in until the blast.

"You should know that Colin took some extraordinary risks to save you. My heart was in my throat and I was shaking the whole time I watched him." She held up a pair of binoculars. "It was truly breathtaking. I've never seen a greater display of love. I can't tell you how proud I am of you, nephew." She smiled warmly at him. Ian clapped him on the back.

"It's just too bad that after all that, I died," Cat said casually.

Colin turned to her and froze. "You're serious. You died?"

She smirked. "Oh, you know. Just something normal for my people. I died, spent some time with my mother, learned some secrets then got resuscitated by your aunt. Just a normal day of archaeological research. I'll

tell you about it later. But you interrupted the story."
She and Clarissa exchanged smiles.

Unable to take his eyes off Cat, Colin sat with Ian, both with their mouths open as Clarissa continued. "Today went according to plan. We disarmed the charges as soon as Vincent put them in. We had snipers everywhere," — she turned to Colin and Ian — "which is why I asked you to move out of the line of fire. And I kept the two of you in the dark until the very last moment — even letting you think I'd intercepted your message for help — because I couldn't have Frank and Vincent getting suspicious. I've been dealing with them for a while as their 'buyer'. And while they're vicious thugs, they're also smart ones. That's why I made you think help was *not* on the way. I couldn't read in the two of you until the last moment. They needed to believe your anger at me was real.

"But while we've protected some artifacts and put away some thieves, the most important thing we want to be grateful for is the two of you. You have made each other better, stronger, more loving individuals. Colin has become the man I always knew he could be. If I'd had a daughter, I would have wanted her to be as courageous, fearless and devoted as Cat has become...except perhaps for the pole dancing." Cat blushed. "But who am I to judge?" Clarissa shrugged. "It was a means to an end. You are now a strong, confident woman and a remarkable climber." She held up an imaginary glass. "So 'cheers' to us all."

They all laughed, cheered and pretended to drink.

"One more thing, Colin. As Cat will tell you, the second set of carvings provided more clues, but not everything you thought they did. They're proof that Cocheta's people lived in these mountains long before anyone thought. They suggest it was a remarkable community. And the images clearly suggest there's something of immense value there. But they don't show the location. For that—" She turned to Cat.

"When I died and visited with my mother, she explained the carvings are stories from when my people lived here in the rocks. When I asked her how to find our home, she told me what I need to do next. I'm going to stay here alone for a few days to discover the final key. If my ancestors think I'm worthy, they'll reveal it in a vision."

"In which case, Ian," Aunt Clarissa stood up, "it's time for us to leave. It's a full moon, and there's plenty of light. I think we could use the practice rappelling down. This young couple has a lot of catching up to do—and Cat has a vision quest to begin."

Chuckling and shaking his head, Ian stood up. "Yes, Aunt Clarissa." He turned to Colin. "I'm about to rappel down the side of a mountain with Aunt Clarissa after she pretended to be a master criminal, called in her SWAT team and double-crossed a pair of thieves and smugglers. How weird is that?"

The two stepped into their gear. Clarissa gave the signal, Ian gave a thumbs-up—and they were gone.

* * * *

In the soft, romantic firelight, Cat sat quietly with Colin, overflowing with relief that the last few months were behind them.

Colin took her hands and a deep breath and looked straight at her. "I was wrong, Cat. I'm sorry. I put you through Hell. I told myself it was okay because I was trying to protect you, but that doesn't matter. It was my fault you got hurt. Hell, you *died* because I was so arrogant. I betrayed your trust." He paused. His voice broke as he finished what he had to say. "If I did so much damage that we can't try again, I understand."

She was moved by such an unambiguous apology. When she'd first met Colin, apologizing about anything likely would have never even crossed his mind. She squeezed his hands but remained somber. "I'm not going to lie. For the last three months, I've been in agony. You broke my heart. You got arrested. All I knew was that you'd become the worst possible version of yourself. I was devastated and angry. After the FBI came to my office and interviewed me, I got a daily dose of suspicious looks everywhere I went in town. The only way I kept my sanity was to disappear into the desert and have no contact with anyone.

"Even when your aunt explained everything, it deeply hurt me that you hadn't even talked to me before you decided what to do. It makes me wonder how much of a partner you can really be. I need time to think. But" — she smirked — "that punch at least helped. We can compare notes about what happened when we were apart some other time. Tonight, I just want to feel grateful to be alive and that this ordeal is behind us."

"Agreed." He nodded. "But you know," he said slyly, "I'd feel a lot better if I could help you with the pain you're feeling from your injuries." As he talked, he slowly unzipped her jacket and slid his hand under her T-shirt. "Let me massage your ribs and make them better."

"Colin!" she giggled, pushing his hand away. "First, I'm really too sore. Second, those aren't my *ribs*!"

"Close enough."

Chapter Twenty-Four

Cat slept with Colin under the star-filled sky. After months of torment, they were finally back together. At first light, they awoke.

"How will I ever make things up to you?" Colin was chastened and serious.

"We'll worry about that later. Right now, I need to do a vision quest. I have instructions from my mother. If I'm judged worthy, I'll be shown the secrets of my people. It's going to take at least three days, so you need to leave."

"But your injuries..." His face was full of concern.

"I'll be fine." She smiled. Taking his hands, she looked into his eyes. "More than anything, you have to trust me. Can you do that for me?

He smiled back. "Of course." Then, adopting a clearly professional tone, he took out a notebook. "I have no doubt your vision quest will succeed. After that, you'll want to go exploring. And I don't want you to have to waste any time. Tell me exactly what you'll need. I'll have it waiting for you in a Jeep when you climb back down."

She ticked off the items — camping supplies for a few days, climbing gear, fresh clothes.

"And two satellite phones, just in case," he added — making it plain that this was nonnegotiable.

She smiled to herself at the mix of respect and concern he showed. They kissed goodbye, and Colin descended from the rocky plateau.

Cat had been given detailed instructions by her mother about how to spend the next three days. She hoped she'd be judged worthy and allowed to have a vision that would reveal the secret to her ancestors' village. This was a test of body, mind and spirit. She had no food with her, only water, and she was to stay awake the entire time. Wearing just shorts and a T-shirt, she had no real protection from the elements. But while it was warm in May, the heat wasn't usually oppressive. She didn't think the weather would be an issue. Her task was to sit in one spot and meditate.

It would be a challenge to concentrate the whole time and not let the pain throughout her body distract her. But even harder to ignore would be the tumult of contradictory feelings about Colin roiling around inside her.

I love him. It was such a relief to find out he wasn't a criminal. I'm so furious he didn't even talk to me. That's such a typical guy thing to do. He was trying to protect me – even if he went about it badly, so that matters... At least he could have gotten word to me about what was going on. Did he think I was so stupid I'd go blabbing it all around? But I've never felt anything close to how much I love him. And the sex! Fanfuckingtastic! He really must love me to risk losing me like that... And now worrying about all this is keeping me from focusing! Damn you, Colin Tucker!

For day one, she was to meditate on 'the people are the rocks'. After a few hours, she realized what that meant. Her ancestors had a powerful connection with the red rocks all around her. It was so strong that it allowed them — and her — to pull some sort of energy from the stones. As the beautifully clear day progressed, her pain diminished and became less of a distraction. Her body was still banged up, but it was healing faster than normal. In the middle of the night, she also felt mended in a different way. The emotional turmoil connected with Colin had faded into the background. It wasn't that she'd forgiven him or that her love for him had blotted out the hurt. She simply felt stronger and more independent than she ever had. She might *want* to get back together with him, but she didn't *need* to. He was no longer irresistible — in a good way. She had more control over her destiny and was confident that whatever choice she made would be entirely hers — and the right one.

'See the people' was the mantra for day two. It had been an unusually cold night, so until she warmed up, she had trouble focusing. For the first few hours, she got nowhere. All she saw were the rocks, ledges, plateaus and various striations in the stones all around her. Finally, she realized the more intense red markings in the rockface opposite her formed a pattern — a pentangle or pentagram. Staring at these spots, however, accomplished nothing, and the harder she worked, the more tired and frustrated she became. But *that* showed her what she was doing wrong. A more relaxed gaze, just off center — like the best way to see something in the dark or to look at the stars — revealed something astonishing — faint, almost ghostlike images. They were snapshots of village life — meals, community gatherings, children playing, people gathering around a well. The last one startled her. *A well? I know every water source for a hundred miles. That's not here.* She sighed. Was she looking in the wrong place? Could the village have been hundreds of miles away? *No. My mother wouldn't have let me be so far off.* She went back to looking at the images to see what she could learn about the village's location. As the sun went down, the images began to fade. But just before she lost the light, an image briefly caught her eye. It was a view of the sun going down as seen by a villager. *That's impossible.* Cat had explored the area so much that she knew the topography of every plateau that allowed a west-facing view. No known location allowed that vista. Again, she worried that the location was miles away.

Her final evening was even colder. And as the day had heated up so quickly, she wondered whether her mother was deliberately making conditions more difficult for her. She'd managed to stay awake the whole time, but her fatigue made the heat feel even worse.

The mantra for her final day was 'follow the people'. She went back to examining the images from the day before, but there was no movement. *How can I follow people who aren't moving?* She persisted for the next few hours to no avail. Then the extreme heat took its toll. She was drenched in sweat and had a terrible headache. She fought hard to stay awake. Her head started spinning. She pitched over and lost consciousness.

When she opened her eyes, she felt wonderful. Her head was clear and her body felt so light and so full of energy that she was sure she could fly if she wanted to. She looked around.

She was someplace different. The cliff dwellings carved into the red rock looked familiar, but as an archaeologist, she knew every location. This was new. She also noticed that the spot was completely surrounded by rock. The opening to the sky was relatively small, but everything was bathed in sunlight. She also noticed the well. Her mother was standing beside it.

Cat quickly looked to see what she was wearing. "Regular clothes," she remarked to her mother, "not the ceremonial robe. At least I'm not dead this time." She smiled.

"Welcome, my daughter," said her mother, walking up to hug her. "You have done well and are being rewarded with the vision that will reveal the secret you seek." They were standing in front of a small group of women, all of whom looked remarkably like Cat.

"Welcome to the sisterhood," said one of them, smiling warmly. "We are all the Cochetas from our village's different times." Then the group turned and headed west.

Her mother pointed to the women and took Cat by the hand. "Follow the people."

The women walked to the base of the far wall and began climbing. Cat was stunned at how skilled they all were – even the women who looked like they were in their eighties. They shot up the wall remarkably fast for climbers with no safety equipment. About five hundred feet up, there was a small opening. Going through, she emerged into a passageway. At the far end was an opening. She noticed the setting sun. Pointing to it, she turned to her mother. "The image from yesterday?"

"Yes, my child. And since you have so many questions, I think you should fly out and see for yourself where you are."

Cat frowned. "Fly?"

Her mother laughed. "Of course, Cocheta White Eagle. *She clapped her hands and Cat was transformed into a beautiful white bird.*

Giddy with excitement, Cat shot out of the opening, filled with joy and wonder. She was so thrilled, and all she wanted to do was experience the amazing freedom of flying. She soared, dove, let herself be lifted by the warm currents and took in the glorious view. After a while, she laughed at how carried away she'd gotten, calmed down and addressed the task at hand. So, where am I? She struggled to locate the entrance. No matter which direction she looked from, she could barely see the opening. If she didn't know it was there, she'd completely miss it. She looked for the opening above the village. It was at the top of what was essentially a rock tower, and it was also very hard to see. And, given how bright the village is, it's surprisingly small. Where does all the light come from?

After figuring out where the entry was, she flew through the small opening and instantly transformed back to herself.

"You have what you need," her mother explained.

"Do I? I have so many questions. There must be an easier entrance. Everyone couldn't come and go through that small opening five hundred feet up."

"In time, my daughter." *Her mother smiled knowingly.* "But for now, you have what you need." *She clapped her hands twice.*

Cat woke up on the plateau, lying on her side. The sun was setting and the day had cooled. She quickly reached for her backpack and pulled out her notebook and a map. Not wanting to forget anything, she marked the entry to the village on the map and frantically jotted down as much as she could remember about what she'd seen in the vision. Then, exhausted, but elated, she went to sleep.

She awoke the following morning feeling better than she had in months. Even sore ribs couldn't dampen her enthusiasm. Excited to confirm that she had correctly identified the location of her people's village, she put everything in her backpack and descended. Colin had provided everything she'd asked for. She climbed into the Jeep and headed out on what she knew would be a life-changing experience.

She camped as close to the location as possible. It was so remote and the terrain so difficult, however, that it would be at least a three-hour hike to the base of the rockface. Realizing she'd have to spend at least one night there, she put the supplies into her backpack and headed out.

For someone who'd recently died then endured a strenuous vision quest, Cat's energy was remarkable. Her spirits couldn't be higher. She barely took a break making her way to the rockface.

Once there, she was all business. She was now too accomplished a climber to leave anything to chance. She cinched her harness and helmet, tightened her shoes and proceeded down the rest of her pre-climb checklist. "Rope. Hardware. Chalk. Water." Next, as she always did, she closed her eyes and squeezed the black obsidian she wore. She moved her lips silently. Her heart rate increased and her mouth went dry. She laughed as she hit the final item. "Stupid archaeologist, *still* afraid of heights!" she yelled out loud.

The five-hundred-foot climb was predictably challenging. Remembering what she'd seen in her vision, however, she knew how to navigate the most difficult spots. Pulling herself through the small opening, she was elated that it was exactly the same as it had appeared. She walked down the passageway, looked out onto the village and was stunned. It was an enormous canyon—but walled in on all sides. There was a large open area—like a central square—with a well in the middle, surrounded by countless dwellings carved into the red rock. Tears flowed freely down her face because it was literally a dream come true. More important than this as an archaeological discovery, however, was that it was the first time in her life that she felt at home. *This is where I come from. This is who I am.* She was overwhelmed with gratitude for having been allowed to find her ancestral home and to have been chosen to make this historic discovery.

After climbing down, she began to explore. She looked up and noted how small the opening to the sky was—just like in her vision. *How can everything be so bright?*

It was immediately apparent it would take years to unlock the site's secrets, so she had no interest in rushing. The most remarkable thing was how neat and organized everything was—even though no one had lived there for thousands of years. *It's as though everyone decided to leave at the same time and wanted it to be easy for another group to move in. Amazing!*

She dutifully took photographs and jotted down notes. Her list of questions needing answers was endless. *There must be another way in and out than an opening hundreds of feet above the ground of a nearly vertical rockface. Where is it? Why is everything so bright? Lots of the rocks glow with a beautiful rosy hue. Some minerals in them must reflect the light. I've never heard of anything like that. Amazing! I see what looks like food preparation areas and eating implements, but I can't tell what they ate. Why did they leave? Could the well have gone dry? Food shortage? Did they plan to return when conditions improved? The pottery is extraordinary. The designs are far more advanced than is supposed to be possible for this time. The piece that Colin saw in London had been stolen! Did it come from here? Or was it the result of this community's influence on others? What about the famous 'treasure'? There's no sign of precious metals or jewels. I've got it! A site this well protected – with a well – would have been priceless. That's how the rumors of a treasure got started!* And that was just page one.

Too excited to sleep, she alternated between imagining what life had been like there thousands of years ago and planning a full-blown archaeological survey. She also brooded about how to make sure the site would be treated with appropriate respect for her people. *Who among the indigenous peoples are our closest relatives? They'll need to be involved in the major decisions. The DNA research will be fascinating. Colin loves doing that sort of thing. He'll be as excited as I am about this. I can't wait to tell him.*

She couldn't help noticing how natural it was for her to want to tell Colin about everything as soon as she could and to assume that he'd be involved in the research. It was impossible for her to imagine him not being part of this. His help with her research and on her dissertation had been immeasurable. Unlike the other faculty, he didn't think she was crazy. He'd believed in her.

More than that, however, somewhere along the way, they'd become partners. Her life was unthinkable without him in it. They may not have gotten legally married, but they were clearly, inseparably, body-mind-heart-and-soul married.

She resolved to be brutally honest with herself. If theirs was a bad relationship, no matter how much she loved him and how big a part of her life he'd become, she'd have to walk away from it. She felt a painful pit in her stomach and groaned out loud.

But then there was her mother's comment – *"You and your partner will keep the people from being forgotten forever."* She couldn't imagine anyone other than Colin as her partner.

She grimaced and went back to writing in her notebook. She'd worry about Colin later.

* * * *

After exploring the village for a couple of days, she decided she couldn't put off her decision about her future with Colin any longer. She would return to the site of the ruins they had visited the day after they'd made love. The spot felt special to her. He had been disarmingly open when they'd talked. He had been honest with her about his past, his desire for a serious relationship with her and his fears. As a result, their lovemaking that night had been among the most tender and intimate they'd enjoyed. She hoped the happy memories would offset some of the anger she couldn't entirely get past and would help her decide what she truly wanted.

The hike was longer and even more difficult because the day was so much hotter. She'd waited until the late afternoon to avoid the worst of the heat, but the consequences were that the light was beginning to fade. She was glad she was carrying supplies that would let her spend the night.

As she made the final turn to the site, she was disappointed to discover an enormous tent. She scowled because she'd wanted the place to herself and grumbled about why anyone would need such a huge tent. *Glampers!* she cursed to herself. Not seeing anyone wandering around the ruins, she called out. "Hello!" Not getting any answer, she peeked inside the tent. Her eyes went wide at what she saw.

A small table was covered with a beautiful white tablecloth. There were candles in silver candlesticks, an ice bucket with a bottle of champagne, multiple huge bouquets of roses all around the tent—and Colin.

When she walked in, he beamed. He took a bottle of water from a cooler and handed it to her.

"Thanks." She frowned. "You'd better not tell me you followed me."

He put up his hand as if taking an oath. "I did not. I was tempted to because I was worried, but I knew you wouldn't like it...so I didn't."

"How did you know I'd be here—and be here *now*?"

"I didn't. I took a chance. Call it an act of faith. I thought that after your vision quest led you somewhere—to your people's lost village, I'd guess— you'd go somewhere to decide about us. I hoped this place felt as special to you as it did to me and that you'd come here. I didn't know when that would be, so I decided to come and wait as long as I had to."

"And how long was that?"

"You told me your vision quest would be at least three days. I came here the next day."

"You've been waiting for me here—in this heat—for two days, on the off chance I'd come here?"

"Yes."

Her mood began to soften at how romantic that seemed.

"What's all this?" She waved her hand at everything in the tent.

"I was sure you'd be uncomfortable after your stretch in the mountains and a tough hike, so I wanted you to have something comfortable. Behind the folding panels,"—he pointed to the far corner of the tent— "you'll find a makeshift shower. The water will be warm because the sun's been heating it up all day. I thought you'd also like a change of clothes. You'll find those back there as well."

"Col—"

"Go," he interrupted, pointing to the other corner. "Relax. You've had a difficult few days. Take a shower...then we'll talk."

She started to walk toward the shower, then turned. "Colin, how did you get everything here? Does Aunt Clarissa have access to a fleet of helicopters? Did she lend you one to airlift all this here?"

"Nope," he answered proudly. "I carried it all in."

She looked at him skeptically. "You expect me to believe that? You brought in all of this, piece by piece, over that rough, rocky terrain in this heat?"

"Yes, I did," he replied proudly.

"Seriously?" She looked around, pointing to items one at a time. "Table. Chairs. Flowers. Candle sticks. Ice bucket. Champagne. Food cooler. Folding panel. The shower. Clothing. This tent. This *humongous* tent? And is that a queen-sized air mattress?"

"Every piece." He laughed.

Her mouth dropped as she pictured him carrying everything in, one item at a time. "Why?"

He ran his hand through his hair, not quite able to look her in the eye. "After everything I put you through, you have every reason to tell me to get lost. And if that's your decision, I'll respect it without arguing. But I was desperate to find a way to say I'm sorry...and that I love you. The sun's getting lower in the sky. I'll meet you outside when you're ready."

His facial expression nearly broke her heart. Everything about him said he was prepared for her not to forgive him. There was no trace of the cocky charmer she'd first met. He'd screwed up and was making no excuses. He would accept the consequences of his mistakes without a defense. Tears welled up in her eyes, and she turned and headed around the panel.

As she stepped into the makeshift shower, she spotted bottles of her favorite shampoo and body wash. Colin's attention to detail made her laugh. As she enjoyed the warm water and lavender-scented bubbles from the lather, she realized that she was no longer struggling with what to do. Her heart had made the decision sometime during the last few days and was simply waiting for her head to catch up. She smiled. *He may be an arrogant, know-it-all, royal pain in the ass — but he's* my *arrogant, know-it-all, royal pain in the ass.*

After dressing, she went outside and found him standing by the ledge. The sun was about to do down. Holding hands, they stood and watched silently as the sky turned a glorious scarlet. He turned to her. "I'm not going to ask for your forgiveness, Cat, because I don't deserve it. But there is one thing I want to know — because I won't be able to live with myself if I don't at least ask."

He knelt down in front of her and took a diamond ring from his pocket. He looked at her with pure devotion and just a glimmer of hope. "Cocheta White Eagle, you are the most remarkable woman I've ever met. I know I don't deserve you, but I promise to love you forever and to spend the rest of my life making up for what a worthless tosser I've been. Will you marry me?"

Cat's heart didn't allow her a moment of doubt about how she'd answer. But she wasn't going to deny herself the opportunity for just a bit of fun at his expense.

She looked at him with worry. "Colin, you might have been farther away from the blast than I was when it went off, but I think you might have been injured." She put her hand on his forehead as though she were checking to see if he had a fever. "You should see a neurologist."

He looked impossibly puzzled. "What are you talking about, Cat? I just asked you to marry me."

"Right, you asked me a question I answered months ago. Did you forget I said yes?" She beamed, burst out laughing and began to cry.

He relaxed and began to tear up as well. He slid the ring onto her finger then stood, kissed her tenderly and hugged her gently.

When they let go of each other, she couldn't help but admire the ring. She loved how much the diamond sparkled. It reminded her of— "Colin! This can't be the same ring! I was so hurt and upset that I threw it away. Where did you get this?"

He smiled broadly. "You're getting an important detail wrong, Dr. White Eagle," he teased. "That's poor form for a scientist. You may have wanted to throw it away, but you didn't. Think again. What did you do with it?"

Cat had been impossibly distraught that frigid winter day. Her life had been shattered. For a moment, she had even been ready to let the storm take her. The pain had been so intense that she'd never wanted to recall it. She closed her eyes, fought through the haze and focused on the images until they snapped into focus. "I gave it to a homeless woman."

"Precisely."

"You mean—?"

"Aunt Clarissa told you she was watching over you. She presents a tough face to the world, but she's a romantic at heart. She returned it to me the day you started your quest and asked me to tell you again how bad she felt keeping you out of the loop."

She sat on the rocks with Colin, enjoying the sunset. The golds and reds were spectacular.

As the colors faded, Colin broke the silence. "So, I know you'll marry me, but with my sketchy reputation," he smiled, "are you willing to hire me?"

"Hire you?"

"You've made the discovery of a lifetime. Organizations will be falling over themselves to fund your research. This site is going to take years to study appropriately. You'll need a staff. I'd like to be first to apply."

"Are you sure that you'll be happy with the desert of Arizona, instead of London or New York?"

"I am desperately, hopelessly in love with you, Cat. As long as we're together, that's all that counts."

A naughty smirk broke out on her face. "Okay, but you get no special consideration. I'll need your CV, samples of your written work and professional references. Plus, I'll need to see first-hand whether you possess the special skillset I'm looking for."

"Skillset?" He looked puzzled.

"Let's put it this way. In five minutes, you'll come into the tent and find me naked on that mattress. Tomorrow morning, I'll evaluate your performance and make my decision about whether there's a spot for you on my team. And remember, for this kind of research" — she winked — "stamina and creativity are especially important. Good luck, Professor Tucker. Let's see what you've got."

Want to see more from this author? Here's a taster for you to enjoy!

Treat or Hex?
Jane Colt

Excerpt

Derek nervously polished off yet another glass of wine and sat beside the chestnut-haired woman.

"I shouldn't tell you this, but I've kept this a secret for so long it's killing me." The desperation in his voice startled her. He swallowed and looked straight at her with his penetrating silver-blue eyes. "I love you, Bobbie. You're the most amazing woman I've ever met. I love you so much. I'll die if I can't have you." He put his hand on her thigh.

Uh-oh. That second bottle was definitely a mistake. She removed his hand.

"Come on, Derek," she laughed. You're drunk and horny. That's all."

The shine in his eyes dimmed. He was hurt. "It may have taken an expensive pinot for me to get up the courage to tell you, but I'm serious. I love you. I've been in love with you since the first day we met. But you were so much out of my league—so beautiful, so confident—I was afraid to tell you. We may never get another opportunity. I finally want to confess my feelings."

She studied his face. She saw both love and pain. *Oh my God! He means it!* Her heart danced and her stomach clenched at the same time. It was everything she'd once dreamed of hearing from him. But it was the last thing she wanted now.

"We can't, Derek. We're friends. Good friends. But this would be wrong." Her tone was unconvincing, however.

It was bad enough she'd fallen in love with him the day they'd met at work. He was illegally handsome— tall, wavy dark brown hair, square-jawed, hypnotic eyes the same color of the most beautiful sky she'd ever seen and large hands that instinctively sparked fantasies. Surely beneath his stylish clothes was a hard body just as glorious. For someone who could have any woman he wanted, he was surprisingly shy, sweet and unassuming. Worst of all—or was it best of all?—she occasionally saw a glint in his eye that said he would be anything but hesitant in bed. She found intoxicating the idea of his wanting her so much that he simply took her—roughly and selfishly using her body to pleasure himself. He was exactly the kind of guy she'd dreamed about falling in love with. And the British accent was frosting on the cake.

What made things even more tortuous was that ever since Derek's wife had confided to Bobbie that he was *amazing* in bed, she absolutely burned for him. She regularly fantasized about him in the middle of the night—their hot, sweaty flesh wrapped in darkness, possessed by lust, her body spent from the number of orgasms he'd commanded out of it.

She nervously pulled her slightly revealing wrap dress against her and tightened the belt. She slid down the couch—as far away as she could get.

"*Wrong?*" he objected. "I'm not talking about a meaningless fuck. I want to make love to you. What could be wrong with that?" His tone was earnest and tempting. He moved in her direction.

"Maybe the fact that you're married" — she glared — "and the ease with which you forget that." She ground her teeth. *You couldn't have told me this before you got married? We met a month before you met Phylicia. And you wait until* now *to tell me you love me?*

She didn't know if she was angrier at him or his wife. Derek had been a reserved co-worker she'd fallen hard for. When it had become clear he was too shy to make a move, she'd invited him for drinks to tell him she was interested. Her roommate had known her plan, but 'coincidentally' showed up at the bar at the same time. When the emergency call had come in from one of Bobbie's patients, causing her to leave for the hospital, Phylicia had said she'd '*take care of him*'. And she did that in spades. She and Derek had spent the weekend in bed and married a few months later.

"I never forget I'm married. I love Phylicia. She's such a sweet person. I'd never do anything to hurt her," he defended himself solemnly. "But I've always regretted not telling you how I felt. And I wouldn't have said anything now if fate hadn't put us together in this hotel room a thousand miles from home when the storm diverted our flight. The airline assigned us to the same room because they assumed 'Bobbie' was a man. By the time we figured out what happened, the hotel was full. It's the universe's way of giving us permission. I love you. You're beautiful. You're so remarkable. I can't help myself." He took her face in his two warm hands. "Please. Just this once. Let me make love to you. I love you more than words can say."

His look of pure devotion made her melt. His full lips were irresistible. Her breathing deepened. They inched their faces toward each other.

No. I can't.

She pulled back and looked away. She wrung her hands. Derek wasn't the kind of guy to casually say he loved someone. He was a deeply emotional and sensitive man — something else that fueled her feelings for him. She was thrilled he felt so much for her — and crushed. It didn't change anything.

"It's just wrong. You know that."

He took her hand and looked at her sincerely. "Don't you think it's possible to love two people at the same time? How can love be wrong? Shouldn't we be able to express that love?" He smiled at her warmly. "There's only one question, Bobbie. Do you want to make love to me as much as I do to you? If you say you don't, I can accept that. Tell me you have no feelings for me, and I won't say another word."

Feelings? Sure. Just the wrong kind.

Answering was pointless. The tension in her face signaled her yearning.

"Come on," he prodded. "At least tell me the truth. If you can honestly say you don't want to, I'll drop it."

His refusal to pressure her made her want him even more. *Crap. He's doing the decent thing. Why can't he be a jerk and force himself on me? I'll pretend I'm too drunk to resist, and we can fuck like bunnies. Afterward, he'll blame it on the alcohol and apologize. I'll forgive him and swear never to tell a soul. At least we can have one hot night together.*

She looked directly into his eyes. The passion she saw there mirrored her own.

Her face was warm. Her breath was short. Her hunger for him was undeniable. She might not be able to have him, but she wanted him at least to know the truth. "I never said I didn't want to. But that doesn't change anything."

He reached over and touched her cheek. He smiled and relaxed. "You love me too. I knew it."

She wanted to deny it, but she was tired of hiding her feelings. She was indeed in love with him. There wasn't a moment they were together that she didn't ache for their bodies to be fused and exploding in rapture — and that she didn't feel heartbroken it would never happen.

She was also tired of pretending she'd forgiven Phylicia. Watching the courtship unfold had been agonizing. *She* was supposed to be the one at the altar. A better person would have taken the high road and let things go. A truly decent person would have accepted Phylicia's explanation that it actually had been coincidental she'd showed up at the bar. But Bobbie didn't want to be that decent a person. And she was exhausted at having pretended to be one.

She knew that sometimes Phylicia laid on the 'sweet and innocent' persona to get what she wanted. What she imagined had taken place between Derek and her roommate — a scene that regularly tortured her — popped into her head.